GREAT JAPANESE SHORT STORIES

Paul Morikawa, a Japanese-born literature enthusiast, has persistently fostered cross-cultural exchange through his work as an author and academic. His overseas studies ignited in him a passion for bridging cultural divides, inspiring him to introduce Japanese literary treasures to English-speaking audiences. Through insightful works and translations, he remains a tireless advocate for the appreciation of world literature.

GREAT JAPANESE SHORT STORIES

Compiled by **PAUL MORIKAWA**

RUPA

Published by
Rupa Publications India Pvt. Ltd 2023
7/16, Ansari Road, Daryaganj
New Delhi 110002

Sales centres:
Bengaluru Chennai
Hyderabad Jaipur Kathmandu
Kolkata Mumbai Prayagraj

P-ISBN: 978-93-5702-746-5
E-ISBN: 978-93-5702-724-3

First impression 2023

10 9 8 7 6 5 4 3 2 1

Printed in India

CONTENTS

THE FARMER AND THE BADGER

Long, long ago, there lived an old farmer and his wife who had made their home in the mountains, far from any town. Their only neighbour was a bad and malicious badger. This badger used to come out every night and run across to the farmer's field and spoil the vegetables and the rice which the farmer spent his time in carefully cultivating. The badger at last grew so ruthless in his mischievous work, and did so much harm everywhere on the farm, that the good-natured farmer could not stand it any longer, and determined to put a stop to it. So he lay in wait day after day and night after night, with a big club, hoping to catch the badger, but all in vain. Then he laid traps for the wicked animal.

The farmer's trouble and patience was rewarded, for one fine day on going his rounds he found the badger caught in a hole he had dug for that purpose. The farmer was delighted at having caught his enemy, and carried him home securely bound with rope. When he reached the house the farmer said to his wife:

'I have at last caught the bad badger. You must keep an eye on him while I am out at work and not let him escape, because I want to make him into soup to-night.'

Saying this, he hung the badger up to the rafters of his storehouse and went out to his work in the fields. The badger was in great distress, for he did not at all like the idea of being made into soup that night, and he thought and thought for a long time, trying to hit upon some plan by which he might escape. It was hard to think clearly in his uncomfortable position, for he had been hung upside down. Very near him, at the entrance to the storehouse, looking out towards the green fields and the trees and the pleasant sunshine, stood the farmer's old wife pounding barley. She looked tired and old. Her face was seamed with many wrinkles, and was as brown as leather, and every now and then she stopped to wipe the perspiration which rolled down her face.

'Dear lady,' said the wily badger, 'you must be very weary doing such heavy work in your old age. Won't you let me do that for you? My arms are very strong, and I could relieve you for a little while!'

'Thank you for your kindness,' said the old woman, 'but I cannot let you do this work for me because I must not untie you, for you might escape if I did, and my husband would be very angry if he came home and found you gone.'

Now, the badger is one of the most cunning of animals, and he said again in a very sad, gentle, voice:

'You are very unkind. You might untie me, for I promise not to try to escape. If you are afraid of your husband, I will let you bind me again before his return when I have finished pounding the barley. I am so tired and sore tied up like this. If you would only let me down for a few minutes I would indeed be thankful!'

The old woman had a good and simple nature, and could not think badly of any one. Much less did she think that the badger was only deceiving her in order to get away. She felt sorry, too, for the animal as she turned to look at him. He looked in such a sad plight hanging downwards from the ceiling by his legs, which were all tied together so tightly that the rope and the knots were cutting into the skin. So in the kindness of her heart, and believing the creature's promise that he would not run away, she untied the cord and let him down.

The old woman then gave him the wooden pestle and told him to do the work for a short time while she rested. He took the pestle, but instead of doing the work as he was told, the badger at once sprang upon the old woman and knocked her down with the heavy piece of wood. He then killed her and cut her up and made soup of her, and waited for the return of the old farmer. The old man worked hard in his fields all day, and as he worked he thought with pleasure that no more now would his labour be spoiled by the destructive badger.

Towards sunset he left his work and turned to go home. He was very tired, but the thought of the nice supper of hot badger soup awaiting his return cheered him. The thought that the badger might get free and take revenge on the poor old woman never once came into his mind.

The badger meanwhile assumed the old woman's form, and as soon as he saw the old farmer approaching came out to greet him on the veranda of the little house, saying:

'So you have come back at last. I have made the badger soup and have been waiting for you for a long time.'

The old farmer quickly took off his straw sandals and sat down before his tiny dinner-tray. The innocent man never even dreamed that it was not his wife but the badger who was waiting upon him, and asked at once for the soup. Then the badger suddenly transformed himself back to his natural form and cried out:

'You wife-eating old man! Look out for the bones in the kitchen!'

Laughing loudly and derisively he escaped out of the house and ran away to his den in the hills. The old man was left behind alone. He could hardly believe what he had seen and heard. Then when he understood the whole truth he was so scared and horrified that he fainted right away. After a while he came round and burst into tears. He cried loudly and bitterly. He rocked himself to and fro in his hopeless grief. It seemed too terrible to be real that his faithful old wife had been killed and cooked by the badger while he was working quietly in the fields, knowing nothing of what was going on at home, and congratulating himself on having once for all got rid of the wicked animal who had so often spoiled his fields. And oh! the horrible thought; he had very nearly drunk the soup which the creature had made of his poor old woman. 'Oh dear, oh dear, oh dear!' he wailed aloud. Now, not far away there lived in the same mountain a kind, good-natured old rabbit. He heard the old man crying and sobbing and at once set out to see what was the matter, and if there was anything he could do to help his neighbour. The old man told him all that had happened. When the rabbit heard the story he was very angry at the wicked and deceitful badger, and told the old man to leave everything to him and he would avenge his wife's death. The farmer was at last comforted, and, wiping away his tears, thanked the rabbit for his goodness in coming to him in his distress.

The rabbit, seeing that the farmer was growing calmer, went back to his home to lay his plans for the punishment of the badger.

The next day the weather was fine, and the rabbit went out to find the badger. He was not to be seen in the woods or on the hillside or in the fields anywhere, so the rabbit went to his den and found the badger hiding there, for the animal had been afraid to show himself ever since he had escaped from the farmer's house, for fear of the old man's wrath.

The rabbit called out:

'Why are you not out on such a beautiful day? Come out with me, and we will go and cut grass on the hills together.'

The badger, never doubting but that the rabbit was his friend, willingly consented to go out with him, only too glad to get away from the neighbourhood of the farmer and the fear of meeting him.

The rabbit led the way miles away from their homes, out on the hills where the grass grew tall and thick and sweet. They both set to work to cut down as much as they could carry home, to store it up for their winter's food. When they had each cut down all they wanted they tied it in bundles and then started homewards, each carrying his bundle of grass on his back. This time the rabbit made the badger go first.

When they had gone a little way the rabbit took out a flint and steel, and, striking it over the badger's back as he stepped along in front, set his bundle of grass on fire. The badger heard the flint striking, and asked:

'What is that noise. "Crack, crack"?'

'Oh, that is nothing.' replied the rabbit; 'I only said "Crack, crack" because this mountain is called Crackling Mountain.'

The fire soon spread in the bundle of dry grass on the badger's back. The badger, hearing the crackle of the burning grass, asked, 'What is that?'

'Now we have come to the "Burning Mountain,"' answered the rabbit.

By this time the bundle was nearly burned out and all the hair had been burned off the badger's back. He now knew what had happened by the smell of the smoke of the burning grass. Screaming with pain the badger ran as fast as he could to his hole. The rabbit followed and found him lying on his bed groaning with pain.

'What an unlucky fellow you are!' said the rabbit. 'I can't

imagine how this happened! I will bring you some medicine which will heal your back quickly!'

The rabbit went away glad and smiling to think that the punishment upon the badger had already begun. He hoped that the badger would die of his burns, for he felt that nothing could be too bad for the animal, who was guilty of murdering a poor helpless old woman who had trusted him. He went home and made an ointment by mixing some sauce and red pepper together.

He carried this to the badger, but before putting it on he told him that it would cause him great pain, but that he must bear it patiently, because it was a very wonderful medicine for burns and scalds and such wounds. The badger thanked him and begged him to apply it at once. But no language can describe the agony of the badger as soon as the red pepper had been pasted all over his sore back. He rolled over and over and howled loudly. The rabbit, looking on, felt that the farmer's wife was beginning to be avenged.

The badger was in bed for about a month; but at last, in spite of the red pepper application, his burns healed and he got well. When the rabbit saw that the badger was getting well, he thought of another plan by which he could compass the creature's death. So he went one day to pay the badger a visit and to congratulate him on his recovery.

During the conversation the rabbit mentioned that he was going fishing, and described how pleasant fishing was when the weather was fine and the sea smooth.

The badger listened with pleasure to the rabbit's account of the way he passed his time now, and forgot all his pains and his month's illness, and thought what fun it would be if he could go fishing too; so he asked the rabbit if he would take him the next time he went out to fish. This was just what the rabbit wanted, so he agreed.

Then he went home and built two boats, one of wood and the other of clay. At last they were both finished, and as the rabbit stood and looked at his work he felt that all his trouble would be well rewarded if his plan succeeded, and he could manage to kill the wicked badger now.

The day came when the rabbit had arranged to take the badger fishing. He kept the wooden boat himself and gave the badger the clay boat. The badger, who knew nothing about boats, was delighted with his new boat and thought how kind it was of the rabbit to give it to him. They both got into their boats and set out. After going some distance from the shore the rabbit proposed that they should try their boats and see which one could go the quickest. The badger fell in with the proposal, and they both set to work to row as fast as they could for some time. In the middle of the race the badger found his boat going to pieces, for the water now began to soften the clay. He cried out in great fear to the rabbit to help him. But the rabbit answered that he was avenging the old woman's murder, and that this had been his intention all along, and that he was happy to think that the badger had at last met his deserts for all his evil crimes, and was to drown with no one to help him. Then he raised his oar and struck at the badger with all his strength till he fell with the sinking clay boat and was seen no more.

Thus at last he kept his promise to the old farmer. The rabbit now turned and rowed shorewards, and having landed and pulled his boat upon the beach, hurried back to tell the old farmer everything, and how the badger, his enemy, had been killed.

The old farmer thanked him with tears in his eyes. He said that till now he could never sleep at night or be at peace in the daytime, thinking of how his wife's death was unavenged, but from this time he would be able to sleep and eat as of old. He begged the rabbit to stay with him and share his home, so from this day the rabbit went to stay with the old farmer and they both lived together as good friends to the end of their days.

THE 'SHINANSHA', OR THE
SOUTH-POINTING CARRIAGE

The compass, with its needle always pointing to the north, is quite a common thing, and no one thinks that it is remarkable now, though when it was first invented it must have been a wonder.

Now long ago in China, there was a still more wonderful invention called the *shinansha*. This was a kind of chariot with the figure of a man on it always pointing to the south. No matter how the chariot was placed the figure always wheeled about and pointed to the south.

This curious instrument was invented by Kotei, one of the three Chinese emperors of the Mythological age. Kotei was the son of the Emperor Yuhi. Before he was born his mother had a vision which foretold that her son would be a great man.

One summer evening she went out to walk in the meadows to seek the cool breezes which blow at the end of the day and to gaze with pleasure at the star-lit heavens above her. As she looked at the North Star, strange to relate, it shot forth vivid flashes of lightning in every direction. Soon after this her son Kotei came into the world.

Kotei in time grew to manhood and succeeded his father the Emperor Yuhi. His early reign was greatly troubled by the rebel Shiyu. This rebel wanted to make himself king, and many were the battles which he fought to this end. Shiyu was a wicked magician, his head was made of iron, and there was no man that could conquer him.

At last Kotei declared war against the rebel and led his army to battle, and the two armies met on a plain called Takuroku. The emperor boldly attacked the enemy, but the magician brought down a dense fog upon the battlefield, and while the royal army were wandering about in confusion, trying to find their way, Shiyu retreated with his troops, laughing at having fooled the royal army.

No matter however strong and brave the emperor's soldiers were, the rebel with his magic could always escape in the end.

Kotei returned to his palace, and thought and pondered deeply as to how he should conquer the magician, for he was determined not to give up yet. After a long time he invented the shinansha with the figure of a man always pointing south, for there were no compasses in those days. With this instrument to show him the way he need not fear the dense fogs raised up by the magician to confound his men.

Kotei again declared war against Shiyu. He placed the shinansha in front of his army and led the way to the battlefield.

The battle began in earnest. The rebel was being driven backward by the royal troops when he again resorted to magic, and upon his saying some strange words in a loud voice, immediately a dense fog came down upon the battlefield.

But this time no soldier minded the fog, not one was confused. Kotei by pointing to the shinansha could find his way and directed the army without a single mistake. He closely pursued the rebel army and drove them backward till they came to a big river. This river Kotei and his men found was swollen by the floods and impossible to cross.

Shiyu by using his magic art quickly passed over with his

army and shut himself up in a fortress on the opposite bank.

When Kotei found his march checked he was wild with disappointment, for he had very nearly overtaken the rebel when the river stopped him.

He could do nothing, for there were no boats in those days, so the emperor ordered his tent to be pitched in the pleasantest spot that the place afforded.

One day he stepped forth from his tent and after walking about for a short time he came to a pond. Here he sat down on the bank and was lost in thought.

It was autumn. The trees growing along the edge of the water were shedding their leaves, which floated hither and thither on the surface of the pond. By and by, Kotei's attention was attracted to a spider on the brink of the water. The little insect was trying to get on to one of the floating leaves near by. It did so at last, and was soon floating over the water to the other side of the pond.

This little incident made the clever emperor think that he might try to make something that could carry himself and his men over the river in the same way that the leaf had carried over the spider. He set to work and persevered till he invented the first boat. When he found that it was a success he set all his men to make more, and in time there were enough boats for the whole army.

Kotei now took his army across the river, and attacked Shiyu's headquarters. He gained a complete victory, and so put an end to the war which had troubled his country for so long.

This wise and good emperor did not rest till he had secured peace and prosperity throughout his whole land. He was beloved by his subjects, who now enjoyed their happiness of peace for many long years under him. He spent a great deal of time in making inventions which would benefit his people, and he succeeded in many besides the boat and the south-pointing shinansha.

He had reigned about a hundred years when one day, as Kotei was looking upwards, the sky became suddenly red, and something came glittering like gold towards the earth. As it came nearer Kotei saw that it was a great dragon. The dragon approached and bowed down its head before the emperor. The empress and the courtiers were so frightened that they ran away screaming.

But the emperor only smiled and called to them to stop, and said:

'Do not be afraid. This is a messenger from Heaven. My time here is finished!' He then mounted the dragon, which began to ascend towards the sky.

When the empress and the courtiers saw this they all cried out together:

'Wait a moment! We wish to come too.' And they all ran and caught hold of the dragon's beard and tried to mount him.

But it was impossible for so many people to ride on the dragon. Several of them hung on to the creature's beard so that when it tried to mount the hair was pulled out and they fell to the ground.

Meanwhile the empress and a few of the courtiers were safely seated on the dragon's back. The dragon flew up so high in the heavens that in a short time the inmates of the palace, who had been left behind disappointed, could see them no more.

After some time a bow and an arrow dropped to the earth in the courtyard of the palace. They were recognized as having belonged to the Emperor Kotei. The courtiers took them up carefully and preserved them as sacred relics in the palace.

THE STORY OF PRINCESS HASE

Many, many years ago there lived in Nara, the ancient capital of Japan, a wise state minister, by name Prince Toyonari Fujiwara. His wife was a noble, good and beautiful woman called Princess Murasaki (Violet). They had been married by their respective families according to Japanese custom when very young, and had lived together happily ever since. They had, however, one cause for great sorrow, for as the years went by no child was born to them. This made them very unhappy, for they both longed to see a child of their own who would grow up to gladden their old age, carry on the family name, and keep up the ancestral rites when they were dead. The prince and his lovely wife, after long consultation and much thought, determined to make a pilgrimage to the temple of Hase-no-Kwannon (Goddess of Mercy at Hase), for they believed, according to the beautiful tradition of their religion, that the Mother of Mercy, Kwannon, comes to answer the prayers of mortals in the form that they need the most. Surely after all these years of prayer she would come to them in the form of a beloved child in answer to their special pilgrimage, for that was the greatest need of their two lives. Everything else they had that this life could give them, but it was all as nothing because the cry of their hearts was unsatisfied.

So the Prince Toyonari and his wife went to the temple of Kwannon at Hase and stayed there for a long time, both daily offering incense and praying to Kwannon, the Heavenly Mother, to grant them the desire of their whole lives. And their prayer was answered.

A daughter was born at last to the Princess Murasaki, and great was the joy of her heart. On presenting the child to her husband, they both decided to call her Hase-Hime, or the Princess of Hase, because she was the gift of the Kwannon at that place. They both reared her with great care and tenderness, and the child grew in strength and beauty.

When the little girl was five years old her mother fell dangerously ill and all the doctors and their medicines could not save her. A little before she breathed her last she called her daughter to her, and gently stroking her head, said:

'Hase-Hime, do you know that your mother cannot live any longer? Though I die, you must grow up a good girl. Do your best not to give trouble to your nurse or any other of your family. Perhaps your father will marry again and some one will fill my place as your mother. If so do not grieve for me, but look upon your father's second wife as your true mother, and be obedient and filial to both her and your father. Remember when you are grown up to be submissive to those who are your superiors, and to be kind to all those who are under you. Don't forget this. I die with the hope that you will grow up a model woman.'

Hase-Hime listened in an attitude of respect while her mother spoke, and promised to do all that she was told. There is a proverb which says 'As the soul is at three so it is at one hundred,' and so Hase-Hime grew up as her mother had wished, a good and obedient little princess, though she was now too young to understand how great was the loss of her mother.

Not long after the death of his first wife, Prince Toyonari married again, a lady of noble birth named Princess Terute.

Very different in character, alas! to the good and wise Princess Murasaki, this woman had a cruel, bad heart. She did not love her step-daughter at all, and was often very unkind to the little motherless girl, saying to herself:

'This is not my child! this is not my child!'

But Hase-Hime bore every unkindness with patience, and even waited upon her step-mother kindly and obeyed her in every way and never gave any trouble, just as she had been trained by her own good mother, so that the Lady Terute had no cause for complaint against her.

The little princess was very diligent, and her favourite studies were music and poetry. She would spend several hours practising every day, and her father had the most proficient of masters he could find to teach her the *koto* (Japanese harp), the art of writing letters and verse. When she was twelve years of age she could play so beautifully that she and her step-mother were summoned to the palace to perform before the emperor.

It was the Festival of the Cherry Flowers, and there were great festivities at the court. The emperor threw himself into the enjoyment of the season, and commanded that Princess Hase should perform before him on the koto, and that her mother Princess Terute should accompany her on the flute.

The emperor sat on a raised dais, before which was hung a curtain of finely-sliced bamboo and purple tassels, so that His Majesty might see all and not be seen, for no ordinary subject was allowed to looked upon his sacred face.

Hase-Hime was a skilled musician though so young, and often astonished her masters by her wonderful memory and talent. On this momentous occasion she played well. But Princess Terute, her step-mother, who was a lazy woman and never took the trouble to practise daily, broke down in her accompaniment and had to request one of the court ladies to take her place. This was a great disgrace, and she was furiously jealous to think that she had failed where her step-daughter succeeded; and to make matters worse the emperor sent many beautiful gifts to the little princess to reward her for playing so well at the palace.

There was also now another reason why Princess Terute hated her step-daughter, for she had had the good fortune to have a son born to her, and in her inmost heart she kept saying:

'If only Hase-Hime were not here, my son would have all the love of his father.'

And never having learned to control herself, she allowed this wicked thought to grow into the awful desire of taking her step-daughter's life.

So one day she secretly ordered some poison and poisoned some sweet wine. This poisoned wine she put into a bottle. Into another similar bottle she poured some good wine. It was the occasion of the Boys' Festival on the fifth of May, and Hase-Hime was playing with her little brother. All his toys of warriors and heroes were spread out and she was telling him wonderful stories about each of them. They were both enjoying themselves and laughing merrily with their attendants when his mother entered with the two bottles of wine and some delicious cakes.

'You are both so good and happy.' said the wicked Princess Terute with a smile, 'that I have brought you some sweet wine as a reward—and here are some nice cakes for my good children.'

And she filled two cups from the different bottles.

Hase-Hime, never dreaming of the dreadful part her step-mother was acting, took one of the cups of wine and gave to her little step-brother the other that had been poured out for him.

The wicked woman had carefully marked the poisoned bottle, but on coming into the room she had grown nervous, and pouring out the wine hurriedly had unconsciously given the poisoned cup to her own child. All this time she was anxiously watching the little princess, but to her amazement no change whatever took place in the young girl's face. Suddenly the little boy screamed and threw himself on the floor, doubled up with pain. His mother flew to him, taking the precaution to upset the two tiny jars of wine which she had brought into the room, and lifted him up. The attendants rushed for the doctor, but nothing could save the child—he died within the hour in his mother's arms. Doctors did not know much in those ancient times, and it was thought that the wine had disagreed with the boy, causing convulsions of which he died.

Thus was the wicked woman punished in losing her own child when she had tried to do away with her step-daughter; but instead of blaming herself she began to hate Hase-Hime more than ever in the bitterness and wretchedness of her own heart, and she eagerly watched for an opportunity to do her harm, which was, however, long in coming.

When Hase-Hime was thirteen years of age, she had already become mentioned as a poetess of some merit. This was an accomplishment very much cultivated by the women of old Japan and one held in high esteem.

It was the rainy season at Nara, and floods were reported every day as doing damage in the neighbourhood. The river Tatsuta, which flowed through the imperial palace grounds, was swollen to the top of its banks, and the roaring of the torrents of water rushing along a narrow bed so disturbed the emperor's rest day and night, that a serious nervous disorder was the result. An Imperial Edict was sent forth to all the Buddhist temples commanding the priests to offer up continuous prayers to Heaven to stop the noise of the flood. But this was of no avail.

Then it was whispered in court circles that the Princess Hase, the daughter of Prince Toyonari Fujiwara, second minister at court, was the most gifted poetess of the day, though still so young, and her masters confirmed the report. Long ago, a beautiful and gifted maiden-poetess had moved Heaven by praying in verse, had brought down rain upon a land famished with drought—so said the ancient biographers of the poetess Ono-no-Komachi. If the Princess Hase were to write a poem and offer it in prayer, might it not stop the noise of the rushing river and remove the cause of the imperial illness? What the court said at last reached the ears of the emperor himself, and he sent an order to the minister Prince Toyonari to this effect.

Great indeed was Hase-Hime's fear and astonishment when her father sent for her and told her what was required of her. Heavy, indeed, was the duty that was laid on her young shoulders—that of saving the emperor's life by the merit of her verse.

At last the day came and her poem was finished. It was written on a leaflet of paper heavily flecked with gold-dust. With her father and attendants and some of the court officials, she proceeded to the bank of the roaring torrent and raising up her heart to Heaven, she read the poem she had composed, aloud, lifting it heavenwards in her two hands.

Strange indeed it seemed to all those standing round. The waters ceased their roaring, and the river was quiet in direct answer to her prayer. After this the emperor soon recovered his health.

His Majesty was highly pleased, and sent for her to the palace and rewarded her with the rank of Chinjo—that of Lieutenant-General—to distinguish her. From that time she was called Chinjo-Hime, or the Lieutenant-General Princess, and respected and loved by all.

There was only one person who was not pleased at Hase-Hime's success. That one was her stepmother. Forever brooding over the death of her own child whom she had killed when trying to poison her step-daughter, she had the mortification of seeing her rise to power and honour, marked by Imperial favour and the admiration of the whole court. Her envy and jealousy burned in her heart like fire. Many were the lies she carried to her husband about Hase-Hime, but all to no purpose. He would listen to none of her tales, telling her sharply that she was quite mistaken.

At last the step-mother, seizing the opportunity of her husband's absence, ordered one of her old servants to take the innocent girl to the Hibari Mountains, the wildest part of the country, and to kill her there. She invented a dreadful story about the little princess, saying that this was the only way to prevent disgrace falling upon the family—by killing her.

Katoda, her vassal, was bound to obey his mistress. Anyhow, he saw that it would be the wisest plan to pretend obedience in the absence of the girl's father, so he placed Hase-Hime in a palanquin and accompanied her to the most solitary place he could find in the wild district. The poor child knew there was no good in protesting to her unkind step-mother at being sent away in this strange manner, so she went as she was told.

But the old servant knew that the young princess was quite innocent of all the things her step-mother had invented to him as reasons for her outrageous orders, and he determined to save her life. Unless he killed her, however, he could not return to his cruel task-mistress, so he decided to stay out in the wilderness. With the help of some peasants he soon built a little cottage, and having sent secretly for his wife to come, these two good old people did all in their power to take care of the now unfortunate princess. She all the time trusted in her father, knowing that as soon as he returned home and found her absent, he would search for her.

Prince Toyonari, after some weeks, came home, and was told by his wife that his daughter hime had done something wrong and had run away for fear of being punished. He was nearly ill with anxiety. Every one in the house told the same story—that Hase-Hime had suddenly disappeared, none of them knew why or whither. For fear of scandal he kept the matter quiet and searched everywhere he could think of, but all to no purpose.

One day, trying to forget his terrible worry, he called all his men together and told them to make ready for a several days' hunt in the mountains. They were soon ready and mounted, waiting at the gate for their lord. He rode hard and fast to the district of the Hibari Mountains, a great company following him. He was soon far ahead of every one, and at last found himself in a narrow picturesque valley.

Looking round and admiring the scenery, he noticed a tiny house on one of the hills quite near, and then he distinctly heard a beautiful clear voice reading aloud. Seized with curiosity as to who could be studying so diligently in such a lonely spot, he dismounted, and leaving his horse to his groom, he walked up the hillside and approached the cottage. As he drew nearer his surprise increased, for he could see that the reader was a beautiful girl. The cottage was wide open and she was sitting facing the view. Listening attentively, he heard her reading the Buddhist scriptures with great devotion. More and more curious, he hurried on to the tiny gate and entered the little garden, and looking up beheld his lost daughter Hase-Hime. She was so intent on what she was saying that she neither heard nor saw her father till he spoke.

'Hase-Hime!' he cried, 'it is you, my Hase-Hime!'

Taken by surprise, she could hardly realize that it was her own dear father who was calling her, and for a moment she was utterly bereft of the power to speak or move.

'My father, my father! It is indeed you—oh, my father!' was all she could say, and running to him she caught hold of his thick sleeve, and burying her face burst into a passion of tears.

Her father stroked her dark hair, asking her gently to tell him all that had happened, but she only wept on, and he wondered if he were not really dreaming.

Then the faithful old servant Katoda came out, and bowing himself to the ground before his master, poured out the long tale of wrong, telling him all that had happened, and how it was that he found his daughter in such a wild and desolate spot with only two old servants to take care of her.

The Prince's astonishment and indignation knew no bounds. He gave up the hunt at once and hurried home with his daughter. One of the company galloped ahead to inform the household of the glad news, and the step-mother hearing what had happened, and fearful of meeting her husband now that her wickedness was discovered, fled from the house and returned in disgrace to her father's roof, and nothing more was heard of her.

The old servant Katoda was rewarded with the highest promotion in his master's service, and lived happily to the end of his days, devoted to the little princess, who never forgot that she owed her life to this faithful retainer. She was no longer troubled by an unkind step-mother, and her days passed happily and quietly with her father.

As Prince Toyonari had no son, he adopted a younger son of one of the court nobles to be his heir, and to marry his daughter Hase-Hime, and in a few years the marriage took place. Hase-Hime lived to a good old age, and all said that she was the wisest, most devout, and most beautiful mistress that had ever reigned in Prince Toyonari's ancient house. She had the joy of presenting her son, the future lord of the family, to her father just before he retired from active life.

To this day there is preserved a piece of needle-work in one of the Buddhist temples of Kioto. It is a beautiful piece of tapestry, with the figure of Buddha embroidered in the silky threads drawn from the stem of the lotus. This is said to have been the work of the hands of the good Princess Hase.

THE STORY OF THE MAN WHO
DID NOT WISH TO DIE

Long, long ago there lived a man called Sentaro. His surname meant 'Millionaire,' but although he was not so rich as all that, he was still very far removed from being poor. He had inherited a small fortune from his father and lived on this, spending his time carelessly, without any serious thoughts of work, till he was about thirty-two years of age.

One day, without any reason whatsoever, the thought of death and sickness came to him. The idea of falling ill or dying made him very wretched.

'I should like to live,' he said to himself, 'till I am five or six hundred years old at least, free from all sickness. The ordinary span of a man's life is very short.'

He wondered whether it were possible, by living simply and frugally henceforth, to prolong his life as long as he wished.

He knew there were many stories in ancient history of emperors who had lived a thousand years, and there was a Princess of Yamato, who, it was said, lived to the age of five hundred. This was the latest story of a very long life record.

Sentaro had often heard the tale of the Chinese king named Shin-no-Shiko. He was one of the most able and powerful rulers in Chinese history. He built all the large palaces, and also the famous great wall of China. He had everything in the world he could wish for, but in spite of all his happiness and the luxury and the splendour of his court, the wisdom of his councillors and the glory of his reign, he was miserable because he knew that one day he must die and leave it all.

When Shin-no-Shiko went to bed at night, when he rose in the morning, as he went through his day, the thought of death was always with him. He could not get away from it. Ah—if only he could find the 'Elixir of Life,' he would be happy.

The emperor at last called a meeting of his courtiers and asked them all if they could not find for him the 'Elixir of Life' of which he had so often read and heard.

One old courtier, Jofuku by name, said that far away across the seas there was a country called Horaizan, and that certain hermits lived there who possessed the secret of the 'Elixir of Life.' Whoever drank of this wonderful draught lived forever.

The emperor ordered Jofuku to set out for the land of Horaizan, to find the hermits, and to bring him back a phial of the magic elixir. He gave Jofuku one of his best junks, fitted it out for him, and loaded it with great quantities of treasures and precious stones for Jofuku to take as presents to the hermits.

Jofuku sailed for the land of Horaizan, but he never returned to the waiting emperor; but ever since that time Mount Fuji has been said to be the fabled Horaizan and the home of hermits who had the secret of the elixir, and Jofuku has been worshipped as their patron god.

Now Sentaro determined to set out to find the hermits, and if he could, to become one, so that he might obtain the water of perpetual life. He remembered that as a child he had been told that not only did these hermits live on Mount Fuji, but that they were said to inhabit all the very high peaks.

So he left his old home to the care of his relatives, and started out on his quest. He travelled through all the mountainous regions of the land, climbing to the tops of the highest peaks, but never a hermit did he find.

At last, after wandering in an unknown region for many days, he met a hunter.

'Can you tell me,' asked Sentaro, 'where the hermits live who have the Elixir of Life?'

'No.' said the hunter; 'I can't tell you where such hermits live, but there is a notorious robber living in these parts. It is said that he is chief of a band of two hundred followers.'

This odd answer irritated Sentaro very much, and he thought how foolish it was to waste more time in looking for the hermits in this way, so he decided to go at once to the shrine of Jofuku, who is worshipped as the patron god of the hermits in the south of Japan.

Sentaro reached the shrine and prayed for seven days, entreating Jofuku to show him the way to a hermit who could give him what he wanted so much to find.

At midnight of the seventh day, as Sentaro knelt in the temple, the door of the innermost shrine flew open, and Jofuku appeared in a luminous cloud, and calling to Sentaro to come nearer, spoke thus:

'Your desire is a very selfish one and cannot be easily granted. You think that you would like to become a hermit so as to find the Elixir of Life. Do you know how hard a hermit's life is? A hermit is only allowed to eat fruit and berries and the bark of pine trees; a hermit must cut himself off from the world so that his heart may become as pure as gold and free from every earthly desire. Gradually after following these strict rules, the hermit ceases to feel hunger or cold or heat, and his body becomes so light that he can ride on a crane or a carp, and can walk on water without getting his feet wet.'

'You, Sentaro, are fond of good living and of every comfort. You are not even like an ordinary man, for you are exceptionally idle, and more sensitive to heat and cold than most people. You would never be able to go barefoot or to wear only one thin dress in the winter time! Do you think that you would ever have the patience or the endurance to live a hermit's life?'

'In answer to your prayer, however, I will help you in another way. I will send you to the country of Perpetual Life, where death never comes—where the people live forever!'

Saying this, Jofuku put into Sentaro's hand a little crane made of paper, telling him to sit on its back and it would carry him there.

Sentaro obeyed wonderingly. The crane grew large enough for him to ride on it with comfort. It then spread its wings, rose high in the air, and flew away over the mountains right out to sea.

Sentaro was at first quite frightened; but by degrees he grew accustomed to the swift flight through the air. On and on they went for thousands of miles. The bird never stopped for rest or food, but as it was a paper bird it doubtless did not require any nourishment, and strange to say, neither did Sentaro.

After several days they reached an island. The crane flew some distance inland and then alighted.

As soon as Sentaro got down from the bird's back, the crane folded up of its own accord and flew into his pocket.

Now Sentaro began to look about him wonderingly, curious to see what the country of Perpetual Life was like. He walked first round about the country and then through the town. Everything was, of course, quite strange, and different from his own land. But both the land and the people seemed prosperous, so he decided that it would be good for him to stay there and took up lodgings at one of the hotels.

The proprietor was a kind man, and when Sentaro told him that he was a stranger and had come to live there, he promised to arrange everything that was necessary with the governor of the city concerning Sentaro's sojourn there. He even found a house for his guest, and in this way Sentaro obtained his great wish and became a resident in the country of Perpetual Life.

Within the memory of all the islanders no man had ever died there, and sickness was a thing unknown. Priests had come over from India and China and told them of a beautiful country called Paradise, where happiness and bliss and contentment fill all men's hearts, but its gates could only be reached by dying. This tradition was handed down for ages from generation to generation—but none knew exactly what death was except that it led to Paradise.

Quite unlike Sentaro and other ordinary people, instead of having a great dread of death, they all, both rich and poor, longed for it as something good and desirable. They were all tired of their long, long lives, and longed to go to the happy land of contentment called Paradise of which the priests had told them centuries ago.

All this Sentaro soon found out by talking to the islanders. He found himself, according to his ideas, in the land of Topsyturvydom. Everything was upside down. He had wished to escape from dying. He had come to the land of Perpetual Life with great relief and joy, only to find that the inhabitants themselves, doomed never to die, would consider it bliss to find death.

What he had hitherto considered poison these people ate as good food, and all the things to which he had been accustomed as food they rejected. Whenever any merchants from other countries arrived, the rich people rushed to them eager to buy poisons. These they swallowed eagerly, hoping for death to come so that they might go to Paradise. But what were deadly poisons in other lands were without effect in this strange place, and people who swallowed them with the hope of dying, only found that in a short time they felt better in health instead of worse.

Vainly they tried to imagine what death could be like. The wealthy would have given all their money and all their goods if they could but shorten their lives to two or three hundred years even. Without any change to live on forever seemed to this people wearisome and sad.

In the chemist shops there was a drug which was in constant demand, because after using it for a hundred years, it was supposed to turn the hair slightly grey and to bring about disorders of the stomach.

Sentaro was astonished to find that the poisonous globe-fish was served up in restaurants as a delectable dish, and hawkers in the streets went about selling sauces made of Spanish flies. He never saw any one ill after eating these horrible things, nor did he ever see any one with as much as a cold.

Sentaro was delighted. He said to himself that he would never grow tired of living, and that he considered it profane to wish for death. He was the only happy man on the island. For his part he wished to live thousands of years and to enjoy life. He set himself up in business, and for the present never even dreamed of going back to his native land.

As years went by, however, things did not go as smoothly as at first. He had heavy losses in business, and several times some affairs went wrong with his neighbours. This caused him great annoyance.

Time passed like the flight of an arrow for him, for he was busy from morning till night. Three hundred years went by in this monotonous way, and then at last he began to grow tired of life in this country, and he longed to see his own land and his old home. However long he lived here, life would always be the same, so was it not foolish and wearisome to stay on here forever?

Sentaro, in his wish to escape from the country of Perpetual Life, recollected Jofuku, who had helped him before when he was wishing to escape from death—and he prayed to the saint to bring him back to his own land again.

No sooner did he pray than the paper crane popped out of his pocket. Sentaro was amazed to see that it had remained undamaged after all these years. Once more the bird grew and grew till it was large enough for him to mount it. As he did so, the bird spread its wings and flew, swiftly out across the sea in the direction of Japan.

Such was the willfulness of the man's nature that he looked back and regretted all he had left behind. He tried to stop the bird in vain. The crane held on its way for thousands of miles across the ocean.

Then a storm came on, and the wonderful paper crane got damp, crumpled up, and fell into the sea. Sentaro fell with it. Very much frightened at the thought of being drowned, he cried out loudly to Jofuku to save him. He looked round, but there was no ship in sight. He swallowed a quantity of sea-water, which only increased his miserable plight. While he was thus struggling to keep himself afloat, he saw a monstrous shark swimming towards him. As it came nearer it opened its huge mouth ready to devour him. Sentaro was all but paralysed with fear now that he felt his end so near, and screamed out as loudly as ever he could to Jofuku to come and rescue him.

Lo, and behold, Sentaro was awakened by his own screams, to find that during his long prayer he had fallen asleep before the shrine, and that all his extraordinary and frightful adventures had been only a wild dream. He was in a cold perspiration with fright, and utterly bewildered.

Suddenly a bright light came towards him, and in the light

stood a messenger. The messenger held a book in his hand, and spoke to Sentaro:

'I am sent to you by Jofuku, who in answer to your prayer, has permitted you in a dream to see the land of Perpetual Life. But you grew weary of living there, and begged to be allowed to return to your native land so that you might die. Jofuku, so that he might try you, allowed you to drop into the sea, and then sent a shark to swallow you up. Your desire for death was not real, for even at that moment you cried out loudly and shouted for help.'

'It is also vain for you to wish to become a hermit, or to find the Elixir of Life. These things are not for such as you—your life is not austere enough. It is best for you to go back to your paternal home, and to live a good and industrious life. Never neglect to keep the anniversaries of your ancestors, and make it your duty to provide for your children's future. Thus will you live to a good old age and be happy, but give up the vain desire to escape death, for no man can do that, and by this time you have surely found out that even when selfish desires are granted they do not bring happiness.'

'In this book I give you there are many precepts good for you to know—if you study them, you will be guided in the way I have pointed out to you.'

The angel disappeared as soon as he had finished speaking, and Sentaro took the lesson to heart. With the book in his hand he returned to his old home, and giving up all his old vain wishes, tried to live a good and useful life and to observe the lessons taught him in the book, and he and his house prospered henceforth.

THE GOBLIN OF ADACHIGAHARA

Long, long ago there was a large plain called Adachigahara, in the province of Mutsu in Japan. This place was said to be haunted by a cannibal goblin who took the form of an old woman. From time to time many travellers disappeared and were never heard of more, and the old women round the charcoal braziers in the evenings, and the girls washing the household rice at the wells in the mornings, whispered dreadful stories of how the missing folk had been lured to the goblin's cottage and devoured, for the goblin lived only on human flesh. No one dared to venture near the haunted spot after sunset, and all those who could, avoided it in the daytime, and travellers were warned of the dreaded place. One day as the sun was setting, a priest came to the plain. He was a belated traveller, and his robe showed that he was a Buddhist pilgrim walking from shrine to shrine to pray for some blessing or to crave for forgiveness of sins. He had apparently lost his way, and as it was late he met no one who could show him the road or warn him of the haunted spot.

He had walked the whole day and was now tired and hungry, and the evenings were chilly, for it was late autumn, and he began to be very anxious to find some house where he could obtain a night's lodging. He found himself lost in the midst of the large plain, and looked about in vain for some sign of human habitation.

At last, after wandering about for some hours, he saw a clump of trees in the distance, and through the trees he caught sight of the glimmer of a single ray of light. He exclaimed with joy:

'Oh. surely that is some cottage where I can get a night's lodging!'

Keeping the light before his eyes he dragged his weary, aching feet as quickly as he could towards the spot, and soon came to a miserable-looking little cottage. As he drew near he saw that it was in a tumble-down condition, the bamboo fence was broken and weeds and grass pushed their way through the gaps. The paper screens which serve as windows and doors in Japan were full of holes, and the posts of the house were bent with age and seemed scarcely able to support the old thatched roof. The hut was open, and by the light of an old lantern an old woman sat industriously spinning.

The pilgrim called to her across the bamboo fence and said:

'*O-baa-san* (old woman), good evening! I am a traveller! Please excuse me, but I have lost my way and do not know what to do, for I have nowhere to rest to-night. I beg you to be good enough to let me spend the night under your roof.'

The old woman as soon as she heard herself spoken to stopped spinning, rose from her seat and approached the intruder.

'I am very sorry for you. You must indeed be distressed to have lost your way in such a lonely spot so late at night. Unfortunately I cannot put you up, for I have no bed to offer you, and no accommodation whatsoever for a guest in this poor place!'

'Oh, that does not matter,' said the priest; 'all I want is a shelter under some roof for the night, and if you will be good enough just to let me lie on the kitchen floor I shall be grateful. I am too tired to walk further to-night, so I hope you will not refuse me, otherwise I shall have to sleep out on the cold plain.' And in this way he pressed the old woman to let him stay.

She seemed very reluctant, but at last she said:

'Very well, I will let you stay here. I can offer you a very poor welcome only, but come in now and I will make a fire, for the night is cold.'

The pilgrim was only too glad to do as he was told. He took off his sandals and entered the hut. The old woman then brought some sticks of wood and lit the fire, and bade her guest draw near and warm himself.

'You must be hungry after your long tramp,' said the old woman. 'I will go and cook some supper for you.' She then went to the kitchen to cook some rice.

After the priest had finished his supper the old woman sat down by the fire-place, and they talked together for a long time. The pilgrim thought to himself that he had been very lucky to come across such a kind, hospitable old woman. At last the wood gave out, and as the fire died slowly down he began to shiver with cold just as he had done when he arrived.

'I see you are cold,' said the old woman; 'I will go out and gather some wood, for we have used it all. You must stay and take care of the house while I am gone.'

'No, no,' said the pilgrim, 'let me go instead, for you are old, and I cannot think of letting you go out to get wood for me this cold night!'

The old woman shook her head and said:

'You must stay quietly here, for you are my guest.' Then she left him and went out.

In a minute she came back and said:

'You must sit where you are and not move, and whatever happens don't go near or look into the inner room. Now mind what I tell you!'

'If you tell me not to go near the back room, of course I won't,' said the priest, rather bewildered.

The old woman then went out again, and the priest was left alone. The fire had died out, and the only light in the hut was that of a dim lantern. For the first time that night he began to feel that he was in a weird place, and the old woman's words, 'Whatever you do don't peep into the back room,' aroused his curiosity and his fear.

What hidden thing could be in that room that she did not wish him to see? For some time the remembrance of his promise to the old woman kept him still, but at last he could no longer resist his curiosity to peep into the forbidden place.

He got up and began to move slowly towards the back room. Then the thought that the old woman would be very angry with him if he disobeyed her made him come back to his place by the fireside.

As the minutes went slowly by and the old woman did not return, he began to feel more and more frightened, and to wonder what dreadful secret was in the room behind him. He must find out.

'She will not know that I have looked unless I tell her. I will just have a peep before she comes back,' said the man to himself.

With these words he got up on his feet (for he had been sitting all this time in Japanese fashion with his feet under him) and stealthily crept towards the forbidden spot. With trembling hands he pushed back the sliding door and looked in. What he saw froze the blood in his veins. The room was full of dead men's bones and the walls were splashed and the floor was covered with human blood. In one corner skull upon skull rose to the ceiling, in another was a heap of arm bones, in another a heap of leg bones. The sickening smell made him faint. He fell backwards with horror, and for some time lay in a heap with fright on the floor, a pitiful sight. He trembled all over and his teeth chattered, and he could hardly crawl away from the dreadful spot.

'How horrible!' he cried out. 'What awful den have I come to in my travels? May Buddha help me or I am lost. Is it possible that that kind old woman is really the cannibal goblin? When she comes back she will show herself in her true character and eat me up at one mouthful!'

With these words his strength came back to him and, snatching up his hat and staff, he rushed out of the house as fast as his legs could carry him. Out into the night he ran, his one thought to get as far as he could from the goblin's haunt. He had not gone far when he heard steps behind him and a voice crying: 'Stop! stop!'

He ran on, redoubling his speed, pretending not to hear. As he ran he heard the steps behind him come nearer and nearer, and at last he recognized the old woman's voice which grew louder and louder as she came nearer.

'Stop! stop, you wicked man, why did you look into the forbidden room?'

The priest quite forgot how tired he was and his feet flew over the ground faster than ever. Fear gave him strength, for he knew that if the goblin caught him he would soon be one of her victims. With all his heart he repeated the prayer to Buddha:

'Namu Amida Butsu, Namu Amida Butsu.'

And after him rushed the dreadful old hag, her hair flying in the wind, and her face changing with rage into the demon that she was. In her hand she carried a large blood-stained knife, and she still shrieked after him, 'Stop! stop!'

At last, when the priest felt he could run no more, the dawn broke, and with the darkness of night the goblin vanished and he was safe. The priest now knew that he had met the Goblin of Adachigahara, the story of whom he had often heard but never believed to be true. He felt that he owed his wonderful escape to the protection of Buddha to whom he had prayed for help, so he took out his rosary and bowing his head as the sun rose he said his prayers and made his thanksgiving earnestly. He then set forward for another part of the country, only too glad to leave the haunted plain behind him.

THE SAGACIOUS MONKEY
AND THE BOAR

L ong, long ago, there lived in the province of Shinshin in
Japan, a traveling monkey-man, who earned his living by
taking round a monkey and showing off the animal's tricks.

One evening the man came home in a very bad temper
and told his wife to send for the butcher the next morning.

The wife was very bewildered and asked her husband:

'Why do you wish me to send for the butcher?'

'It's no use taking that monkey round any longer, he's too
old and forgets his tricks. I beat him with my stick all I know
how, but he won't dance properly. I must now sell him to the
butcher and make what money out of him I can. There is
nothing else to be done.'

The woman felt very sorry for the poor little animal, and
pleaded for her husband to spare the monkey, but her pleading
was all in vain, the man was determined to sell him to the
butcher.

Now the monkey was in the next room and overheard every
word of the conversation. He soon understood that he was to
be killed, and he said to himself:

'Barbarous, indeed, is my master! Here I have served him
faithfully for years, and instead of allowing me to end my days
comfortably and in peace, he is going to let me be cut up by
the butcher, and my poor body is to be roasted and stewed and

eaten? Woe is me! What am I to do. Ah! a bright thought has struck me! There is, I know, a wild boar living in the forest near by. I have often heard tell of his wisdom. Perhaps if I go to him and tell him the strait I am in he will give me his counsel. I will go and try.'

There was no time to lose. The monkey slipped out of the house and ran as quickly as he could to the forest to find the boar. The boar was at home, and the monkey began his tale of woe at once.

'Good Mr Boar, I have heard of your excellent wisdom. I am in great trouble, you alone can help me. I have grown old in the service of my master, and because I cannot dance properly now he intends to sell me to the butcher. What do you advise me to do? I know how clever you are!'

The boar was pleased at the flattery and determined to help the monkey. He thought for a little while and then said:

'Hasn't your master a baby?'

'Oh, yes,' said the monkey, 'he has one infant son.'

'Doesn't it lie by the door in the morning when your mistress begins the work of the day? Well, I will come round early and when I see my opportunity I will seize the child and run off with it.'

'What then?' said the monkey.

'Why the mother will be in a tremendous scare, and before your master and mistress know what to do, you must run after me and rescue the child and take it home safely to its parents, and you will see that when the butcher comes they won't have the heart to sell you.'

The monkey thanked the boar many times and then went home. He did not sleep much that night, as you may imagine, for thinking of the morrow. His life depended on whether the boar's plan succeeded or not. He was the first up, waiting anxiously for what was to happen. It seemed to him a very long time before his master's wife began to move about and open the shutters to let in the light of day. Then all happened as the boar had planned. The mother placed her child near the porch as usual while she tidied up the house and got her breakfast ready.

The child was crooning happily in the morning sunlight, dabbing on the mats at the play of light and shadow. Suddenly there was a noise in the porch and a loud cry from the child. The mother ran out from the kitchen to the spot, only just in time to see the boar disappearing through the gate with her child in its clutch. She flung out her hands with a loud cry of despair and rushed into the inner room where her husband was still sleeping soundly.

He sat up slowly and rubbed his eyes, and crossly demanded what his wife was making all that noise about. By the time that the man was alive to what had happened, and they both got outside the gate, the boar had got well away, but they saw the monkey running after the thief as hard as his legs would carry him.

Both the man and wife were moved to admiration at the plucky conduct of the sagacious monkey, and their gratitude knew no bounds when the faithful monkey brought the child safely back to their arms.

'There!' said the wife. 'This is the animal you want to kill— if the monkey hadn't been here we should have lost our child forever.'

'You are right, wife, for once,' said the man as he carried the child into the house. 'You may send the butcher back when he comes, and now give us all a good breakfast and the monkey too.'

When the butcher arrived he was sent away with an order for some boar's meat for the evening dinner, and the monkey was petted and lived the rest of his days in peace, nor did his master ever strike him again.

THE HAPPY HUNTER AND
THE SKILFUL FISHER

Long, long ago Japan was governed by Hohodemi, the fourth *Mikoto* (or Augustness) in descent from the illustrious Amaterasu, the Sun Goddess. He was not only as handsome as his ancestress was beautiful, but he was also very strong and brave, and was famous for being the greatest hunter in the land. Because of his matchless skill as a hunter, he was called '*Yama-sachi-hiko*' or 'The Happy Hunter of the Mountains.'

His elder brother was a very skilful fisher, and as he far surpassed all rivals in fishing, he was named '*Unii-sachi-hiko*' or the 'Skilful Fisher of the Sea.' The brothers thus led happy lives, thoroughly enjoying their respective occupations, and the days passed quickly and pleasantly while each pursued his own way, the one hunting and the other fishing.

One day the Happy Hunter came to his brother, the Skilful Fisher, and said:

'Well, my brother, I see you go to the sea every day with your fishing rod in your hand, and when you return you come laden with fish. And as for me, it is my pleasure to take my bow and arrow and to hunt the wild animals up the mountains and down in the valleys. For a long time we have each followed our favourite occupation, so that now we must both be tired, you of your fishing and I of my hunting. Would it not be wise for us to make a change? Will you try hunting in the mountains and I will go and fish in the sea?'

The Skilful Fisher listened in silence to his brother, and for a moment was thoughtful, but at last he answered:

'O yes, why not? Your idea is not a bad one at all. Give me your bow and arrow and I will set out at once for the mountains and hunt for game.'

So the matter was settled by this talk, and the two brothers each started out to try the other's occupation, little dreaming of all that would happen. It was very unwise of them, for the Happy Hunter knew nothing of fishing, and the Skilful Fisher, who was bad tempered, knew as much about hunting.

The Happy Hunter took his brother's much-prized fishing hook and rod and went down to the seashore and sat down on the rocks. He baited his hook and then threw it into the sea clumsily. He sat and gazed at the little float bobbing up and down in the water, and longed for a good fish to come and be caught. Every time the buoy moved a little he pulled up his rod, but there was never a fish at the end of it, only the hook and the bait. If he had known how to fish properly, he would have been able to catch plenty of fish, but although he was the greatest hunter in the land he could not help being the most bungling fisher.

The whole day passed in this way, while he sat on the rocks holding the fishing rod and waiting in vain for his luck to turn. At last the day began to darken, and the evening came; still he had caught not a single fish. Drawing up his line for the last time before going home, he found that he had lost his hook without even knowing when he had dropped it.

He now began to feel extremely anxious, for he knew that his brother would be angry at his having lost his hook, for, it being his only one, he valued it above all other things. The Happy Hunter now set to work to look among the rocks and on the sand for the lost hook, and while he was searching to and fro, his brother, the Skilful Fisher, arrived on the scene. He had failed to find any game while hunting that day, and was not only in a bad temper, but looked fearfully cross. When he saw the Happy Hunter searching about on the shore he knew that something must have gone wrong, so he said at once:

'What are you doing, my brother?'

The Happy Hunter went forward timidly, for he feared his brother's anger, and said:

'Oh, my brother, I have indeed done badly.'

'What is the matter?—what have you done?' asked the elder brother impatiently.

'I have lost your precious fishing hook—'

While he was still speaking his brother stopped him, and cried out fiercely:

'Lost my hook! It is just what I expected. For this reason, when you first proposed your plan of changing over our occupations I was really against it, but you seemed to wish it so much that I gave in and allowed you to do as you wished. The mistake of our trying unfamiliar tasks is soon seen! And you have done badly. I will not return you your bow and arrow till you have found my hook. Look to it that you find it and return it to me quickly.'

The Happy Hunter felt that he was to blame for all that had come to pass, and bore his brother's scornful scolding with humility and patience. He hunted everywhere for the hook most diligently, but it was nowhere to be found. He was at last obliged to give up all hope of finding it. He then went home, and in desperation broke his beloved sword into pieces and made five hundred hooks out of it.

He took these to his angry brother and offered them to him, asking his forgiveness, and begging him to accept them in the place of the one he had lost for him. It was useless; his brother would not listen to him, much less grant his request.

The Happy Hunter then made another five hundred hooks, and again took them to his brother, beseeching him to pardon him.

'Though you make a million hooks,' said the Skilful Fisher, shaking his head, 'they are of no use to me. I cannot forgive you unless you bring me back my own hook.'

Nothing would appease the anger of the Skilful Fisher, for he had a bad disposition, and had always hated his brother because of his virtues, and now with the excuse of the lost fishing hook he planned to kill him and to usurp his place as ruler of Japan. The Happy Hunter knew all this full well, but he could say nothing, for being the younger he owed his elder brother obedience; so he returned to the seashore and once more began to look for the missing hook. He was much cast down, for he had lost all hope of ever finding his brother's hook now. While he stood on the beach, lost in perplexity and wondering what he had best do next, an old man suddenly appeared carrying a stick in his hand. The Happy Hunter afterwards remembered that he did not see from whence the old man came, neither did he know how he was there—he happened to look up and saw the old man coming towards him.

'You are Hohodemi, the Augustness, sometimes called the Happy Hunter, are you not?' asked the old man. 'What are you doing alone in such a place?'

'Yes, I am he,' answered the unhappy young man. 'Unfortunately, while fishing I lost my brother's precious fishing hook. I have hunted this shore all over, but alas! I cannot find it, and I am very troubled, for my brother won't forgive me till I restore it to him. But who are you?'

'My name is Shiwozuchino Okina, and I live near by on

this shore. I am sorry to hear what misfortune has befallen you. You must indeed be anxious. But if I tell you what I think, the hook is nowhere here—it is either at the bottom of the sea or in the body of some fish who has swallowed it, and for this reason, though you spend your whole life in looking for it here, you will never find it.'

'Then what can I do?' asked the distressed man.

'You had better go down to Riu Gu and tell Riu Jin, the Dragon King of the Sea, what your trouble is and ask him to find the hook for you. I think that would be the best way.'

'Your idea is a splendid one,' said the Happy Hunter, 'but I fear I cannot get to the Sea King's realm, for I have always heard that it is situated at the bottom of the sea.'

'Oh, there will be no difficulty about your getting there,' said the old man; 'I can soon make something for you to ride on through the sea.'

'Thank you,' said the Happy Hunter, 'I shall be very grateful to you if you will be so kind.'

The old man at once set to work, and soon made a basket and offered it to the Happy Hunter. He received it with joy, and taking it to the water, mounted it, and prepared to start. He bade good by to the kind old man who had helped him so much, and told him that he would certainly reward him as soon as he found his hook and could return to Japan without fear of his brother's anger. The old man pointed out the direction he must take, and told him how to reach the realm of Riu Gu, and watched him ride out to sea on the basket, which resembled a small boat.

The Happy Hunter made all the haste he could, riding on the basket which had been given him by his friend. His queer boat seemed to go through the water of its own accord, and the distance was much shorter than he had expected, for in a few hours he caught sight of the gate and the roof of the Sea King's palace. And what a large place it was, with its numberless sloping roofs and gables, its huge gateways, and its grey stone walls! He soon landed, and leaving his basket on the beach, he walked up to the large gateway. The pillars of the gate were made of beautiful red coral, and the gate itself was adorned with glittering gems of all kinds. Large katsura trees overshadowed it. Our hero had often heard of the wonders of the Sea King's palace beneath the sea, but all the stories he had ever heard fell short of the reality which he now saw for the first time.

The Happy Hunter would have liked to enter the gate there and then, but he saw that it was fast closed, and also that there was no one about whom he could ask to open it for him, so he stopped to think what he should do. In the shade of the trees before the gate he noticed a well full of fresh spring water. Surely some one would come out to draw water from the well some time, he thought. Then he climbed into the tree overhanging the well, and seated himself to rest on one of the branches, and waited for what might happen. Ere long he saw the huge gate swing open, and two beautiful women came out. Now the Mikoto (Augustness) had always heard that Riu Gu was the realm of the Dragon King Under the Sea, and had naturally supposed that the place was inhabited by dragons and similar terrible creatures, so that when he saw these two lovely princesses, whose beauty would be rare even in the world from which he had just come, he was exceedingly surprised, and wondered what it could mean.

He said not a word, however, but silently gazed at them through the foliage of the trees, waiting to see what they would do. He saw that in their hands they carried golden buckets. Slowly and gracefully in their trailing garments they approached the well, standing in the shade of the katsura trees, and were about to draw water, all unknowing of the stranger who was watching them, for the Happy Hunter was quite hidden among the branches of the tree where he had posted himself.

As the two ladies leaned over the side of the well to let down their golden buckets, which they did every day in the year, they saw reflected in the deep still water the face of a handsome youth gazing at them from amidst the branches of the tree in whose shade they stood. Never before had they seen the face of mortal man; they were frightened, and drew back quickly with their golden buckets in their hands. Their curiosity, however, soon gave them courage, and they glanced timidly upwards to see the cause of the unusual reflection, and then they beheld the Happy Hunter sitting in the tree looking down at them with surprise and admiration. They gazed at him face to face, but their tongues were still with wonder and could not find a word to say to him.

When the Mikoto saw that he was discovered, he sprang down lightly from the tree and said:

'I am a traveller, and as I was very thirsty I came to the well in the hopes of quenching my thirst, but I could find no bucket with which to draw the water. So I climbed into the tree, much vexed, and waited for some one to come. Just at that moment, while I was thirstily and impatiently waiting, you noble ladies appeared, as if in answer to my great need. Therefore I pray you of your mercy give me some water to drink, for I am a thirsty traveller in a strange land.'

His dignity and graciousness overruled their timidity, and bowing in silence they both once more approached the well, and letting down their golden buckets drew up some water and poured it into a jewelled cup and offered it to the stranger.

He received it from them with both hands, raising it to the height of his forehead in token of high respect and pleasure, and then drank the water quickly, for his thirst was great. When he had finished his long draught he set the cup down on the edge of the well, and drawing his short sword he cut off one of the strange curved jewels (*magatama*), a necklace of which hung round his neck and fell over his breast. He placed the jewel in the cup and returned it to them, and said, bowing deeply:

'This is a token of my thanks!'

The two ladies took the cup, and looking into it to see what he had put inside—for they did not yet know what it was—they gave a start of surprise, for there lay a beautiful gem at the bottom of the cup.

'No ordinary mortal would give away a jewel so freely. Will you not honour us by telling us who you are?' said the elder damsel.

'Certainly,' said the Happy Hunter, 'I am Hohodemi, the fourth Mikoto, also called in Japan, the Happy Hunter.'

'Are you indeed Hohodemi, the grandson of Amaterasu, the Sun Goddess?' asked the damsel who had spoken first. 'I am the eldest daughter of Riu Jin, the King of the Sea, and my name is Princess Tayotama.'

'And,' said the younger maiden, who at last found her tongue, 'I am her sister, the Princess Tamayori.'

'Are you indeed the daughters of Riu Jin, the King of the Sea? I cannot tell you how glad I am to meet you,' said the Happy Hunter. And without waiting for them to reply he went on:

'The other day I went fishing with my brother's hook and dropped it, how, I am sure I can't tell. As my brother prizes his fishing hook above all his other possessions, this is the greatest calamity that could have befallen me. Unless I find it again I can never hope to win my brother's forgiveness, for he is very angry at what I have done. I have searched for it many, many times, but I cannot find it, therefore I am much troubled. While I was hunting for the hook, in great distress, I met a wise old man, and he told me that the best thing I could do was to come to Riu Gu, and to Riu Jin, the Dragon King of the Sea, and ask him to help me. This kind old man also showed me how to come. Now you know how it is I am here and why. I want to ask Riu Jin, if he knows where the lost hook is. Will you be so kind as to take me to your father? And do you think he will see me?' asked the Happy Hunter anxiously.

Princess Tayotama listened to this long story, and then said:

'Not only is it easy for you to see my father, but he will be much pleased to meet you. I am sure he will say that good fortune has befallen him, that so great and noble a man as you, the grandson of Amaterasu, should come down to the bottom of the sea.' And then turning to her younger sister, she said:

'Do you not think so, Tamayori?'

'Yes, indeed,' answered the Princess Tamayori, in her sweet voice. 'As you say, we can know no greater honour than to welcome the Mikoto to our home.'

'Then I ask you to be so kind as to lead the way,' said the Happy Hunter.

'Condescend to enter, Mikoto (Augustness),' said both the sisters, and bowing low, they led him through the gate.

The younger princess left her sister to take charge of the Happy Hunter, and going faster than they, she reached the Sea King's palace first, and running quickly to her father's room, she told him of all that had happened to them at the gate, and that her sister was even now bringing the Augustness to him. The Dragon King of the Sea was much surprised at the news, for it was but seldom, perhaps only once in several hundred years, that the Sea King's palace was visited by mortals.

Riu Jin at once clapped his hands and summoned all his

courtiers and the servants of the palace, and the chief fish of the sea together, and solemnly told them that the grandson of the Sun Goddess, Amaterasu, was coming to the palace, and that they must be very ceremonious and polite in serving the august visitor. He then ordered them all to the entrance of the palace to welcome the Happy Hunter.

Riu Jin then dressed himself in his robes of ceremony, and went out to welcome him. In a few moments the Princess Tayotama and the Happy Hunter reached the entrance, and the Sea King and his wife bowed to the ground and thanked him for the honour he did them in coming to see them. The Sea King then led the Happy Hunter to the guest room, and placing him in the uppermost seat, he bowed respectfully before him, and said:

'I am Riu Jin, the Dragon King of the Sea, and this is my wife. Condescend to remember us forever!'

'Are you indeed Riu Jin, the King of the Sea, of whom I have so often heard?' answered the Happy Hunter, saluting his host most ceremoniously. 'I must apologize for all the trouble I am giving you by my unexpected visit.' And he bowed again, and thanked the Sea King.

'You need not thank me,' said Riu Jin. 'It is I who must thank you for coming. Although the Sea Palace is a poor place, as you see, I shall be highly honoured if you will make us a long visit.'

There was much gladness between the Sea King and the Happy Hunter, and they sat and talked for a long time. At last the Sea King clapped his hands, and then a huge retinue of fishes appeared, all robed in ceremonial garments, and bearing in their fins various trays on which all kinds of sea delicacies were served. A great feast was now spread before the king and his royal guest. All the fishes-in-waiting were chosen from amongst the finest fish in the sea, so you can imagine what a wonderful array of sea creatures it was that waited upon the Happy Hunter that day. All in the palace tried to do their best to please him and to show him that he was a much honoured guest. During the long repast, which lasted for hours, Riu Jin commanded his daughters to play some music, and the two princesses came in and performed on the koto (the Japanese harp), and sang and danced in turns. The time passed so pleasantly that the Happy Hunter seemed to forget his trouble and why he had come at all to the Sea King's Realm, and he gave himself up to the enjoyment of this wonderful place, the land of fairy fishes! Who has ever heard of such a marvellous place? But the Mikoto soon remembered what had brought him to Riu Gu, and said to his host:

'Perhaps your daughters have told you, King Riu Jin, that I have come here to try and recover my brother's fishing hook, which I lost while fishing the other day. May I ask you to be so kind as to inquire of all your subjects if any of them have seen a fishing hook lost in the sea?'

'Certainly,' said the obliging Sea King, 'I will immediately summon them all here and ask them.'

As soon as he had issued his command, the octopus, the cuttlefish, the bonito, the oxtail fish, the eel, the jellyfish, the shrimp, and the plaice, and many other fishes of all kinds came in and sat down before Riu Jin their king, and arranged themselves and their fins in order. Then the Sea King said solemnly:

'Our visitor who is sitting before you all is the august grandson of Amaterasu. His name is Hohodemi, the fourth Augustness, and he is also called the Happy Hunter of the Mountains. While he was fishing the other day upon the shore of Japan, some one robbed him of his brother's fishing hook. He has come all this way down to the bottom of the sea to our kingdom because he thought that one of you fishes may have taken the hook from him in mischievous play. If any of you have done so you must immediately return it, or if any of you know who the thief is you must at once tell us his name and where he is now.'

All the fishes were taken by surprise when they heard these words, and could say nothing for some time. They sat looking at each other and at the Dragon King. At last the cuttlefish came forward and said:

'I think the *tai* (the red bream) must be the thief who has stolen the hook!'

'Where is your proof?' asked the king.

'Since yesterday evening the tai has not been able to eat anything, and he seems to be suffering from a bad throat! For this reason I think the hook may be in his throat. You had better send for him at once!'

All the fish agreed to this, and said: 'It is certainly strange that the tai is the only fish who has not obeyed your summons. Will you send for him and inquire into the matter. Then our innocence will be proved.'

'Yes,' said the Sea King, 'it is strange that the tai has not come, for he ought to be the first to be here. Send for him at once!'

Without waiting for the king's order the cuttlefish had already started for the tai's dwelling, and he now returned, bringing the tai with him. He led him before the king.

The tai sat there looking frightened and ill. He certainly was in pain, for his usually red face was pale, and his eyes were nearly closed and looked but half their usual size.

'Answer, O tai!' cried the Sea King, 'why did you not come in answer to my summons today?'

'I have been ill since yesterday,' answered the tai; 'that is why I could not come.'

'Don't say another word!' cried out Riu Jin angrily. 'Your illness is the punishment of the gods for stealing the Mikoto's hook.'

'It is only too true!' said the tai; 'the hook is still in my throat, and all my efforts to get it out have been useless. I can't eat, and I can scarcely breathe, and each moment I feel that it will choke me, and sometimes it gives me great pain. I had no intention of stealing the Mikoto's hook. I heedlessly snapped at the bait which I saw in the water, and the hook came off and stuck in my throat. So I hope you will pardon me.'

The cuttlefish now came forward, and said to the king:

'What I said was right. You see the hook still sticks in the tai's throat. I hope to be able to pull it out in the presence of the Mikoto, and then we can return it to him safely!'

'O please make haste and pull it out!' cried the tai, pitifully, for he felt the pains in his throat coming on again; 'I do so want to return the hook to the Mikoto.'

'All right, Tai-san,' said his friend the cuttlefish, and then opening the tai's mouth as wide as he could and putting one of his feelers down the tai's throat, he quickly and easily drew the hook out of the sufferer's large mouth. He then washed it and brought it to the king.

Riu Jin took the hook from his subject, and then respectfully returned it to the Happy Hunter (the Mikoto or Augustness, the fishes called him), who was overjoyed at getting back his hook. He thanked Riu Jin many times, his face beaming with gratitude, and said that he owed the happy ending of his quest to the Sea King's wise authority and kindness.

Riu Jin now desired to punish the tai, but the Happy Hunter begged him not to do so; since his lost hook was thus happily recovered he did not wish to make more trouble for the poor tai. It was indeed the tai who had taken the hook, but he had already suffered enough for his fault, if fault it could be called. What had been done was done in heedlessness and not by intention. The Happy Hunter said he blamed himself; if he had understood how to fish properly he would never have lost his hook, and therefore all this trouble had been caused in the first place by his trying to do something which he did not know how to do. So he begged the Sea King to forgive his subject.

Who could resist the pleading of so wise and compassionate a judge? Riu Jin forgave his subject at once at the request of his august guest. The tai was so glad that he shook his fins for joy, and he and all the other fish went out from the presence of their king, praising the virtues of the Happy Hunter. Now that the hook was found the Happy Hunter had nothing to keep him in Riu Gu, and he was anxious to get back to his own kingdom and to make peace with his angry brother, the Skilful Fisher; but the Sea King, who had learnt to love him and would fain have kept him as a son, begged him not to go so soon, but to make the Sea Palace his home as long as ever he liked. While the Happy Hunter was still hesitating, the two lovely princesses, Tayotama and Tamayori, came, and with the sweetest of bows and voices joined with their father in pressing him to stay, so that without seeming ungracious he could not say them 'Nay,' and was obliged to stay on for some time.

Between the Sea Realm and the Earth there was no difference in the night of time, and the Happy Hunter found that three years went fleeting quickly by in this delightful land. The years pass swiftly when any one is truly happy. But though the wonders of that enchanted land seemed to be new every day, and though the Sea King's kindness seemed rather to increase than to grow less with time, the Happy Hunter grew more and more homesick as the days passed, and he could not repress a great anxiety to know what had happened to his home and his country and his brother while he had been away.

So at last he went to the Sea King and said:

'My stay with you here has been most happy and I am very grateful to you for all your kindness to me, but I govern Japan, and, delightful as this place is, I cannot absent myself forever from my country. I must also return the fishing hook to my brother and ask his forgiveness for having deprived him of it for so long. I am indeed very sorry to part from you, but this time it cannot be helped. With your gracious permission, I will take my leave to-day. I hope to make you another visit some day. Please give up the idea of my staying longer now.'

King Riu Jin was overcome with sorrow at the thought that he must lose his friend who had made a great diversion in the Palace of the Sea, and his tears fell fast as he answered:

'We are indeed very sorry to part with you, Mikoto, for we have enjoyed your stay with us very much. You have been a noble and honoured guest and we have heartily made you welcome. I quite understand that as you govern Japan you ought to be there and not here, and that it is vain for us to try and keep you longer with us, much as we would like to have you stay. I hope you will not forget us. Strange circumstances have brought us together and I trust the friendship thus begun between the Land and the Sea will last and grow stronger than it has ever been before.'

When the Sea King had finished speaking he turned to his two daughters and bade them bring him the two Tide-Jewels of the Sea. The two princesses bowed low, rose and glided out of the hall. In a few minutes they returned, each one carrying in her hands a flashing gem which filled the room with light. As the Happy Hunter looked at them he wondered what they could be. The Sea King took them from his daughters and said to his guest:

'These two valuable talismans we have inherited from our ancestors from time immemorial. We now give them to you as a parting gift in token of our great affection for you. These two gems are called the *nanjiu* and the *kanjiu*.'

The Happy Hunter bowed low to the ground and said:

'I can never thank you enough for all your kindness to me. And now will you add one more favour to the rest and tell me what these jewels are and what I am to do with them?'

'The nanjiu,' answered the Sea King, 'is also called the Jewel of the Flood Tide, and whoever holds it in his possession can command the sea to roll in and to flood the land at any time that he wills. The kanjiu is also called the Jewel of the Ebbing Tide, and this gem controls the sea and the waves thereof, and will cause even a tidal wave to recede.'

Then Riu Jin showed his friend how to use the talismans one by one and handed them to him. The Happy Hunter was very glad to have these two wonderful gems, the Jewel of the Flood Tide and the Jewel of the Ebbing Tide, to take back with him, for he felt that they would preserve him in case of danger from enemies at any time. After thanking his kind host again and again, he prepared to depart. The Sea King and the two princesses, Tayotama and Tamayori, and all the inmates of the palace, came out to say 'Good-by,' and before the sound of the last farewell had died away the Happy Hunter passed out from under the gateway, past the well of happy memory standing in the shade of the great katsura trees on his way to the beach.

Here he found, instead of the queer basket on which he had come to the Realm of Riu Gu, a large crocodile waiting for him. Never had he seen such a huge creature. It measured eight fathoms in length from the tip of its tail to the end of its long mouth. The Sea King had ordered the monster to carry the Happy Hunter back to Japan. Like the wonderful basket which Shiwozuchino Okina had made, it could travel faster than any steamboat, and in this strange way, riding on the back of a crocodile, the Happy Hunter returned to his own land.

As soon as the crocodile landed him, the Happy Hunter hastened to tell the Skilful Fisher of his safe return. He then gave him back the fishing hook which had been found in the mouth of the tai and which had been the cause of so much trouble between them. He earnestly begged his brother's forgiveness, telling him all that had happened to him in the Sea King's palace and what wonderful adventures had led to the finding of the hook.

Now the Skilful Fisher had used the lost hook as an excuse for driving his brother out of the country. When his brother had left him that day three years ago, and had not returned, he had been very glad in his evil heart and had at once usurped his brother's place as ruler of the land, and had become powerful and rich. Now in the midst of enjoying what did not belong to him, and hoping that his brother might never return to claim his rights, quite unexpectedly there stood the Happy Hunter before him.

The Skilful Fisher feigned forgiveness, for he could make no more excuses for sending his brother away again, but in his heart he was very angry and hated his brother more and more, till at last he could no longer bear the sight of him day after day, and planned and watched for an opportunity to kill him.

One day when the Happy Hunter was walking in the rice fields his brother followed him with a dagger. The Happy Hunter knew that his brother was following him to kill him, and he felt that now, in this hour of great danger, was the time to use the Jewels of the Flow and Ebb of the Tide and prove whether what the Sea King had told him was true or not.

So he took out the Jewel of the Flood Tide from the bosom of his dress and raised it to his forehead. Instantly over the fields and over the farms the sea came rolling in wave upon wave till it reached the spot where his brother was standing. The Skilful Fisher stood amazed and terrified to see what was happening. In another minute he was struggling in the water and calling on his brother to save him from drowning.

The Happy Hunter had a kind heart and could not bear the sight of his brother's distress. He at once put back the Jewel of the Flood Tide and took out the Jewel of the Ebb Tide. No sooner did he hold it up as high as his forehead than the sea ran back and back, and ere long the tossing rolling floods had vanished, and the farms and fields and dry land appeared as before.

The Skilful Fisher was very frightened at the peril of death in which he had stood, and was greatly impressed by the wonderful things he had seen his brother do. He learned now that he was making a fatal mistake to set himself against his brother, younger than he thought he was, for he now had become so powerful that the sea would flow in and the tide ebb at his word of command. So he humbled himself before the Happy Hunter and asked him to forgive him all the wrong he had done him. The Skilful Fisher promised to restore his brother to his rights and also swore that though the Happy Hunter was the younger brother and owed him allegiance by right of birth, that he, the Skilful Fisher, would exalt him as his superior and bow before him as Lord of all Japan.

Then the Happy Hunter said that he would forgive his brother if he would throw into the receding tide all his evil ways. The Skilful Fisher promised and there was peace between the two brothers. From this time he kept his word and became a good man and a kind brother.

The Happy Hunter now ruled his kingdom without being disturbed by family strife, and there was peace in Japan for a long, long time. Above all the treasures in his house he prized the wonderful Jewels of the Flow and Ebb of the Tide which had been given him by Riu Jin, the Dragon King of the Sea.

This is the congratulatory ending of the Happy Hunter and the Skilful Fisher.

THE STORY OF THE OLD MAN WHO MADE WITHERED TREES TO FLOWER

Long, long ago there lived an old man and his wife who supported themselves by cultivating a small plot of land. Their life had been a very happy and peaceful one save for one great sorrow, and this was they had no child. Their only pet was a dog named Shiro, and on him they lavished all the affection of their old age. Indeed, they loved him so much that whenever they had anything nice to eat they denied themselves to give it to Shiro. Now Shiro means 'white,' and he was so called because of his colour. He was a real Japanese dog, and very like a small wolf in appearance.

The happiest hour of the day both for the old man and his dog was when the man returned from his work in the field, and having finished his frugal supper of rice and vegetables, would take what he had saved from the meal out to the little veranda that ran round the cottage. Sure enough, Shiro was waiting for his master and the evening tit-bit. Then the old man said 'Chin, chin!' and Shiro sat up and begged, and his master gave him the food. Next door to this good old couple there lived another old man and his wife who were both wicked and cruel, and who hated their good neighbours and the dog Shiro with all their might. Whenever Shiro happened to look into their kitchen they at once kicked him or threw something at him, sometimes even wounding him.

One day Shiro was heard barking for a long time in the field at the back of his master's house. The old man, thinking that perhaps some birds were attacking the corn, hurried out to see what was the matter. As soon as Shiro saw his master he ran to meet him, wagging his tail, and, seizing the end of his kimono, dragged him under a large yenoki tree. Here he began to dig very industriously with his paws, yelping with joy all the time. The old man, unable to understand what it all meant, stood looking on in bewilderment. But Shiro went on barking and digging with all his might. The thought that something might be hidden beneath the tree, and that the dog had scented it, at last struck the old man. He ran back to the house, fetched his spade and began to dig the ground at that spot. What was his astonishment when, after digging for some time, he came upon a heap of old and valuable coins, and the deeper he dug the more gold coins did he find. So intent was the old man on his work that he never saw the cross face of his neighbour peering at him through the bamboo hedge. At last all the gold coins lay shining on the ground. Shiro sat by erect with pride and looking fondly at his master as if to say, 'You see, though only a dog, I can make some return for all the kindness you show me.'

The old man ran in to call his wife, and together they carried home the treasure. Thus in one day the poor old man became rich. His gratitude to the faithful dog knew no bounds, and he loved and petted him more than ever, if that were possible.

The cross old neighbour, attracted by Shiro's barking, had been an unseen and envious witness of the finding of the treasure. He began to think that he, too, would like to find a fortune. So a few days later he called at the old man's house and very ceremoniously asked permission to borrow Shiro for a short time.

Shiro's master thought this a strange request, because he knew quite well that not only did his neighbour not love his pet dog, but that he never lost an opportunity of striking and tormenting him whenever the dog crossed his path. But the good old man was too kind-hearted to refuse his neighbour, so he consented to lend the dog on condition that he should be taken great care of.

The wicked old man returned to his home with an evil smile on his face, and told his wife how he had succeeded in his crafty intentions. He then took his spade and hastened to his own field, forcing the unwilling Shiro to follow him. As soon as he reached a yenoki tree, he said to the dog, threateningly:

'If there were gold coins under your master's tree, there must also be gold coins under my tree. You must find them for me! Where are they? Where? Where?'

And catching hold of Shiro's neck he held the dog's head to the ground, so that Shiro began to scratch and dig in order to free himself from the horrid old man's grasp.

The old man was very pleased when he saw the dog begin to scratch and dig, for he at once supposed that some gold coins lay buried under his tree as well as under his neighbour's, and that the dog had scented them as before; so pushing Shiro away he began to dig himself, but there was nothing to be found. As he went on digging a foul smell was noticeable, and he at last came upon a refuse heap.

The old man's disgust can be imagined. This soon gave way to anger. He had seen his neighbour's good fortune, and hoping for the same luck himself, he had borrowed the dog Shiro; and now, just as he seemed on the point of finding what he sought, only a horrid smelling refuse heap had rewarded him for a morning's digging. Instead of blaming his own greed for his disappointment, he blamed the poor dog. He seized his spade, and with all his strength struck Shiro and killed him on the spot. He then threw the dog's body into the hole which he had dug in the hope of finding a treasure of gold coins, and covered it over with the earth. Then he returned to the house, telling no one, not even his wife, what he had done.

After waiting several days, as the dog Shiro did not return, his master began to grow anxious. Day after day went by and the good old man waited in vain. Then he went to his neighbour and asked him to give him back his dog. Without any shame or hesitation, the wicked neighbour answered that he had killed Shiro because of his bad behavior. At this dreadful news Shiro's master wept many sad and bitter tears. Great indeed, was his woeful surprise, but he was too good and gentle to reproach his bad neighbour. Learning that Shiro was buried under the yenoki tree in the field, he asked the old man to give him the tree, in remembrance of his poor dog Shiro.

Even the cross old neighbour could not refuse such a simple request, so he consented to give the old man the tree under which Shiro lay buried. Shiro's master then cut the tree down and carried it home. Out of the trunk he made a mortar. In this his wife put some rice, and he began to pound it with the intention of making a festival to the memory of his dog Shiro.

A strange thing happened! His wife put the rice into the mortar, and no sooner had he begun to pound it to make the cakes, than it began to increase in quantity gradually till it was about five times the original amount, and the cakes were turned out of the mortar as if an invisible hand were at work.

When the old man and his wife saw this, they understood that it was a reward to them from Shiro for their faithful love to him. They tasted the cakes and found them nicer than any other food. So from this time they never troubled about food, for they lived upon the cakes with which the mortar never ceased to supply them.

The greedy neighbour, hearing of this new piece of good luck, was filled with envy as before, and called on the old man and asked leave to borrow the wonderful mortar for a short time, pretending that he, too, sorrowed for the death of Shiro, and wished to make cakes for a festival to the dog's memory.

The old man did not in the least wish to lend it to his cruel neighbour, but he was too kind to refuse. So the envious man carried home the mortar, but he never brought it back.

Several days passed, and Shiro's master waited in vain for the mortar, so he went to call on the borrower, and asked him to be good enough to return the mortar if he had finished with it. He found him sitting by a big fire made of pieces of wood. On the ground lay what looked very much like pieces of a broken mortar. In answer to the old man's inquiry, the wicked neighbour answered haughtily:

'Have you come to ask me for your mortar? I broke it to pieces, and now I am making a fire of the wood, for when I tried to pound cakes in it only some horrid smelling stuff came out.'

The good old man said:

'I am very sorry for that. It is a great pity you did not ask me for the cakes if you wanted them. I would have given you as many as ever you wanted. Now please give me the ashes of the mortar, as I wish to keep them in remembrance of my dog.'

The neighbour consented at once, and the old man carried home a basket full of ashes.

Not long after this the old man accidentally scattered some of the ashes made by the burning of the mortar on the trees of his garden. A wonderful thing happened!

It was late in autumn and all the trees had shed their leaves, but no sooner did the ashes touch their branches than the cherry trees, the plum trees and all other blossoming shrubs burst into bloom, so that the old man's garden was suddenly transformed into a beautiful picture of spring. The old man's delight knew no bounds, and he carefully preserved the remaining ashes. The story of the old man's garden spread far and wide, and people from far and near came to see the wonderful sight.

One day, soon after this, the old man heard some one knocking at his door, and going to the porch to see who it was he was surprised to see a knight standing there. This knight told him that he was a retainer of a great daimio (Earl); that one of the favourite cherry trees in this nobleman's garden had withered, and that though every one in his service had tried all manner of means to revive it, none took effect. The knight was sore perplexed when he saw what great displeasure the loss of his favourite cherry tree caused the daimio. At this point, fortunately, they had heard that there was a wonderful old man who could make withered trees to blossom, and that his Lord had sent him to ask the old man to come to him.

'And,' added the knight, 'I shall be very much obliged if you will come at once.'

The good old man was greatly surprised at what he heard, but respectfully followed the knight to the nobleman's palace.

The daimio, who had been impatiently awaiting the old man's coming, as soon as he saw him asked him at once:

'Are you the old man who can make withered trees flower even out of season?'

The old man made an obeisance, and replied:

'I am that old man!'

Then the daimio said:

'You must make that dead cherry tree in my garden blossom again by means of your famous ashes. I shall look on.'

Then they all went into the garden—the daimio and his retainers and the ladies-in waiting, who carried the daimio's sword.

The old man now tucked up his kimono and made ready to climb the tree. Saying 'Excuse me,' he took the pot of ashes which he had brought with him, and began to climb the tree, every one watching his movements with great interest.

At last he climbed to the spot where the tree divided into two great branches, and taking up his position here, the old man sat down and scattered the ashes right and left all over the branches and twigs.

Wonderful, indeed, was the result! The withered tree at once burst into full bloom! The daimio was so transported with joy that he looked as if he would go mad. He rose to his feet and spread out his fan, calling the old man down from the tree. He himself gave the old man a wine cup filled with the best *saké*, and rewarded him with much silver and gold and many other precious things. The daimio ordered that henceforth the old man should call himself by the name of *Hana-Saka-Jijii*, or 'The Old Man who makes the Trees to Blossom,' and that henceforth all were to recognize him by this name, and he sent him home with great honour.

The wicked neighbour, as before, heard of the good old man's fortune, and of all that had so auspiciously befallen him, and he could not suppress all the envy and jealousy that filled his heart. He called to mind how he had failed in his attempt to find the gold coins, and then in making the magic cakes; this time surely he must succeed if he imitated the old man, who made withered trees to flower simply by sprinkling ashes on them. This would be the simplest task of all.

So he set to work and gathered together all the ashes which remained in the fire-place from the burning of the wonderful mortar. Then he set out in the hope of finding some great man to employ him, calling out loudly as he went along:

'Here comes the wonderful man who can make withered trees blossom! Here comes the old man who can make dead trees blossom!'

The daimio in his palace heard this cry, and said:

'That must be the Hana-Saka-Jijii passing. I have nothing to do to-day. Let him try his art again; it will amuse me to look on.'

So the retainers went out and brought in the impostor before their Lord. The satisfaction of false old man can now be imagined.

But the daimio looking at him, thought it strange that he was not at all like the old man he had seen before, so he asked him:

'Are you the man whom I named Hana-Saka-Jijii?'

And the envious neighbour answered with a lie:

'Yes, my Lord!'

'That is strange!' said the daimio. 'I thought there was only one Hana-Saka-Jijii in the world! Has he now some disciples?'

'I am the true Hana-Saka-Jijii. The one who came to you before was only my disciple!' replied the old man again.

'Then you must be more skilful than the other. Try what you can do and let me see!'

The envious neighbour, with the daimio and his court following, then went into the garden, and approaching a dead tree, took out a handful of the ashes which he carried with him, and scattered them over the tree.

But not only did the tree not burst into flower, but not even a bud came forth. Thinking that he had not used enough ashes, the old man took handfuls and again sprinkled them over the withered tree. But all to no effect. After trying several times, the ashes were blown into the daimio's eyes. This made him very angry, and he ordered his retainers to arrest the false Hana-Saka-Jijii at once and put him in prison for an impostor. From this imprisonment the wicked old man was never freed. Thus did he meet with punishment at last for all his evil doings.

The good old man, however, with the treasure of gold coins which Shiro had found for him, and with all the gold and the silver which the daimio had showered on him, became a rich and prosperous man in his old age, and lived a long and happy life, beloved and respected by all.

THE WHITE HARE AND
THE CROCODILES

Long, long ago, when all the animals could talk, there lived in the province of Inaba in Japan, a little white hare. His home was on the island of Oki, and just across the sea was the mainland of Inaba.

Now the hare wanted very much to cross over to Inaba. Day after day he would go out and sit on the shore and look longingly over the water in the direction of Inaba, and day after day he hoped to find some way of getting across.

One day as usual, the hare was standing on the beach, looking towards the mainland across the water, when he saw a great crocodile swimming near the island.

'This is very lucky!' thought the hare. 'Now I shall be able to get my wish. I will ask the crocodile to carry me across the sea!'

But he was doubtful whether the crocodile would consent to do what he wanted. So he thought instead of asking a favour he would try to get what he wanted by a trick.

So with a loud voice he called to the crocodile, and said:

'Oh, Mr Crocodile, isn't it a lovely day?'

The crocodile, who had come out all by itself that day to enjoy the bright sunshine, was just beginning to feel a bit lonely when the hare's cheerful greeting broke the silence. The crocodile swam nearer the shore, very pleased to hear some one speak.

'I wonder who it was that spoke to me just now! Was it you, Mr Hare? You must be very lonely all by yourself!'

'Oh, no, I am not at all lonely,' said the hare, 'but as it was such a fine day I came out here to enjoy myself. Won't you stop and play with me a little while?'

The crocodile came out of the sea and sat on the shore, and the two played together for some time.

Then the hare said:

'Mr Crocodile, you live in the sea and I live on this island, and we do not often meet, so I know very little about you. Tell me, do you think the number of your company is greater than mine?'

'Of course, there are more crocodiles than hares,' answered the crocodile. 'Can you not see that for yourself? You live on this small island, while I live in the sea, which spreads through all parts of the world, so if I call together all the crocodiles who dwell in the sea you hares will be as nothing compared to us!' The crocodile was very conceited.

The hare, who meant to play a trick on the crocodile, said:

'Do you think it possible for you to call up enough crocodiles to form a line from this island across the sea to Inaba?'

The crocodile thought for a moment and then answered:

'Of course, it is possible.'

'Then do try,' said the artful hare, 'and I will count the number from here!'

The crocodile, who was very simple-minded, and who hadn't the least idea that the hare intended to play a trick on him, agreed to do what the hare asked, and said:

'Wait a little while I go back into the sea and call my company together!'

The crocodile plunged into the sea and was gone for some

time. The hare, meanwhile, waited patiently on the shore. At last the crocodile appeared, bringing with him a large number of other crocodiles.

'Look, Mr Hare!' said the crocodile, 'it is nothing for my friends to form a line between here and Inaba. There are enough crocodiles to stretch from here even as far as China or India. Did you ever see so many crocodiles?'

Then the whole company of crocodiles arranged themselves in the water so as to form a bridge between the Island of Oki and the mainland of Inaba. When the hare saw the bridge of crocodiles, he said:

'How splendid! I did not believe this was possible. Now let me count you all! To do this, however, with your permission, I must walk over on your backs to the other side, so please be so good as not to move, or else I shall fall into the sea and be drowned!'

So the hare hopped off the island on to the strange bridge of crocodiles, counting as he jumped from one crocodile's back to the other:

'Please keep quite still, or I shall not be able to count. One, two, three, four, five, six, seven, eight, nine—'

Thus the cunning hare walked right across to the mainland of Inaba. Not content with getting his wish, he began to jeer at the crocodiles instead of thanking them, and said, as he leapt off the last one's back:

'Oh! you stupid crocodiles, now I have done with you!'

And he was just about to run away as fast as he could. But he did not escape so easily, for so soon as the crocodiles understood that this was a trick played upon them by the hare so as to enable him to cross the sea, and that the hare was now laughing at them for their stupidity, they became furiously angry and made up their minds to take revenge. So some of them ran after the hare and caught him. Then they all surrounded the poor little animal and pulled out all his fur. He cried out loudly and entreated them to spare him, but with each tuft of fur they pulled out they said:

'Serve you right!'

When the crocodiles had pulled out the last bit of fur, they threw the poor hare on the beach, and all swam away laughing at what they had done.

The hare was now in a pitiful plight, all his beautiful white fur had been pulled out, and his bare little body was quivering with pain and bleeding all over. He could hardly move, and all he could do was to lie on the beach quite helpless and weep over the misfortune that had befallen him. Notwithstanding that it was his own fault that had brought all this misery and suffering upon the white hare of Inaba, any one seeing the poor little creature could not help feeling sorry for him in his sad condition, for the crocodiles had been very cruel in their revenge.

Just at this time a number of men, who looked like king's sons, happened to pass by, and seeing the hare lying on the beach crying, stopped and asked what was the matter.

The hare lifted up his head from between his paws, and answered them, saying:

'I had a fight with some crocodiles, but I was beaten, and they pulled out all my fur and left me to suffer here—that is why I am crying.'

Now one of these young men had a bad and spiteful disposition. But he feigned kindness, and said to the hare:

'I feel very sorry for you. If you will only try it, I know of a remedy which will cure your sore body. Go and bathe yourself in the sea, and then come and sit in the wind. This will make your fur grow again, and you will be just as you were before.'

Then all the young men passed on. The hare was very pleased, thinking that he had found a cure. He went and bathed in the sea and then came out and sat where the wind could blow upon him.

But as the wind blew and dried him, his skin became drawn and hardened, and the salt increased the pain so much that he rolled on the sand in his agony and cried aloud.

Just then another king's son passed by, carrying a great bag on his back. He saw the hare, and stopped and asked why he was crying so loudly.

But the poor hare, remembering that he had been deceived by one very like the man who now spoke to him, did not answer, but continued to cry.

But this man had a kind heart, and looked at the hare very pityingly, and said:

'You poor thing! I see that your fur is all pulled out and that your skin is quite bare. Who can have treated you so cruelly?'

When the hare heard these kind words he felt very grateful to the man, and encouraged by his gentle manner the hare told him all that had befallen him. The little animal hid nothing from his friend, but told him frankly how he had played a trick on the crocodiles and how he had come across the bridge they had made, thinking that he wished to count their number: how he had jeered at them for their stupidity, and then how the crocodiles had revenged themselves on him. Then he went on to say how he had been deceived by a party of men who looked very like his kind friend: and the hare ended his long tale of woe by begging the man to give him some medicine that would cure him and make his fur grow again.

When the hare had finished his story, the man was full of pity towards him, and said:

'I am very sorry for all you have suffered, but remember,

it was only the consequence of the deceit you practised on the crocodiles.'

'I know,' answered the sorrowful hare, 'but I have repented and made up my mind never to use deceit again, so I beg you to show me how I may cure my sore body and make the fur grow again.'

'Then I will tell you of a good remedy,' said the man. 'First go and bathe well in that pond over there and try to wash all the salt from your body. Then pick some of those kaba flowers that are growing near the edge of the water, spread them on the ground and roll yourself on them. If you do this the pollen will cause your fur to grow again, and you will be quite well in a little while.'

The hare was very glad to be told what to do, so kindly. He crawled to the pond pointed out to him, bathed well in it, and then picked the kaba flowers growing near the water, and rolled himself on them.

To his amazement, even while he was doing this, he saw his nice white fur growing again, the pain ceased, and he felt just as he had done before all his misfortunes.

The hare was overjoyed at his quick recovery, and went hopping joyfully towards the young man who had so helped him, and kneeling down at his feet, said:

'I cannot express my thanks for all you have done for me! It is my earnest wish to do something for you in return. Please tell me who you are?'

'I am no king's son as you think me. I am a fairy, and my name is Okuni-nushi-no-Mikoto,' answered the man, 'and those beings who passed here before me are my brothers. They have heard of a beautiful princess called Yakami who lives in this province of Inaba, and they are on their way to find her and to ask her to marry one of them. But on this expedition I am only an attendant, so I am walking behind them with this great big bag on my back.'

The hare humbled himself before this great fairy Okuni-nushi-no-Mikoto, whom many in that part of the land worshipped as a god.

'Oh, I did not know that you were Okuni-nushi-no-Mikoto. How kind you have been to me! It is impossible to believe that that unkind fellow who sent me to bathe in the sea is one of your brothers. I am quite sure that the princess, whom your brothers have gone to seek, will refuse to be the bride of any of them, and will prefer you for your goodness of heart. I am quite sure that you will win her heart without intending to do so, and she will ask to be your bride.'

Okuni-nushi-no-Mikoto took no notice of what the hare said, but bidding the little animal goodby, went on his way quickly and soon overtook his brothers. He found them just entering the princess's gate.

Just as the hare had said, the princess could not be persuaded to become the bride of any of the brothers, but when she looked at the kind brother's face she went straight up to him and said:

'To you I give myself,' and so they were married.

This is the end of the story. Okuni-nushi-no-Mikoto is worshipped by the people in some parts of Japan, as a god, and the hare has become famous as 'The White Hare of Inaba.' But what became of the crocodiles nobody knows.

THE STORY OF PRINCE YAMATO TAKE

The insignia of the great Japanese Empire is composed of three treasures which have been considered sacred, and guarded with jealous care from time immemorial. These are the *Yatano-no-Kagami* or the Mirror of Yata, the *Yasakami-no-Magatama* or the Jewel of Yasakami, and the *Murakumo-no-Tsurugi* or the Sword of Murakumo.

Of these three treasures of the Empire, the sword of Murakumo, afterwards known as *Kusanagi-no-Tsurugi*, or the grass-cleaving sword, is considered the most precious and most highly to be honoured, for it is the symbol of strength to this nation of warriors and the talisman of invincibility for the emperor, while he holds it sacred in the shrine of his ancestors.

Nearly two thousand years ago this sword was kept at the shrines of Ite, the temples dedicated to the worship of Amaterasu, the great and beautiful Sun Goddess from whom the Japanese emperors are said to be descended.

There is a story of knightly adventure and daring which explains why the name of the sword was changed from that of Murakumo to Kusanagi, which means grass clearing.

Once, many, many years ago, there was born a son to the Emperor Keiko, the twelfth in descent from the great Jimmu, the founder of the Japanese dynasty. This prince was the second son of the Emperor Keiko, and he was named Yamato. From his childhood he proved himself to be of remarkable strength, wisdom and courage, and his father noticed with pride that he gave promise of great things, and he loved him even more than he did his elder son.

Now when Prince Yamato had grown to manhood (in the olden days of Japanese history, a boy was considered to have reached man's estate at the early age of sixteen) the realm was much troubled by a band of outlaws whose chiefs were two brothers, Kumaso and Takeru. These rebels seemed to delight in rebelling against the king, in breaking the laws and defying all authority.

At last King Keiko ordered his younger son Prince Yamato to subdue the brigands and, if possible, to rid the land of their evil lives. Prince Yamato was only sixteen years of age, he had but reached his manhood according to the law, yet though he was such a youth in years he possessed the dauntless spirit of a warrior of fuller age and knew not what fear was. Even then there was no man who could rival him for courage and bold deeds, and he received his father's command with great joy.

He at once made ready to start, and great was the stir in the precincts of the palace as he and his trusty followers gathered together and prepared for the expedition, and polished up their armour and donned it. Before he left his father's court he went to pray at the shrine of Ise and to take leave of his aunt the Princess Yamato, for his heart was somewhat heavy at the thought of the dangers he had to face, and he felt that he needed the protection of his ancestress, Amaterasu, the Sun Goddess. The princess his aunt came out to give him glad welcome, and congratulated him on being trusted with so great a mission by his father the king. She then gave him one of her gorgeous robes as a keepsake to go with him and to bring him good luck, saying that it would surely be of service to him on this adventure. She then wished him all success in his undertaking and bade him good speed. The young prince bowed low before his aunt, and received her gracious gift with much pleasure and many respectful bows.

'I will now set out,' said the prince, and returning to the palace he put himself at the head of his troops. Thus cheered by his aunt's blessing, he felt ready for all that might befall, and marching through the land he went down to the southern island of Kiushiu, the home of the brigands.

Before many days had passed he reached the Southern Island, and then slowly but surely made his way to the head-quarters of the chiefs Kumaso and Takeru. He now met with great difficulties, for he found the country exceedingly wild and rough. The mountains were high and steep, the valleys dark and deep, and huge trees and bowlders of rock blocked up the road and stopped the progress of his army. It was all but impossible to go on.

Though the prince was but a youth he had the wisdom of years, and, seeing that it was vain to try and lead his men further, he said to himself:

'To attempt to fight a battle in this impassable country unknown to my men only makes my task harder. We cannot clear the roads and fight as well. It is wiser for me to resort to stratagem and come upon my enemies unawares. In that way I may be able to kill them without much exertion.'

So he now bade his army halt by the way. His wife, the Princess Ototachibana, had accompanied him, and he bade her bring him the robe his aunt the priestess of Ise had given him, and to help him attire himself as a woman. With her help he put on the robe, and let his hair down till it flowed over his shoulders. Ototachibana then brought him her comb, which he put in his black tresses, and then adorned himself with strings of strange jewels just as you see in the picture. When he had finished his unusual toilet, Ototachibana brought him her mirror. He smiled as he gazed at himself—the disguise was so perfect.

He hardly knew himself, so changed was he. All traces of the warrior had disappeared, and in the shining surface only a beautiful lady looked back at him.

Thus completely disguised, he set out for the enemy's camp alone. In the folds of his silk gown, next his strong heart, was hidden a sharp dagger.

The two chiefs Kumaso and Takeru were sitting in their tent, resting in the cool of the evening, when the prince approached. They were talking of the news which had recently been carried to them, that the king's son had entered their country with a large army determined to exterminate their band. They had both heard of the young warrior's renown, and for the first time in their wicked lives they felt afraid. In a pause in their talk they happened to look up, and saw through the door of the tent a beautiful woman robed in sumptuous garments coming towards them. Like an apparition of loveliness she appeared in the soft twilight. Little did they dream that it was their enemy whose coming they so dreaded who now stood before them in this disguise.

'What a beautiful woman! Where has she come from?' said the astonished Kumaso, forgetting war and council and everything as he looked at the gentle intruder.

He beckoned to the disguised prince and bade him sit down and serve them with wine. Yamato Take felt his heart swell with a fierce glee for he now knew that his plan would succeed. However, he dissembled cleverly, and putting on a sweet air of shyness he approached the rebel chief with slow steps and eyes glancing like a frightened deer. Charmed to distraction by the girl's loveliness Kumaso drank cup after cup of wine for the pleasure of seeing her pour it out for him, till at last he was quite overcome with the quantity he had drunk. This was the moment for which the brave prince had been waiting. Flinging down the wine jar, he seized the tipsy and astonished Kumaso and quickly stabbed him to death with the dagger which he had secretly carried hidden in his breast.

Takeru, the brigand's brother, was terror-struck as soon as he saw what was happening and tried to escape, but Prince Yamato was too quick for him. Ere he could reach the tent door the prince was at his heel, his garments were clutched by a hand of iron, and a dagger flashed before his eyes and he lay stabbed to the earth, dying but not yet dead.

'Wait one moment!' gasped the brigand painfully, and he seized the Prince's hand.

Yamato relaxed his hold somewhat and said.

'Why should I pause, thou villain?'

The brigand raised himself fearfully and said:

'Tell me from whence you come, and whom I have the honour of addressing? Hitherto I believed that my dead brother and I were the strongest men in the land, and that there was no one who could overcome us. Alone you have ventured into our stronghold, alone you have attacked and killed us! Surely you are more than mortal?'

Then the young prince answered with a proud smile:—'I am the son of the king and my name is Yamato, and I have been sent by my father as the avenger of evil to bring death to all rebels! No longer shall robbery and murder hold my people in terror!' and he held the dagger dripping red above the rebel's head.

'Ah,' gasped the dying man with a great effort, 'I have often heard of you. You are indeed a strong man to have so easily overcome us. Allow me to give you a new name. From henceforth you shall be known as Yamato Take. Our title I bequeath to you as the bravest man in Yamato.'

And with these noble words, Takeru fell back and died.

The prince having thus successfully put an end to his father's enemies in the world, was prepared to return to the capital. On the way back he passed through the province of Idum. Here he met with another outlaw named Idzumo Takeru who he knew had done much harm in the land. He again resorted to stratagem, and feigned friendship with the rebel under an assumed name. Having done this he made a sword of wood and jammed it tightly in the shaft of his own strong sword. This he purposedly buckled to his side and wore on every occasion when he expected to meet the third robber Takeru.

He now invited Takeru to the bank of the river Hinokawa, and persuaded him to try a swim with him in the cool refreshing waters of the river.

As it was a hot summer's day, the rebel was nothing loath to take a plunge in the river, while his enemy was still swimming down the stream the prince turned back and landed with all possible haste. Unperceived, he managed to change swords, putting his wooden one in place of the keen steel sword of Takeru.

Knowing nothing of this, the brigand came up to the bank shortly. As soon as he had landed and donned his clothes, the prince came forward and asked him to cross swords with him to prove his skill, saying:

'Let us two prove which is the better swordsman of the two!'

The robber agreed with delight, feeling certain of victory, for he was famous as a fencer in his province and he did not know who his adversary was. He seized quickly what he thought was his sword and stood on guard to defend himself. Alas! for the rebel the sword was the wooden one of the young prince and in vain Takeru tried to unsheathe it—it was jammed fast, not all his exerted strength could move it. Even if his efforts had been successful the sword would have been of no use to him for it was of wood. Yamato Take saw that his enemy was in his power, and swinging high the sword he had taken from Takeru he brought it down with great might and dexterity and cut off the robber's head.

In this way, sometimes by using his wisdom and sometimes by using his bodily strength, and at other times by resorting to craftiness, which was as much esteemed in those days as it is despised in these, he prevailed against all the king's foes one by one, and brought peace and rest to the land and the people.

When he returned to the capital the king praised him for his brave deeds, and held a feast in the palace in honour of his safe coming home and presented him with many rare gifts. From this time forth the king loved him more than ever and would not let Yamato Take go from his side, for he said that his son was now as precious to him as one of his arms.

But the prince was not allowed to live an idle life long. When he was about thirty years old, news was brought that the Ainu race, the aborigines of the islands of Japan, who had been conquered and pushed northwards by the Japanese, had rebelled in the eastern provinces, and leaving the vicinity which had been allotted to them were causing great trouble in the land. The king decided that it was necessary to send an army to do battle with them and bring them to reason. But who was to lead the men?

Prince Yamato Take at once offered to go and bring the newly arisen rebels into subjection. Now as the king loved the prince dearly, and could not bear to have him go out of his sight even for the length of one day, he was of course very loath to send him on his dangerous expedition. But in the whole army there was no warrior so strong or so brave as the prince his son, so that His Majesty, unable to do otherwise, reluctantly complied with Yamato's wish.

When the time came for the prince to start, the king gave him a spear called the Eight-Arms-Length-Spear of the Holly Tree (the handle was probably made from the wood of the holly tree), and ordered him to set out to subjugate the Eastern Barbarians as the Ainu were then called.

The Eight-Arms-Length-Spear of the Holly Tree of those old days, was prized by warriors just as much as the standard or banner is valued by a regiment in these modern days, when given by the king to his soldiers on the occasion of setting out for war.

The prince respectfully and with great reverence received the king's spear, and leaving the capital, marched with his army to the East. On his way he visited first of all the temples of Ise for worship, and his aunt the Princess of Yamato and High Priestess came out to greet him. She it was who had given him her robe which had proved such a boon to him before in helping him to overcome and slay the brigands of the West.

He told her all that had happened to him, and of the great part her keepsake had played in the success of his previous undertaking, and thanked her very heartily. When she heard that he was starting out once again to do battle with his father's enemies, she went into the temple, and reappeared bearing a sword and a beautiful bag which she had made herself, and which was full of flints, which in those times people used instead of matches for making fire. These she presented to him as a parting gift.

The sword was the sword of Murakumo, one of the three sacred treasures which comprise the insignia of the Imperial

House of Japan. No more auspicious talisman of luck and success could she have given her nephew, and she bade him use it in the hour of his greatest need.

Yamato Take now bade farewell to his aunt, and once more placing himself at the head of his men he marched to the farthest east through the province of Owari, and then he reached the province of Suruga. Here the governor welcomed the prince right heartily and entertained him royally with many feasts. When these were over, the governor told his guest that his country was famous for its fine deer, and proposed a deer hunt for the prince's amusement. The prince was utterly deceived by the cordiality of his host, which was all feigned, and gladly consented to join in the hunt.

The governor then led the prince to a wild and extensive plain where the grass grew high and in great abundance. Quite ignorant that the governor had laid a trap for him with the desire to compass his death, the prince began to ride hard and hunt down the deer, when all of a sudden to his amazement he saw flames and smoke bursting out from the bush in front of him. Realizing his danger he tried to retreat, but no sooner did he turn his horse in the opposite direction than he saw that even there the prairie was on fire. At the same time the grass on his left and right burst into flames, and these began to spread swiftly towards him on all sides. He looked round for a chance of escape. There was none. He was surrounded by fire.

'This deer hunt was then only a cunning trick of the enemy!' said the prince, looking round on the flames and the smoke that crackled and rolled in towards him on every side. 'What a fool I was to be lured into this trap like a wild beast!' and he ground his teeth with rage as he thought of the governor's smiling treachery.

Dangerous as was his situation now, the prince was not in the least confounded. In his dire extremity he remembered the gifts his aunt had given him when they parted, and it seemed to him as if she must, with prophetic foresight, have divined this hour of need. He coolly opened the flint-bag that his aunt had given him and set fire to the grass near him. Then drawing the sword of Murakumo from its sheath he set to work to cut down the grass on either side of him with all speed. He determined to die, if that were necessary, fighting for his life and not standing still waiting for death to come to him.

Strange to say the wind began to change and to blow from the opposite direction, and the fiercest portion of the burning bush which had hitherto threatened to come upon him was now blown right away from him, and the prince, without even a scratch on his body or a single hair burned, lived to tell the tale of his wonderful escape, while the wind rising to a gale overtook the governor, and he was burned to death in the flames he had set alight to kill Yamato Take.

Now the prince ascribed his escape entirely to the virtue of the sword of Murakumo, and to the protection of Amaterasu, the Sun Goddess of Ise, who controls the wind and all the elements and insures the safety of all who pray to her in the hour of danger. Lifting the precious sword he raised it above his head many times in token of his great respect, and as he did this he re-named it Kusanagi-no-Tsurugi or the Grass-Cleaving Sword, and the place where he set fire to the grass round him and escaped from death in the burning prairie, he called Yaidzu. To this day there is a spot along the great Tokaido railway named Yaidzu, which is said to be the very place where this thrilling event took place.

Thus did the brave Prince Yamato Take escape out of the snare laid for him by his enemy. He was full of resource and courage, and finally outwitted and subdued all his foes. Leaving Yaidzu he marched eastward, and came to the shore at Idzu from whence he wished to cross to Kadzusa.

In these dangers and adventures he had been followed by his faithful loving wife the Princess Ototachibana. For his sake she counted the weariness of the long journeys and the dangers of war as nothing, and her love for her warrior husband was so great that she felt well repaid for all her wanderings if she could but hand him his sword when he sallied forth to battle, or minister to his wants when he returned weary to the camp.

But the heart of the prince was full of war and conquest and he cared little for the faithful Ototachibana. From long exposure in travelling, and from care and grief at her lord's coldness to her, her beauty had faded, and her ivory skin was burnt brown by the sun, and the prince told her one day that her place was in the palace behind the screens at home and not with him upon the warpath. But in spite of rebuffs and indifference on her husband's part, Ototachibana could not find it in her heart to leave him. But perhaps it would have been better for her if she had done so, for on the way to Idzu, when they came to Owari, her heart was well-nigh broken.

Here dwelt in a palace shaded by pine-trees and approached by imposing gates, the Princess Miyadzu, beautiful as the cherry blossom in the blushing dawn of a spring morning. Her garments were dainty and bright, and her skin was white as snow, for she had never known what it was to be weary along the path of duty or to walk in the heat of a summer's sun. And the prince was ashamed of his sunburnt wife in her travel-stained garments, and bade her remain behind while he went to visit the Princess Miyadzu. Day after day he spent hours in the gardens and the palace of his new friend, thinking only of his pleasure, and caring little for his poor wife who remained behind to weep in the tent at the misery which had come into her life. Yet she was so faithful a wife, and her character so patient, that she never allowed a reproach to escape her lips, or a frown to mar the sweet sadness of her face, and she was ever ready with a smile to welcome her husband back or usher him forth wherever he went.

At last the day came when the Prince Yamato Take must depart for Idzu and cross over the sea to Kadzusa, and he bade his wife follow in his retinue as an attendant while he went to take a ceremonious farewell of the Princess Miyadzu. She came out to greet him dressed in gorgeous robes, and she seemed more beautiful than ever, and when Yamato Take saw her he forgot his wife, his duty, and everything except the joy of the idle present, and swore that he would return to Owari and marry her when the war was over. And as he looked up when he had said these words he met the large almond eyes of Ototachibana fixed full upon him in unspeakable sadness and wonder, and he knew that he had done wrong, but he hardened his heart and rode on, caring little for the pain he had caused her.

When they reached the seashore at Idzu his men sought for boats in which to cross the straits to Kadzusa, but it was difficult to find boats enough to allow all the soldiers to embark. Then the prince stood on the beach, and in the pride of his strength he scoffed and said:

'This is not the sea! This is only a brook! Why do you men want so many boats? I could jump this if I would.'

When at last they had all embarked and were fairly on their way across the straits, the sky suddenly clouded and a great storm arose. The waves rose mountains high, the wind howled, the lightning flashed and the thunder rolled, and the boat which held Ototachibana and the prince and his men was tossed from crest to crest of the rolling waves, till it seemed that every moment must be their last and that they must all be swallowed up in the angry sea. For Riu Jin, the Dragon King of the Sea, had heard Yamato Take jeer, and had raised this terrible storm in anger, to show the scoffing prince how awful the sea could be though it did but look like a brook.

The terrified crew lowered the sails and looked after the rudder, and worked for their dear lives' sake, but all in vain— the storm only seemed to increase in violence, and all gave themselves up for lost. Then the faithful Ototachibana rose, and forgetting all the grief that her husband had caused her, forgetting even that he had wearied of her, in the one great desire of her love to save him, she determined to sacrifice her life to rescue him from death if it were possible.

While the waves dashed over the ship and the wind whirled round them in fury she stood up and said:

'Surely all this has come because the prince has angered Riu Jin, the God of the Sea, by his jesting. If so, I, Ototachibana, will appease the wrath of the Sea God who desires nothing less than my husband's life!'

Then addressing the sea she said:

'I will take the place of His Augustness, Yamato Take. I will now cast myself into your outraged depths, giving my life for his. Therefore hear me and bring him safely to the shore of Kadzusa.'

With these words she leaped quickly into the boisterous sea, and the waves soon whirled her away and she was lost to sight. Strange to say, the storm ceased at once, and the sea became as calm and smooth as the matting on which the astonished onlookers were sitting. The gods of the sea were now appeased, and the weather cleared and the sun shone as on a summer's day.

Yamato Take soon reached the opposite shore and landed

safely, even as his wife Ototachibana had prayed. His prowess in war was marvellous, and he succeeded after some time in conquering the Eastern Barbarians, the Ainu.

He ascribed his safe landing wholly to the faithfulness of his wife, who had so willingly and lovingly sacrificed herself in the hour of his utmost peril. His heart was softened at the remembrance of her, and he never allowed her to pass from his thoughts even for a moment. Too late had he learned to esteem the goodness of her heart and the greatness of her love for him.

As he was returning on his homeward way he came to the high pass of the Usui Toge, and here he stood and gazed at the wonderful prospect beneath him. The country, from this great elevation, all lay open to his sight, a vast panorama of mountain and plain and forest, with rivers winding like silver ribbons through the land; then far off he saw the distant sea, which shimmered like a luminous mist in the great distance, where Ototachibana had given her life for him, and as he turned towards it he stretched out his arms, and thinking of her love which he had scorned and his faithlessness to her, his heart burst out into a sorrowful and bitter cry:

'*Azuma, Azuma, Ya!*' (Oh! my wife, my wife!) And to this day there is a district in Tokio called Azuma, which commemorates the words of Prince Yamato Take, and the place where his faithful wife leapt into the sea to save him is still pointed out. So, though in life the Princess Ototachibana was unhappy, history keeps her memory green, and the story of her unselfishness and heroic death will never pass away.

Yamato Take had now fulfilled all his father's orders, he had subdued all rebels, and rid the land of all robbers and enemies to the peace, and his renown was great, for in the whole land there was no one who could stand up against him, he was so strong in battle and wise in council.

He was about to return straight for home by the way he had come, when the thought struck him that he would find it more interesting to take another route, so he passed through the province of Owari and came to the province of Omi.

When the prince reached Omi he found the people in a state of great excitement and fear. In many houses as he passed along he saw the signs of mourning and heard loud lamentations. On inquiring the cause of this he was told that a terrible monster had appeared in the mountains, who daily came down from thence and made raids on the villages, devouring whoever he could seize. Many homes had been made desolate and the men were afraid to go out to their daily work in the fields, or the women to go to the rivers to wash their rice.

When Yamato Take heard this his wrath was kindled, and he said fiercely:

'From the western end of Kiushiu to the eastern corner of Yezo I have subdued all the king's enemies—there is no one who dares to break the laws or to rebel against the king. It is indeed a matter for wonder that here in this place, so near the capital, a wicked monster has dared to take up his abode and be the terror of the king's subjects. Not long shall it find pleasure in devouring innocent folk. I will start out and kill it at once.'

With these words he set out for the Ibuki Mountain, where the monster was said to live. He climbed up a good distance, when all of a sudden, at a winding in the path, a monster serpent appeared before him and stopped the way.

'This must be the monster,' said the prince; 'I do not need my sword for a serpent. I can kill him with my hands.'

He thereupon sprang upon the serpent and tried to strangle it to death with his bare arms. It was not long before his prodigious strength gained the mastery and the serpent lay dead at his feet. Now a sudden darkness came over the mountain and rain began to fall, so that for the gloom and the rain the prince could hardly see which way to take. In a short time, however, while he was groping his way down the pass, the weather cleared, and our brave hero was able to make his way quickly down the mountain.

When he got back he began to feel ill and to have burning pains in his feet, so he knew that the serpent had poisoned him. So great was his suffering that he could hardly move, much less walk, so he had himself carried to a place in the mountains famous for its hot mineral springs, which rose bubbling out of the earth, and almost boiling from the volcanic fires beneath.

Yamato Take bathed daily in these waters, and gradually he felt his strength come again, and the pains left him, till at last one day he found with great joy that he was quite recovered. He now hastened to the temples of Ise, where you will remember that he prayed before undertaking this long expedition. His aunt, priestess of the shrine, who had blessed him on his setting out, now came to welcome him back. He told her of the many dangers he had encountered and of how marvellously his life had been preserved through all—and she praised his courage and his warrior's prowess, and then putting on her most magnificent robes she returned thanks to their ancestress the Sun Goddess Amaterasu, to whose protection they both ascribed the Prince's wonderful preservation.

Here ends the story of Prince Yamato Take of Japan.

HOW AN OLD MAN LOST HIS WEN

Many, many years ago there lived a good old man who had a wen like a tennis-ball growing out of his right cheek. This lump was a great disfigurement to the old man, and so annoyed him that for many years he spent all his time and money in trying to get rid of it. He tried everything he could think of. He consulted many doctors far and near, and took all kinds of medicines both internally and externally. But it was all of no use. The lump only grew bigger and bigger till it was nearly as big as his face, and in despair he gave up all hopes of ever losing it, and resigned himself to the thought of having to carry the lump on his face all his life.

One day the firewood gave out in his kitchen, so, as his wife wanted some at once, the old man took his axe and set out for the woods up among the hills not very far from his home. It was a fine day in the early autumn, and the old man enjoyed the fresh air and was in no hurry to get home. So the whole afternoon passed quickly while he was chopping wood, and he had collected a goodly pile to take back to his wife. When the day began to draw to a close, he turned his face homewards.

The old man had not gone far on his way down the mountain pass when the sky clouded and rain began to fall heavily. He looked about for some shelter, but there was not even a charcoal-burner's hut near. At last he espied a large hole in the hollow trunk of a tree. The hole was near the ground, so he crept in easily, and sat down in hopes that he had only been overtaken by a mountain shower, and that the weather would soon clear.

But much to the old man's disappointment, instead of clearing the rain fell more and more heavily, and finally a heavy thunderstorm broke over the mountain. The thunder roared so terrifically, and the heavens seemed to be so ablaze with lightning, that the old man could hardly believe himself to be alive. He thought that he must die of fright. At last, however, the sky cleared, and the whole country was aglow in the rays of the setting sun. The old man's spirits revived when he looked out at the beautiful twilight, and he was about to step out from his strange hiding-place in the hollow tree when the sound of what seemed like the approaching steps of several people caught his ear. He at once thought that his friends had come to look for him, and he was delighted at the idea of having some jolly companions with whom to walk home. But on looking out from the tree, what was his amazement to see, not his friends, but hundreds of demons coming towards the spot. The more he looked, the greater was his astonishment. Some of these demons were as large as giants, others had great big eyes out of all proportion to the rest of their bodies, others again had absurdly long noses, and some had such big mouths that they seemed to open from ear to ear. All had horns growing on their foreheads. The old man was so surprised at what he saw that he lost his balance and fell out of the hollow tree. Fortunately for him the demons did not see him, as the tree was in the background. So he picked himself up and crept back into the tree.

While he was sitting there and wondering impatiently when he would be able to get home, he heard the sounds of gay music, and then some of the demons began to sing.

'What are these creatures doing?' said the old man to himself. 'I will look out, it sounds very amusing.'

On peeping out, the old man saw that the demon chief himself was actually sitting with his back against the tree in which he had taken refuge, and all the other demons were sitting round, some drinking and some dancing. Food and wine was spread before them on the ground, and the demons were evidently having a great entertainment and enjoying themselves immensely.

It made the old man laugh to see their strange antics.

'How amusing this is!' laughed the old man to himself 'I am now quite old, but I have never seen anything so strange in all my life.'

He was so interested and excited in watching all that the demons were doing, that he forgot himself and stepped out of the tree and stood looking on.

The demon chief was just taking a big cup of saké and watching one of the demons dancing. In a little while he said with a bored air:

'Your dance is rather monotonous. I am tired of watching it. Isn't there any one amongst you all who can dance better than this fellow?'

Now the old man had been fond of dancing all his life, and was quite an expert in the art, and he knew that he could do much better than the demon.

'Shall I go and dance before these demons and let them see what a human being can do? It may be dangerous, for if I don't please them they may kill me!' said the old fellow to himself.

His fears, however, were soon overcome by his love of dancing. In a few minutes he could restrain himself no longer, and came out before the whole party of demons and began to dance at once. The old man, realizing that his life probably depended on whether he pleased these strange creatures or not, exerted his skill and wit to the utmost.

The demons were at first very surprised to see a man so fearlessly taking part in their entertainment, and then their surprise soon gave place to admiration.

'How strange!' exclaimed the horned chief. 'I never saw such a skilful dancer before! He dances admirably!'

When the old man had finished his dance, the big demon said:

'Thank you very much for your amusing dance. Now give us the pleasure of drinking a cup of wine with us,' and with these words he handed him his largest wine-cup.

The old man thanked him very humbly:

'I did not expect such kindness from your lordship. I fear I have only disturbed your pleasant party by my unskilful dancing.'

'No, no,' answered the big demon. 'You must come often and dance for us. Your skill has given us much pleasure.'

The old man thanked him again and promised to do so.

'Then will you come again to-morrow, old man?' asked the demon.

'Certainly, I will,' answered the old man.

'Then you must leave some pledge of your word with us,' said the demon.

'Whatever you like,' said the old man.

'Now what is the best thing he can leave with us as a pledge?' asked the demon, looking round.

Then said one of the demon's attendants kneeling behind the chief:

'The token he leaves with us must be the most important thing to him in his possession. I see the old man has a wen on his right cheek. Now mortal men consider such a wen very fortunate.

Let my lord take the lump from the old man's right cheek, and he will surely come to-morrow, if only to get that back.'

'You are very clever,' said the demon chief, giving his horns an approving nod. Then he stretched out a hairy arm and claw-like hand, and took the great lump from the old man's right cheek. Strange to say, it came off as easily as a ripe plum from the tree at the demon's touch, and then the merry troop of demons suddenly vanished.

The old man was lost in bewilderment by all that had happened. He hardly knew for some time where he was. When he came to understand what had happened to him, he was delighted to find that the lump on his face, which had for so many years disfigured him, had really been taken away without any pain to himself. He put up his hand to feel if any scar remained, but found that his right cheek was as smooth as his left.

The sun had long set, and the young moon had risen like a silver crescent in the sky. The old man suddenly realized how late it was and began to hurry home. He patted his right cheek all the time, as if to make sure of his good fortune in having lost the wen. He was so happy that he found it impossible to walk quietly—he ran and danced the whole way home.

He found his wife very anxious, wondering what had happened to make him so late. He soon told her all that had passed since he left home that afternoon. She was quite as happy as her husband when he showed her that the ugly lump had disappeared from his face, for in her youth she had prided herself on his good looks, and it had been a daily grief to her to see the horrid growth.

Now next door to this good old couple there lived a wicked and disagreeable old man. He, too, had for many years been troubled with the growth of a wen on his left cheek, and he, too, had tried all manner of things to get rid of it, but in vain.

He heard at once, through the servant, of his neighbour's good luck in losing the lump on his face, so he called that very evening and asked his friend to tell him everything that concerned the loss of it. The good old man told his disagreeable neighbour all that had happened to him. He described the place where he would find the hollow tree in which to hide, and advised him to be on the spot in the late afternoon towards the time of sunset.

The old neighbour started out the very next afternoon, and after hunting about for some time, came to the hollow tree just as his friend had described. Here he hid himself and waited for the twilight.

Just as he had been told, the band of demons came at that hour and held a feast with dance and song. When this had gone on for some time the chief of the demons looked around and said:

'It is now time for the old man to come as he promised us. Why doesn't he come?'

When the second old man heard these words he ran out of his hiding-place in the tree and, kneeling down before the *oni*, said:

'I have been waiting for a long time for you to speak!'

'Ah, you are the old man of yesterday,' said the demon chief. 'Thank you for coming, you must dance for us soon.'

The old man now stood up and opened his fan and began to dance. But he had never learned to dance, and knew nothing about the necessary gestures and different positions. He thought that anything would please the demons, so he just hopped about, waving his arms and stamping his feet, imitating as well as he could any dancing he had ever seen.

The oni were very dissatisfied at this exhibition, and said amongst themselves:

'How badly he dances to-day!'

Then to the old man the demon chief said:

'Your performance to-day is quite different from the dance of yesterday. We don't wish to see any more of such dancing. We will give you back the pledge you left with us. You must go away at once.'

With these words he took out from a fold of his dress the lump which he had taken from the face of the old man who had danced so well the day before, and threw it at the right cheek of the old man who stood before him. The lump immediately attached itself to his cheek as firmly as if it had grown there always, and all attempts to pull it off were useless. The wicked old man, instead of losing the lump on his left cheek as he had hoped, found to his dismay that he had but added another to his right cheek in his attempt to get rid of the first.

He put up first one hand and then the other to each side of his face to make sure if he were not dreaming a horrible nightmare. No, sure enough there was now a great wen on the right side of his face as on the left. The demons had all disappeared, and there was nothing for him to do but to return home. He was a pitiful sight, for his face, with the two large lumps, one on each side, looked just like a Japanese gourd.

THE MEETING OF THE STAR-LOVERS

One of the greatest days in the calendar of old Japan was the seventh of July; or, as the Japanese people put it, 'the seventh day of the seventh month.' It was a vermilion day in the almanacs, to which every child looked forward with eyes sparkling, hands clapping and fingers counting, as each night rolled the time nearer. All manner of fruits and other eatable vegetables were prepared, and cakes baked, in the household. The boys plucked bamboo stalks, and strung on their branches bright-coloured ribbons, tinkling bells, and long streamers of paper, on which poetry was written. On this night, mothers hoped for wealth, happiness, good children and wisdom. The girls made a wish that they might become skilled in needlework. Only one wish a year, however, could be made. So, if any one wanted several things—health, wealth, skill in needlework, wisdom, etc.—they must wait many years before all the favours could be granted. Above all things, rainy weather was not desired. It was a 'good sign' when a spider spun his web over a melon, or, if put in a square box he should weave a circular web. Now, the cause of all this preparation was that on the seventh of July the Herd-boy star and the Spinning Maiden star cross the Milky Way to meet each other. These are the stars which we call Capricornus and Alpha Lyra. These stars that shine and glitter so far up in the zenith, are the boy with an ox and the girl with a shuttle, about whom the story runs as follows:

On the banks of the Silver River of Heaven (which we call the Milky Way) there lived a beautiful maiden, who was the daughter of the sun. Her name was Shokujo. She did not care for games or play, like her companions, and, thinking nothing of vain display, wore only the simplest of dress. Yet she was very diligent, and made many garments for others. Indeed, so busy was she that all called her the Weaving or Spinning Princess.

The sun-king noticed the serious disposition and close habits of his daughter, and tried in various ways to get her to be more lively. At last he thought to marry her. As marriages in the star-land are usually planned by the parents, and not by the foolish lover-boys and girls, he arranged the union without consulting his daughter. The young man on whom the sun-king thus bestowed his daughter's hand was Kingin, who kept a herd of cows on the banks of the celestial stream. He had always been a good neighbour, and, living on the same side of the river, the father thought he would get a nice son-in-law, and at the same time improve his daughter's habits and disposition.

No sooner did the maiden become wife than her habits and character utterly changed for the worse, and the father had a very vexatious case of *tadashiku suguru* ('too much of a good thing') on his hands. The wife became not only very merry and lively, but utterly forsook loom and needle. She gave up her nights and days to play and idleness, and no silly lover could have been more foolish than she.

The sun-king became very much offended at all this, and thinking that the husband was the cause of it, he determined to separate the couple. So he ordered the husband to remove to the other side of the river of stars, and told him that hereafter they should meet only once a year, on the seventh night of the seventh month. To make a bridge over the flood of stars, the sun-king called myriads of magpies, which thereupon flew together, and, making a bridge, supported him on their wings and backs as if it were a roadway of solid land. So, bidding his weeping wife farewell, the lover-husband sorrowfully crossed the River of Heaven. No sooner had he set foot on the opposite side than the magpies flew away, filling all the heavens with their chatter. The weeping wife and lover-husband stood for a long time wistfully gazing at each other from afar. Then they separated, the one to lead his ox, the other to ply her shuttle during the long hours of the day with diligent toil. Thus they filled the hours, and the sun-king again rejoiced in his daughter's industry.

But when night fell, and all the lamps of heaven were lighted, the lovers would come and stand by the banks of the starry river, and gaze longingly at each other, waiting for the seventh night of the seventh month.

At last the time drew near, and only one fear possessed the loving wife. Every time she thought of it her heart played pit-a-pat faster. What if it should rain? For the River of Heaven is always full to the brim, and one extra drop of rain causes a flood which sweeps away even the bird-bridge.

But not a drop fell. The seventh month, seventh night, came, and all the heavens were clear. The magpies flew joyfully in myriads, making one way for the tiny feet of the little lady. Trembling with joy, and with heart fluttering more than the bridge of wings, she crossed the River of Heaven, and was in the arms of her husband. This she did every year. The lover-husband stayed on his side of the river, and the wife came to him on the magpie bridge, save on the sad occasion when it rained. So every year the people hope for clear weather, and the happy festival is celebrated alike by old and young.

THE TRAVELS OF TWO FROGS

Forty miles apart, as the cranes fly, stand the great cities of Ozaka and Kioto. The one is the city of canals and bridges. Its streets are full of bustling trade, and its waterways are ever alive with gondolas, shooting hither and thither like the wooden shuttles in a loom. The other is the sacred city of the mikado's empire, girdled with green hills and a nine-fold circle of flowers. In its quiet, clean streets, laid out like a chessboard, walk the shaven monks and gowned scholars. And very beautiful is Kioto, with pretty girls, and temple gardens, and castle walls, and towers, and moats in which the white lotus blooms.

Long, long ago, in the good old days before the hairy-faced and pale-cheeked men from over the Sea of Great Peace (Pacific Ocean) came to Japan; before the black coal-smoke and snorting engine scared the white heron from the rice-fields; before black crows and fighting sparrows, which fear not man, perched on telegraph wires, or ever a railway was thought of, there lived two frogs—one in a well in Kioto, the other in a lotus-pond in Ozaka.

Now it is a common proverb in the Land of the Gods (Japan) that 'the frog in the well knows not the great ocean,' and the Kioto frog had so often heard this scornful sneer from the maids who came to draw out water, with their long bamboo-handled buckets that he resolved to travel abroad and see the world, and especially the *Tai-kai* (the great ocean).

'I'll see for myself,' said Mr Frog, as he packed his wallet and wiped his spectacles, 'what this great ocean is that they talk about. I'll wager it isn't half as deep or wide as well, where I can see the stars even at daylight.'

Now the truth was, a recent earthquake had greatly reduced the depth of the well and the water was getting very shallow. Mr Frog informed his family of his intentions. Mrs Frog wept a great deal; but, drying her eyes with her paper handkerchief, she declared she would count the hours on her fingers till he came back, and at every morning and evening meal would set out his table with food on it, just as if he were home. She tied up a little lacquered box full of boiled rice and snails for his journey, wrapped it around with a silk napkin, and, putting his extra clothes in a bundle, swung it on his back. Tying it over his neck, he seized his staff and was ready to go.

'*Sayonara*' ('Good-bye') cried he, as, with a tear in his eye, he walked away.

'Sayonara. *Oshidzukani*' ('Good-bye. Walk slowly'), croaked Mrs Frog and the whole family of young frogs in a chorus.

Two of the froggies were still babies, that is, they were yet polywogs, with a half inch of tail still on them; and, of course, were carried about by being strapped on the back of their older brothers.

Mr Frog being now on land, out of his well, noticed that the other animals did not leap, but walked on their legs. And, not wishing to be eccentric, he likewise began briskly walking upright on his hind legs or waddling on all fours.

Now it happened that about the same time the Ozaka father frog had become restless and dissatisfied with life on the edges of his lotus-ditch. He had made up his mind to 'cast the lion's cub into the valley.'

'Why! that *is* tall talk for a frog, I must say,' exclaims the reader. 'What did he mean?'

I must tell you that the Ozaka frog was a philosopher. Right at the edge of his lotus-pond was a monastery, full of Buddhist monks, who every day studied their sacred rolls and droned over the books of Confucius, to learn them by heart. Our frog had heard them so often that he could (in frog language, of course) repeat many of their wise sentences and intone responses to their evening prayers put up by the great idol Amida. Indeed, our frog had so often listened to their debates on texts from the classics that he had himself become a sage and a philosopher. Yet, as the proverb says, 'the sage is not happy.'

Why not? In spite of a soft mud-bank, plenty of green scum, stagnant water, and shady lotus leaves, a fat wife and a numerous family; in short, everything to make a frog happy, his forehead, or rather gullet, was wrinkled with care from long pondering of knotty problems, such as the following:

The monks often come down to the edge of the pond to look at the pink and white lotus. One summer day, as a little frog, hardly out of his tadpole state, with a small fragment of tail still left, sat basking on a huge round leaf, one monk said to the other:

'Of what does that remind you?'

'The babies of frogs will become but frogs,' said one shaven pate, laughing.

'What think you?'

'The white lotus flower springs out of the black mud,' said the other, solemnly, as both walked away.

The old frog, sitting near by, overheard them and began to philosophize: 'Humph! The babies of frogs will become but frogs, hey? If mud becomes lotus, why shouldn't a frog become a man? Why not? If my pet son should travel abroad and see the world—go to Kioto, for instance—why shouldn't he be as wise as those shining-headed men, I wonder? I shall try it, anyhow. I'll send my son on a journey to Kioto. I'll "cast the lion's cub into the valley" (send the pet son abroad in the world, to see and study) at once. I'll deny myself for the sake of my offspring.'

Flump! splash! sounded the water, as a pair of webby feet disappeared. The 'lion's cub' was soon ready, after much paternal advice, and much counsel to beware of being gobbled up by long-legged storks, and trod on by impolite men, and struck at by bad boys. '*Kio ni no inaka*' ('Even in the capital there are boors') said Father Frog.

Now it so happened that the old frog from Kioto and the 'lion's cub' from Ozaka started each from his home at the same time. Nothing of importance occurred to either of them until, as luck would have it, they met on a hill near Hashimoto, which is half way between the two cities. Both were footsore, and websore, and very tired, especially about the hips, on account of the unfroglike manner of walking, instead of hopping, as they had been used to.

'*Ohio gozarimasu*' ('Good-morning') said the 'lion's cub' to the old frog, as he fell on all fours and bowed his head to the ground three times, squinting up over his left eye, to see if the other frog was paying equal deference in return.

'*He, konnichi wa*' ('Yes, good-day') replied the Kioto frog.

'*O tenki*' ('It is rather fine weather to-day') said the 'cub.'

'*He, yoi tenki gozence*' ('Yes, it is very fine') replied the old fellow.

'I am Gamataro, from Ozaka, the oldest son of Hiki Dono, Sensui no Kami' (Lord Bullfrog, Prince of the Lotus-Ditch).

'Your Lordship must be weary with your journey. I am Kayeru-san of Idomidzu (Sir Frog of the Well) in Kioto. I started out to see the 'great ocean' from Ozaka; but, I declare, my hips are so dreadfully tired that I believe that I'll give up my plan and content myself with a look from this hill.'

The truth must be owned that the old frog was not only on his hind legs, but also on his last legs, when he stood up to look at Ozaka; while the 'cub' was tired enough to believe anything. The old fellow, wiping his face, spoke up:

'Suppose we save ourselves the trouble of the journey. This hill is half way between the two cities, and while I see Ozaka and the sea you can get a good look of the Kio' (Capital, or Kioto).

'Happy thought!' said the Ozaka frog.

Then both reared themselves upon their hind-legs, and stretching upon their toes, body to body, and neck to neck, propped each other up, rolled their goggles and looked steadily, as they supposed, on the places which they each wished to see. Now everyone knows that a frog has eyes mounted in that part of his head which is front when he is down and back when he stands up. They are set like a compass on gimbals.

Long and steadily they gazed, until, at last, their toes being tired, they fell down on all fours.

'I declare!' said the old *yaze* (daddy) 'Ozaka looks just like Kioto; and as for "the great ocean" those stupid maids talked about, I don't see any at all, unless they mean that strip of river that looks for all the world like the Yodo. I don't believe there is any "great ocean"!'

'As for my part,' said the 'cub', 'I am satisfied that it's all folly to go further; for Kioto is as like Ozaka as one grain of rice is like another.' Then he said to himself: 'Old Totsu-san (my father) is a fool, with all his philosophy.'

Thereupon both congratulated themselves upon the happy labour-saving expedient by which they had spared themselves a long journey, much leg-weariness, and some danger. They departed, after exchanging many compliments; and, dropping again into a frog's hop, they leaped back in half the time—the one to his well and the other to his pond. There each told the story of both cities looking exactly alike; thus demonstrating the folly of those foolish folks called men. As for the old gentleman in the lotus-pond, he was so glad to get the 'cub' back again that he never again tried to reason out the problems of philosophy. And to this day the frog in the well knows not and believes not in the 'great ocean.' Still do the babies of frogs become but frogs. Still is it vain to teach the reptiles philosophy; for all such labour is 'like pouring water in a frog's face.' Still out of the black mud springs the glorious white lotus in celestial purity, unfolding its stainless petals to the smiling heavens, the emblem of life and resurrection.

THE CHILD OF THE THUNDER

In among the hills of Echizen, within sight of the snowy mountain called Hakuzan, lived a farmer named Bimbo. He was very poor, but frugal and industrious. He was very fond of children though he had none himself. He longed to adopt a son to bear his name, and often talked the matter over with his old dame. But being so dreadfully poor both thought it best not to adopt, until they had bettered their condition and increased the area of their land. For all the property Bimbo owned was the earth in a little gully, which he himself was reclaiming. A tiny rivulet, flowing from a spring in the crevice of the rocks above, after trickling over the boulders, rolled down the gully to join a brook in the larger valley below. Bimbo had with great labour, after many years, made dams or terraces of stone, inside which he had thrown soil, partly got from the mountain sides, but mainly carried in baskets on the backs of himself and his wife, from the valley below. By such weary toil, continued year in and year out, small beds of soil were formed, in which rice could be planted and grown. The little rivulet supplied the needful water; for rice, the daily food of labourer and farmer, must be planted and cultivated in soft mud under water. So the little rivulet, which once leaped over the rock and cut its way singing to the valley, now spread itself quietly over each terrace, making more than a dozen descents before it reached the fields below.

Yet after all his toil for a score of years, working every

day from the first croak of the raven, until the stars came out, Bimbo and his wife owned only three tan (three-fourth acre) of terrace land. Sometimes a summer would pass, and little or no rain fall. Then the rivulet dried up and crops failed. It seemed all in vain that their backs were bent and their foreheads seamed and wrinkled with care. Many a time did Bimbo have hard work of it even to pay his taxes, which sometimes amounted to half his crop. Many a time did he shake his head, muttering the discouraged farmer's proverb 'A new field gives a scant crop,' the words of which mean also, 'Human life is but fifty years.'

One summer day after a long drought, when the young rice sprouts, just transplanted were turning yellow at the tips, the clouds began to gather and roll, and soon a smart shower fell, the lightning glittered, and the hills echoed with claps of thunder. But Bimbo, hoe in hand, was so glad to see the rain fall, and the pattering drops felt so cool and refreshing, that he worked on, strengthening the terrace to resist the little flood about to come.

Pretty soon the storm rattled very near him, and he thought he had better seek shelter, lest the thunder should strike and kill him. For Bimbo, like all his neighbours, had often heard stories of Raijin, the god of the thunder-drums, who lives in the skies and rides on the storm, and sometimes kills people by throwing out of the clouds at them a terrible creature like a cat, with iron-like claws and a hairy body.

Just as Bimbo threw his hoe over his shoulder and started to move, a terrible blinding flash of lightning dazzled his eyes. It was immediately followed by a deafening crash, and the thunder fell just in front of him. He covered his eyes with his hands, but finding himself unhurt, uttered a prayer of thanks to Buddha for safety. Then he uncovered his eyes and looked down at his feet.

There lay a little boy, rosy and warm, and crowing in the most lively manner, and never minding the rain in the least. The farmer's eyes opened very wide, but happy and nearly surprised out of his senses, he picked up the child tenderly in his arms, and took him home to his old wife.

'Here's a gift from Raijin,' said Bimbo. 'We'll adopt him as our own son and call him Rai-taro,' (the first-born darling of the thunder).

So the boy grew up and became a very dutiful and loving child. He was as kind and obedient to his foster-parents as though he had been born in their house. He never liked to play with other children, but kept all day in the fields with his father, sporting with the rivulet and looking at the clouds and sky. Even when the strolling players of the *Dai Kagura* (the comedy which makes the gods laugh) and the 'Lion of Corea' came into the village, and every boy and girl and nurse and woman was sure to be out in great glee, the child of the thunder stayed up in the field, or climbed on the high rocks to watch the sailing of the birds and the flowing of the water and the river far away.

Great prosperity seemed to come to the farmer, and he laid it all to the sweet child that fell to him from the clouds. It was very curious that rain often fell on Bimbo's field when none fell elsewhere; so that Bimbo grew rich and changed his name to Kanemochi. He believed that the boy Raitaro beckoned to the clouds, and they shed their rain for him.

A good many summers passed by, and Raitaro had grown to be a tall and handsome lad, almost a man and eighteen years old. On his birthday the old farmer and the good wife made a little feast for their foster-child. They ate and drank and talked of the thunder-storm, out of which Raitaro was born.

Finally the young man said solemnly:

'My dear parents, I thank you very much for your kindness to me, but I must now say farewell. I hope you will always be happy.'

Then, in a moment, all trace of a human form disappeared, and floating in the air, they saw a tiny white dragon, which hovered for a moment above them, and then flew away. The old couple went out of doors to watch it, when it grew bigger and bigger, taking its course to the hills above, where the piled-up white clouds, which form on a summer's afternoon, seemed built up like towers and castles of silver. Towards one of these the dragon moved, until, as they watched his form, now grown to a mighty size, it disappeared from view.

After this Kanemochi and his wife, who were now old and white-headed, ceased from their toil and lived in comfort all their days. When they died and their bodies were reduced to a heap of white cinders in the stone furnace of the village cremation-house, their ashes were mixed, and being put into one urn, were laid away in the cemetery of the temple yard. Their tomb was carved in the form of a white dragon, which to this day, in spite of mosses and lichens, may still be seen among the ancient monuments of the little hamlet.

THE TONGUE-CUT SPARROW

There was once an old man who had a wife with a very bad temper. She had never borne him any children, and would not take the trouble to adopt a son. So for a little pet he kept a tiny sparrow, and fed it with great care. The old dame not satisfied with scolding her husband hated the sparrow.

Now the old woman's temper was especially bad on wash days, when her old back and knees were well strained over the low tub, which rested on the ground.

It happened once that she had made some starch, and set it in a red wooden bowl to cool. While her back was turned, the sparrow hopped down on the edge of the bowl, and pecked at some of the starch. In a rage the old hag seized a pair of scissors and cut the sparrow's tongue out. Flinging the bird in the air she cried out, 'Now be off.' So the poor sparrow, all bleeding, flew away.

When the old man came back and found his pet gone, he made a great ado. He asked his wife, and she told him what she had done and why. The sorrowful old man grieved sorely for his pet, and after looking in every place and calling it by name, gave it up as lost.

Long after this, old man while wandering on the mountains met his old friend the sparrow. They both cried 'Ohio!' (good morning,) to each other, and bowing low offered many mutual congratulations and inquiries as to health, etc. Then the sparrow begged the old man to visit his humble abode, promising to introduce his wife and two daughters.

The old man went in and found a nice little house with a bamboo garden, tiny waterfall, stepping stone and everything complete. Then Mrs Sparrow brought in slices of sugar-jelly, rock-candy, sweet potato custard, and a bowl of hot starch sprinkled with sugar and a pair of chopsticks on a tray. Miss Suzumi, the elder daughter brought the tea caddy and tea-pot, and in a snap of the fingers had a good cup of tea ready, which she offered on a tray, kneeling.

'Please take up and help yourself. The refreshments are very poor, but I hope you will excuse our plainness,' said Mother Sparrow. The delighted old man, wondering in himself at such a polite family of sparrows, ate heartily, and drank several cups of tea. Finally, on being pressed he remained all night.

For several days the old man enjoyed himself at the sparrow's home. He looked at the landscapes and the moonlight, feasted to his heart's content, and played go (the game of 360 checkers) with Ko-suzumi the little daughter. In the evening Mrs Sparrow would bring out the refreshments and the wine, and seat the old man on a silken cushion, while she played the guitar. Mr Sparrow and his two daughters danced, sung and made merry. The delighted old man leaning on the velvet arm-rest forgot his cares, his old limbs and his wife's tongue, and felt like a youth again.

On the fifth day the old man said he must go home. Then the sparrow brought out two baskets made of plaited rattan, such as are used in travelling and carried on men's shoulders. Placing them before their guest, the sparrow said, 'Please accept a parting gift.'

Now one basket was very heavy, and the other very light. The old man, not being greedy, said he would take the lighter one. So with many thanks and bows and good-byes, he set off homewards.

He reached his hut safely, but instead of a kind welcome the old hag began to scold him for being away so long. He begged her to be quiet, and telling of his visit to the sparrows, opened the basket, while the scowling old woman held her tongue, out of sheer curiosity.

Oh, what a splendid sight! There were gold and silver coin, and gems, and coral, and crystal, and amber, and the never-failing bag of money, and the invisible coat and hat, and rolls of books, and all manner of precious things.

At the sight of so much wealth, the old hag's scowl changed to a smile of greedy joy. 'I'll go right off and get a present from the sparrows,' said she.

So binding on her straw sandals, and tucking up her skirts, and adjusting her girdle, tying the bow in front, she seized her staff and set off on the road. Arriving at the sparrow's house she began to flatter Mr Sparrow by soft speeches. Of course the polite sparrow invited her into his house, but nothing but a cup of tea was offered her, and wife and daughters kept away. Seeing she was not going to get any good-bye gift, the brazen hussy asked for one. The sparrow then brought out and set before her two baskets, one heavy and the other light. Taking the heavier one without so much as saying 'thank you,' she carried it back with her. Then she opened it, expecting all kinds of riches.

She took off the lid, when a horrible cuttlefish rushed at her, and a horned oni snapped his tusks at her, a skeleton poked his bony fingers in her face, and finally a long, hairy serpent, with a big head and lolling tongue, sprang out and coiled around her, cracking her bones, and squeezing out her breath, till she died.

After the good old man had buried his wife, he adopted a son to comfort his old age, and with his treasures lived at ease all his days.

THE FIREFLY'S LOVERS

In Japan the night-flies emit so brilliant a light and are so beautiful that ladies go out in the evenings and catch the insects for amusement, as may be seen represented on Japanese fans. They imprison them in tiny cages made of bamboo threads, and hang them up in their rooms or suspend them from the eaves of their houses. At their picnic parties, the people love to sit on August evenings, fan in hand, looking over the lovely landscape, spangled by ten thousand brilliant spots of golden light. Each flash seems like a tiny blaze of harmless lightning.

One of the species of night-flies, the most beautiful of all, is a source of much amusement to the ladies. Hanging the cage of glittering insects on their verandahs, they sit and watch the crowd of winged visitors attracted by the firefly's light. What brings them there, and why the firefly's parlour is filled with suitors as a queen's court with courtiers, let this love story tell.

On the southern and sunny side of the castle moats of the Fukui castle, in Echizen, the water had long ago become shallow so that lotus lilies grew luxuriantly. Deep in the heart of one of the great flowers whose petals were as pink as the lining of a sea-shell, lived the King of the Fireflies, Hi-o, whose only daughter was the lovely princess Hotaru-Hime While still a child the hime (princess) was carefully kept at home within the pink petals of the lily, never going even to the edges except to see her father fly off on his journey. Dutifully she waited until of age, when the fire glowed in her own body, and shone, beautifully illuminating the lotus, until its light at night was like a lamp within a globe of coral.

Every night her light grew brighter and brighter, until at last it was as mellow as gold. Then her father said:

'My daughter is now of age, she may fly abroad with me sometimes, and when the proper suitor comes she may marry whom she will.'

So Hotaru-Hime flew forth in and out among the lotus lilies of the moat, then into rich rice fields, and at last far off to the indigo meadows.

Whenever she went a crowd of suitors followed her, for she had the singular power of attracting all the night-flying insects to herself. But she cared for none of their attentions, and though she spoke politely to them all she gave encouragement to none. Yet some of the sheeny-winged gallants called her a coquette.

One night she said to her mother, the queen:

'I have met many admirers, but I don't wish a husband from any of them. Tonight I shall stay at home, and if any of them love me truly they will come and pay me court here. Then I shall lay an impossible duty on them. If they are wise they will not try to perform it; and if they love their lives more than they love me, I do not want any of them. Whoever succeeds may have me for his bride.'

'As you will my child,' said the queen mother, who arrayed her daughter in her most resplendent robes, and set her on her throne in the heart of the lotus.

Then she gave orders to her bodyguard to keep all suitors at a respectful distance lest some stupid gallant, a hornbug or a cockchafer dazzled by the light should approach too near and hurt the princess or shake her throne.

No sooner had twilight faded away, than forth came the golden beetle, who stood on a stamen and making obeisance, said:—

'I am Lord Green-Gold, I offer my house, my fortune and my love to Princess Hotaru.'

'Go and bring me fire and I will be your bride' said Hotaru-Hime.

With a bow of the head the beetle opened his wings and departed with a stately whirr.

Next came a shining bug with wings and body as black as lamp-smoke, who solemnly professed his passion.

'Bring me fire and you may have me for your wife.'

Off flew the bug with a buzz.

Pretty soon came the scarlet dragonfly, expecting so to dazzle the princess by his gorgeous colours that she would accept him at once.

'I decline your offer' said the princess, 'but if you bring me a flash of fire, I'll become your bride.'

Swift was the flight of the dragonfly on his errand, and in came the Beetle with a tremendous buzz, and ardently plead his suit.

'I'll say "yes" if you bring me fire' said the glittering princess.

Suitor after suitor appeared to woo the daughter of the King of the Fireflies until every petal was dotted with them. One after another in a long troop they appeared. Each in his own way, proudly, humbly, boldly, mildly, with flattery, with boasting, even with tears, each proffered his love, told his rank or expatiated on his fortune or vowed his constancy, sang his tune or played his music. To every one of her lovers the princess in modest voice returned the same answer:

'Bring me fire and I'll be your bride.'

So without telling his rivals, each one thinking he had the secret alone sped away after fire.

But none ever came back to wed the princess. Alas for the poor suitors! The beetle whizzed off to a house near by through the paper windows of which light glimmered. So full was he of his passion that thinking nothing of wood or iron, he dashed his head against a nail, and fell dead on the ground.

The black bug flew into a room where a poor student was reading. His lamp was only a dish of earthenware full of rape seed oil with a wick made of pith. Knowing nothing of oil the love-lorn bug crawled into the dish to reach the flame and in a few seconds was drowned in the oil.

'*Nan jaro?*' (What's that?) said a thrifty housewife, sitting with needle in hand, as her lamp flared up for a moment, smoking the chimney, and then cracking it; while picking out the scorched bits she found a roasted dragonfly, whose scarlet wings were all burned off.

Mad with love the brilliant hawk-moth, afraid of the flame yet determined to win the fire for the princess, hovered round and round the candle flame, coming nearer and nearer each time. 'Now or never, the princess or death,' he buzzed, as he darted forward to snatch a flash of flame, but singeing his wings, he fell helplessly down, and died in agony.

'What a fool he was, to be sure,' said the ugly clothes moth, coming on the spot, 'I'll get the fire. I'll crawl up inside the candle.' So he climbed up the hollow paper wick, and was nearly to the top, and inside the hollow blue part of the flame, when the man, snuffing the wick, crushed him to death.

Sad indeed was the fate of the lovers of Hi-o's daughter. Some hovered around the beacons on the headland, some fluttered about the great wax candles which stood eight feet high in their brass sockets in Buddhist temples; some burned their noses at the top of incense sticks, or were nearly choked by the smoke; some danced all night around the lanterns in the shrines; some sought the sepulchral lamps in the graveyard; one visited the cremation furnace; another the kitchen, where a feast was going on; another chased the sparks that flew out of the chimney; but none brought fire to the princess, or won the lover's prize. Many lost their feelers, had their shining bodies scorched or their wings singed, but most of them alas! lay dead, black and cold next morning.

As the priests trimmed the lamps in the shrines, and the servant maids the lanterns, each said alike:

'The Princess Hotaru must have had many lovers last night.'

Alas! alas! poor suitors. Some tried to snatch a streak of green fire from the cat's eyes, and were snapped up for their pains. One attempted to get a mouthful of bird's breath, but was swallowed alive. A carrion beetle (the ugly lover) crawled off to the sea shore, and found some fish scales that emitted light. The stag-beetle climbed a mountain, and in a rotten tree stump found some bits of glowing wood like fire, but the distance was so great that long before they reached the castle moat it was daylight, and the fire had gone out; so they threw their fish scales and old wood away.

The next day was one of great mourning and there were so many funerals going on, that Hi-maro the Prince of the Fireflies on the north side of the castle moat inquired of his servants the cause. Then he learned for the first time of the glittering princess. Upon this the prince who had just succeeded his father upon the throne fell in love with the princess and resolved to marry her. He sent his chamberlain to ask of her father his daughter in marriage according to true etiquette. The father agreed to the prince's proposal, with the condition that the prince should obey her behest in one thing, which was to come in person bringing her fire.

Then the prince at the head of his glittering battalions came in person and filled the lotus palace with a flood of golden light. But Hotaru-Hime was so beautiful that her charms paled not their fire even in the blaze of the prince's glory. The visit ended in wooing, and the wooing in wedding. On the night appointed, in a palanquin made of the white lotus-petals, amid the blazing torches of the prince's battalions of warriors, Hotaru-Hime was borne to the prince's palace and there, prince and princess were joined in the wedlock.

Many generations have passed since Hi-maro and Hotaru-Hime were married, and still it is the whim of all Firefly princesses that their base-born lovers must bring fire as their love-offering or lose their prize. Else would the glittering fair ones be wearied unto death by the importunity of their lovers. Great indeed is the loss, for in this quest of fire many thousand insects, attracted by the firefly, are burned to death in the vain hope of winning the fire that shall gain the cruel but beautiful one that fascinates them. It is for this cause that each night insects hover around the lamp flame, and every morning a crowd of victims drowned in the oil, or scorched in the flame, must be cleaned from the lamp. This is the reason why young ladies catch and imprison the fireflies to watch the war of insect-love, in the hope that they may have human lovers who will dare as much, through fire and flood, as they.

THE BATTLE OF THE APE AND THE CRAB

In the land where neither the monkeys or the cats have tails, and the persimmons grow to be as large as apples and with seeds bigger than a melon's, there once lived a land crab in the side of a sand hill. One day an ape came along having a persimmon seed, which he offered to swap with the crab for a rice-cake. The crab agreed, and planting the seed in his garden went out every day to watch it grow.

By-and-by the ape came to visit the crab, and seeing the fine tree laden with the yellow-brown fruit, begged a few. The crab, asking pardon of the ape, said he could not climb the tree to offer him any, but agreed to give the ape half, if he would mount the tree and pluck them.

So the monkey ran up the tree, while the crab waited below, expecting to eat the ripe fruit. But the monkey sitting on a limb first filled his pockets full, and then picking off all the best ones, greedily ate the pulp, and threw the skin and stones in the crab's face. Every once in a while, he would pull off a green sour persimmon and hit the crab hard, until his shell was nearly cracked. At last the crab thought he would get the best of the ape. So when his enemy had eaten his fill until he was bulged out, he cried out,

'Now Mister Ape, I dare you to come down head-foremost. You can't do it.'

So the ape began to descend, head downward. This was just

what the crab wanted, for all the finest persimmons rolled out of his pockets on the ground. The crab quickly gathered them up, and with both arms full ran off to his hole. Then the ape was very angry. He kindled a fire, and blew the smoke down the hole, until the crab was nearly choked. The poor crab to save his life had to crawl out.

Then the monkey beat him soundly, and left him for dead.

The crab had not been long thus, when three travellers, a rice-mortar, an egg, and a wasp found him lying on the ground. They carried him into the house, bound up his wounds and while he lay in bed they planned how they might destroy the ape. They all talked of the matter over their cups of tea, and after the mortar had smoked several pipes of tobacco, a plan was agreed on.

So taking the crab along, stiff and sore as he was, they marched to the monkey's castle. The wasp flew inside, and found that their enemy was away from home. Then all entered and hid themselves. The egg cuddled up under the ashes in the hearth. The wasp flew into the closet. The mortar hid behind the door. They then waited for the ape to come home. The crab sat beside the fire.

Towards evening the monkey arrived, and throwing off his coat (which was just what the wasp wanted) he lighted a sulphur match, and kindling a fire, hung on the kettle for a cup of tea, and pulled out his pipe for a smoke. Just as he sat down by the hearth to salute the crab, the egg burst and the hot yolk flew all over him and in his eye, nearly blinding him. He rushed out to the bath-room to plunge in the tub of cold water, when the wasp flew at him and stung his nose. Slipping down, he fell flat on the floor, when the mortar rolled on him and crushed him to death. Then the whole party congratulated the crab on their victory. Grateful for the friendship thus shown, the whole party, crab, mortar and wasp lived in peace together.

The crab married the daughter of a rich crab that lived over the hill, and a great feast of persimmons was spread before the bride's relatives who came to see the ceremony. By-and-by a little crab was born which became a great pet with the mortar and wasp. With no more apes to plague them, they lived very happily.

THE WONDERFUL TEA-KETTLE

A long time ago there was an old priest who lived in the temple of Morinji in the province of Hitachi. He cooked his own rice, boiled his own tea, swept his own floor and lived frugally as an honest priest should do.

One day he was sitting near the square fire-place in the middle of the floor. A rope and chain to hold the pot and kettle hung down from the covered hole in the ceiling which did duty as a chimney. A pair of brass tongs was stuck in the ashes and the fire blazed merrily. At the side of the fire-place, on the floor, was a tray filled with tiny tea-cups, a pewter tea-caddy, a bamboo tea-stirrer, and a little dipper. The priest having finished sweeping the ashes off the edges of the hearth with a little whisk of hawk's feathers, was just about to put on the tea when 'suzz,' 'suzz,' sang the tea-kettle spout; and then 'pattari—pattari' said the lid, as it flapped up and down, and the kettle swung backwards and forwards.

'What does this mean?' said the old bonze. '*Naru hodo*,' said he, with a start as the spout of the kettle turned into a badger's nose with its big whiskers, while from the other side sprouted out a long bushy tail.

'*Yohodo medzurashi*,' shouted the priest dropping the tea-caddy and spilling the green tea all over the matting as four hairy legs appeared under the kettle, and the strange compound, half badger and half kettle, jumped off the fire, and began running around the room. To the priest's horror it leaped on a shelf, puffed out its belly and began to beat a tune with its fore-paws as if it were a drum. The old bonze's pupils, hearing the racket rushed in, and after a lively chase, upsetting piles of books and breaking some of the tea-cups, secured the badger, and squeezed him in a keg used for storing the pickled radishes called *daikon*, (or Japanese sauer-kraut.) They fastened down the lid with a heavy stone. They were sure that the strong odor of the radishes would kill the beast, for no man could possibly survive such a smell, and it was not likely a badger could.

The next morning the tinker of the village called in and the priest told him about his strange visitor. Wishing to show him the animal, he cautiously lifted the lid of the cask, lest the badger, might after all, be still alive, in spite of the stench of the sour mess, when lo! there was nothing but the old iron tea-kettle. Fearing that the utensil might play the same prank again, the priest was glad to sell it to the tinker who bought the kettle for a few iron cash. He carried it to his junk shop, though he thought it felt unusually heavy.

The tinker went to bed as usual that night with his *andon*, or paper shaded lamp, just back of his head. About midnight, hearing a strange noise like the flapping up and down of an iron pot-lid, he sat up in bed, rubbed his eyes, and there was the iron pot covered with fur and sprouting out legs. In short, it was turning into a hairy beast. Going over to the recess and taking a fan from the rack, the badger climbed up on the frame of the lamp, and began to dance on its one hind leg, waving the fan with its fore-paw. It played many other tricks, until the man started up, and then the badger turned into a tea-kettle again.

'I declare,' said the tinker as he woke up next morning, and talked the matter over with his wife. 'I'll just "raise a mountain" (earn my fortune) on this kettle. It certainly is a very highly accomplished tea-kettle. I'll call it the *Bumbuku Chagama* (The Tea-Kettle accomplished in literature and military art) and exhibit it to the public.'

So the tinker hired a professional show-man for his business agent, and built a little theatre and stage. Then he gave an order to a friend of his, an artist, to paint scenery, with Fujiyama and cranes flying in the air, and a crimson sun shining through the bamboo, and a red moon rising over the waves, and golden clouds and tortoises, and the Sumiyoshi couple, and the grasshopper's picnic, and the Procession of Lord Long-legs, and such like. Then he stretched a tight rope of rice-straw across the stage, and the handbills being stuck up in all the barber shops in town, and wooden tickets branded with 'Accomplished and Lucky Tea-Kettle Performance, Admit one,'—the show was opened. The house was full and the people came in parties bringing their tea-pots full of tea and picnic boxes full of rice and eggs, and dumplings, made of millet meal, sugared roast-pea cakes, and other refreshments; because they came to stay all day. Mothers brought their babies with them for the children enjoyed it most of all.

Then the tinker, dressed up in his wide ceremonial clothes, with a big fan in his hand, came out on the platform, made his bow and set the wonderful tea-kettle on the stage. Then at a wave of his fan, the kettle ran around on four legs, half badger and half iron, clanking its lid and wagging its tail. Next it turned into a badger, swelled out its body and beat a tune on it like a drum. It danced a jig on the tight rope, and walked the slack rope, holding a fan, or an umbrella in his paw, stood on his head, and finally at a flourish of his master's fan became a cold and rusty tea-kettle again. The audience were wild with delight, and as the fame of the wonderful tea-kettle spread, many people came from great distances.

Year after year the tinker exhibited the wonder until he grew immensely rich. Then he retired from the show business, and out of gratitude took the old kettle to the temple again and deposited it there as a precious relic. It was then named *Bumbuku Dai Mio Jin* (The Great Illustrious, Accomplished in Literature and the Military Art).

PEACH-PRINCE, AND THE
TREASURE ISLAND

Very long, long ago, there lived an old man and woman in a village near a mountain, from which flowed a stream of purest water. This old couple loved each other so dearly and lived together so happily, that the neighbours called them *oshidori fu-fu* (a love-bird couple), after the mandarin ducks which always dwell together in pairs, and are so affectionate that they are said to pine and die if one be taken from the other. The old man was a woodcutter, and the old woman kept house, but they were very lonely for they had no child, and often grieved over their hard lot.

One day while the man was out on the mountain cutting brush, his old crone took her shallow tub and clothes down to the brook to wash. She had not yet begun, when she saw a peach floating with its stem and two leaves in the stream. She picked up the fruit and set it aside to take home and share it with her old man. When he returned she set it before him, not dreaming what was in it. He was just about to cut it open, when the peach fell in half, and there lay a little baby boy. The happy old couple rejoiced over him and reared him tenderly. Because he was their first child (*taro*) and born of a peach (*momo*) they called him Momotaro or Peach-Darling.

The most wonderful thing in the child, was his great strength! Even when still a baby, he would astonish his foster-mother by standing on the mats, and lifting her wash tub, or kettle of hot tea, which he would balance above his head without spilling a drop. The little fellow grew to be strong and brave and good. He was always kind to his parents and saved them many a step and much toil. He practised archery, wrestling, and handling the iron club, until he was not afraid of anybody or anything. He even laughed at the oni, who, were demons living in the clouds or on lonely islands in the sea. Momotaro was also very kind to birds and animals, so that they were very tame, and became his friends, knew him and called him by name.

Now there was an island far out in the ocean, inhabited by onis with horns in their heads, and big sharp tusks in their mouths, who ravaged the shores of Japan and ate up the people. In the centre of the island was the giant oni's castle, built inside a great cave which was full of all kinds of treasures such as every one wants. These are:

1. The hat which makes the one who puts it on invisible. It looks just like a straw hat, but has a tuft of fine grass on the top, and a pink fringe like the lining of shells, around the brim.
2. A coat like a farmer's grass rain-cloak, which makes the wearer invisible.
3. The crystal jewels which flash fire, and govern the ebb and flow of the tide.
4. Shippo, or 'the seven jewels,' namely gold and silver, branch of red coral, agate, emerald, crystal and pearl. All together called *takare mono*, or precious treasures.

Momotaro made up his mind to conquer these demons, and get their treasures. He prepared his weapons and asked the old woman to make him some millet dumplings. So the old lady ground the millet seeds into meal, the old man kneaded the dough, and both made the dumplings which the little hero carefully stuck on skewers and stowed away in a bamboo basket-box. This he wrapped in a silk napkin, and flung it over his shoulder. Seizing his iron club he stuck his flag in his back as the sign of war. The flag was of white silk, crossed by two black bars at the top, and underneath these, was embroidered the device of a peach with a stem and two leaves floating on a running stream. This was his crest or *sashimono* (banneret). Then he bade the old folks good-bye and walked off briskly. He took his little dog with him, giving him a millet dumpling now and then.

As he passed along he met a monkey chattering and showing his teeth. The monkey said,

'Where are you going, Mr Peach-Darling?'

'I'm going to the oni's island to get his treasures.'

'What have you got good in your package?'

'Millet dumplings. Have one?'

'Yes, give me one, and I'll go with you,' said the monkey.

So the monkey ate the dumpling, and boy, dog and monkey all trudged on together. A little further on a pheasant met them and said:

'Ohio, Momotaro, *doko?*' (Good morning, Mr Peach-Prince, where are you going?). Peach-Prince told him, and at the same time offered him a dumpling. This made the pheasant his friend.

Peach-Prince and his little army of three retainers journeyed on until they reached the sea-shore. There they found a big boat into which Peach-Prince with the dog and monkey embarked, while the pheasant flew over to the island to find a safe place to land, so as to take the onis by surprise.

They quietly reached the door of the cave, and then Momotaro beat in the gate with his iron club. Rushing into the castle, he put the small onis to flight, and dashing forward, the little hero would nearly have reached the room where the giant oni was just waking up after a nights' drunkenness. With a terrible roar he advanced to gobble up Peach-Prince, when the dog ran behind and bit the oni in the leg. The monkey climbed up his back and blinded him with his paws while the pheasant flew in his face. Then Peach-Prince beat him with his iron club, until he begged for his life and promised to give up all his treasures.

The onis brought all their precious things out of the storehouse and laid them on great tables or trays before the little hero and his little army.

Momotaro sat on a rock, with his little army of three retainers around him, holding his fan, with his hands akimbo on his knees, just as mighty generals do after a battle, when they receive the submission of their enemies. On his right sat kneeling on the ground his faithful monkey, while the pheasant and dog sat on the left.

After the onis had surrendered all, they fell down on their hands and knees with their faces in the dust, and acknowledged Peach-Prince as their master, and swore they would ever henceforth be his slaves. Then Peach-Prince, with a wave of his fan bade them rise up and carry the treasures to the largest ship they had, and to point the prow to the land. This done, Momotaro and his company got on board, and the onis bowed farewell.

A stiff breeze sprang up and sent the ship plowing through the waters, and bent out the great white sail like a bow. On the prow was a long black tassel like the mane of a horse, that at every lurch dipped in the waves, and as it rose flung off the spray.

The old couple becoming anxious after their Peach-Darling,

had traveled down to the sea shore, and arrived just as the treasure ship hove in sight. Oh how beautiful it looked with its branches of red coral, and shining heaps of gold and silver, and the invisible coat and hat, the dazzling sheen of the jewels of the ebbing and the flowing tide, the glistening pearls, and piles of agate and crystal.

Momotaro came home laden with riches enough to keep the old couple in comfort all their lives, and he himself lived in great state. He knighted the monkey, the dog and the pheasant, and made them his bodyguard. Then he married a beautiful princess and lived happily till he died.

THE FOX AND THE BADGER

There is a certain mountainous district in Shikoku in which a skilful hunter had trapped or shot so many foxes and badgers that only a few were left. These were an old grey badger and a female fox with one cub. Though hard pressed by hunger, neither dared to touch a loose piece of food, lest a trap might be hidden under it. Indeed they scarcely stirred out of their holes except at night, lest the hunter's arrow should strike them. At last the two animals held a council together to decide what to do, whether to emigrate or to attempt to outwit their enemy. They thought a long while, when finally the badger having hit upon a good plan, cried out:

'I have it. Do you transform yourself into a man. I'll pretend to be dead. Then you can bind me up and sell me in the town. With the money paid you can buy some food. Then I'll get loose and come back. The next week I'll sell you and you can escape.'

'Ha! ha! ha! *yoroshiu, yoroshiu,*' (good, good,) cried both together. 'It's a capital plan,' said Mrs Fox.

So the Fox changed herself into a human form, and the badger, pretending to be dead, was tied up with straw ropes.

Slinging him over her shoulder, the fox went to town, sold the badger, and buying a lot of tofu (bean-cheese) and one or two chickens, made a feast. By this time the badger had got loose, for the man to whom he was sold, thinking him dead, had not watched him carefully. So scampering away to the mountains he met the fox, who congratulated him, while both feasted merrily.

The next week the badger took human form, and going to town sold the fox, who made believe to be dead. But the badger being an old skin-flint, and very greedy, wanted all the money and food for himself. So he whispered in the man's ear to watch the fox well as she was only feigning to be dead. So the man taking up a club gave the fox a blow on the head, which finished her. The badger, buying a good dinner, ate it all himself, and licked his chops, never even thinking of the fox's cub.

The cub after waiting a long time for its mother to come back, suspected foul play, and resolved on revenge. So going to the badger he challenged him to a trial of skill in the art of transformation. The badger accepted right off, for he despised the cub and wished to be rid of him.

'Well what do you want to do first? said Sir Badger.'

'I propose that you go and stand on the Big Bridge leading to the city,' said the cub, 'and wait for my appearance. I shall come in splendid garments, and with many followers in my train. If you recognize me, you win, and I lose. If you fail, I win.'

So the badger went and waited behind a tree. Soon a daimio riding in a palanquin, with a splendid retinue of courtiers appeared, coming up the road. Thinking this was the fox-cub changed into a nobleman, although wondering at the skill of the young fox, the badger went up to the palanquin and told the person inside that he was recognized and had lost the game.

'What!' said the daimio's followers, who were real men, and surrounding the badger, they beat him to death.

The fox-cub, who was looking on from a hill near by, laughed in derision, and glad that treachery was punished, scampered away.

THE SEVEN PATRONS OF HAPPINESS

Every child knows who the *Shichi fuku Fin* or seven Patrons of Happiness are. They have charge of Long Life, Riches, Daily Food, Contentment, Talents, Glory and Love. Their images carved in ivory, wood, stone or cast in bronze are found in every house or sold in the stores or are painted on shop signs or found in picture books. They are a jolly company and make a happy family. On New Year's Eve a picture of the Treasure-ship (*Takare-bune*) laden with *shippo* (the seven jewels) and all the good things of life which men most desire is hung up in houses. The ship is coming into port and the passengers are the seven happy fairies who will make gifts to the people. These seven jewels are the same as those which Momotaro brought back from the oni's island.

First there is Fukuroku Jin the patron of Long Life or Length of Days. He has an enormously high forehead rounded at the top which makes his head look like a sugar-loaf. It is bald and shiny. A few stray white hairs sometimes sprout up, and the barber to reach them has to prop a ladder against his head to climb up and apply his razor. This big head comes from thinking so much. His eyebrows are cotton-white, and a long snowy beard falls down over his breast.

Once in a while in a good humour he ties a handkerchief over his high slippery crown and allows little boys to climb up on top—that is if they are good and can write well.

When he wants to show how strong and lively he is even though so old, he lets Daikoku the fat fellow ride on top of his head, while he smokes his pipe and wades across a river. Daikoku has to hold on tightly or he will slip down and get a ducking.

Usually the old shiny head is a very solemn gentleman, and walks slowly along with his staff in one hand while with the other he strokes his long eyebrows. The tortoise and the crane are always with him, for these are his pets. Sometimes a stag with hair white with age, walks behind him. Every body likes Fukoruku Jin because every one wants to get his favour and live long; until, like a lobster, their backs are bent with age. At a wedding you will always see a picture of white-bearded and shiny-pated Fukoruku Jin.

Daikoku is a short chubby fellow with eyes half sunk in fat but twinkling with fun. He has a flat cap set on his head like the kind which babies wear, a loose sack over his shoulders, and big boots on his feet. His throne is two straw bags of rice, and his badge of office is a mallet or hammer, which makes people rich when he shakes it. The hammer is the symbol of labour, showing that people may expect to get rich only by hard work. One end of it is carved to represent the jewel of the ebbing and the flowing tides, because merchants get rich by commerce on the sea and must watch the tides. He is often seen holding the arithmetic frame on which you can count, do sums, subtract, multiply or divide, by sliding balls up and down a row of sticks set in a frame, instead of writing figures. Beside him is a ledger and day-book. His favourite animal is the rat, which like some rich men's pets, eats or runs away with his wealth.

The great silver-white radish called daikon, two feet long and as big as a man's calf is always seen near him because it signifies flourishing prosperity.

He keeps his bag tightly shut, for money easily runs away when the purse is once opened. He never lets go his hammer, for it is only by constant care that any one can keep money after he gets it. Even when he frolics with Fukuroku Jin, and rides on his head, he keeps his hammer ready swinging at his belt. He has huge lop ears.

Once in a while, when he wishes to take exercise, and Fukuroku Jin wants to show how frisky he can be, even if he is old, they have a wrestling match together. Daikoku nearly always beats, because Fukuroku Jin is so tall that he has to bend down to grip Daikoku, who is fat and short, and thus he becomes top-heavy. Then Daikoku gets his rival's long head under his left arm, seizes him over his back by the belt, and throws him over his shoulder flat on the ground. But if Fukuroku Jin can only get hold of Daikoku's lop ears, both fall together. Then they laugh heartily and try it again.

Ebisu is the patron of daily food, which is rice and fish, and in old times was chiefly fish. He is nearly as fat as Daikoku, but wears a court noble's high cap. He is always fishing or enjoying his game. When very happy, he sits on a rock by the sea, with his right leg bent under him, and a big red fish, called the tai, under his left arm. He carries a straw wallet on his back to hold his fish and keep it fresh. Often he is seen standing knee-deep in the water, pole in hand, watching for a nibble. Some say that Ebisu is the same scamp that goes by the other name of Sosanoo.

Hotei is the patron of contentment, and of course is the father of happiness. He does not wear much clothing, for the truth is that all his property consists of an old, ragged wrapper, a fan and a wallet. He is as round as a pudding, and as fat as if rolled out of dough. His body is like a lump of mochi pastry, and his limbs like *dango* dumplings. He has lop ears that hang down over his shoulders, a tremendous double chin, and a round belly. Though he will not let his beard grow long, the slovenly old fellow never has it shaven when he ought to. He is a jolly vagabond, and never fit for company; but he is a great friend of the children, who romp over his knees and shoulders, pull his ears and climb up over his shaven head. He always keeps something good for them in his wallet. Sometimes he opens it wide, and then makes them guess what is inside. They try to peep in but are not tall enough to look over the edge. He makes tops, paints pictures or kites for the boys, and is the children's greatest friend. When the seven patrons meet together, Hotei is apt to drink more wine than is good for him.

Toshitoku is almost the only one of the seven who never lays aside his dignity. He has a very grave countenance. He is the patron of talents. His pet animal is a spotted fawn. He travels about a good deal to find and reward good boys, who are diligent in their studies, and men who are fitted to rule. In one hand he carries a crooked staff of bamboo, at the top of which is hung a book or roll of manuscript. His dress is like that of a learned doctor, with square cap, stole and high-toed slippers.

Bishamon is the patron of glory and fame. He is a mighty soldier, with a golden helmet, breastplate and complete armour. He is the protector of priests and warriors. He gives them skill in fencing, horsemanship and archery. He holds a pagoda in one hand and a dragon sword in the other. His pet animal is the tiger.

Six out of the jolly seven worthies are men. Benten is the only lady. She is the patron of the family and of the sea. She plays the flute and the guitar for the others, and amuses them at their feasts, sometimes even dancing for them. Her real home is in Riu Gu, and she is the Queen of the World Under the Sea. She often dwells in the sea or ocean caves. Her favourite animal is the snake, and her servants are the dragons.

Once a year the jolly seven meet together to talk over old times, relate their adventures, and have a supper together. Then they proceed to business, which is to arrange all the marriages for the coming year. They have a great many hanks of red and white silk, which are the threads of fate of those to be married: The white threads are the men, the red are the women. At first they select the threads very carefully, and tie a great many pairs or couples neatly and strongly together, so that the matches are perfect. All such marriages of threads make happy marriages among human beings. But by-and-by they get tired, and lazy, and instead of tying the knots carefully, they hurry up the work and then jumble them carelessly, and finally toss and tangle up all the rest in a muss.

This is the reason why so many marriages are unhappy.

Then they begin to frolic like big boys. Benten plays the guitar, and Bishamon lies down on the floor resting with his elbows to hear it. Hotei drinks wine out of a shallow red cup as wide as a dinner plate. Daikoku and Fukuroku Jin begin to wrestle, and when Daikoku gets his man down, he pounds his big head with an empty gourd while Toshitoku and Ebisu begin to eat tai fish. When this fun is over, Benten and Fukuroku Jin play a game of checkers, while the others look on and bet; except Hotei the fat fellow, who is asleep. Then they get ashamed of themselves for gambling, and after a few days the party breaks up and each one goes to his regular business again.

DAIKOKU AND THE ONI

A long while ago, when the idols of Buddha and his host of disciples came to Japan, after travelling through China from India, they were very much vexed because the people still liked the little black fellow named Daikoku. Even when they became Buddhists they still burned incense to Daikoku, because he was the patron of wealth; for everybody then, as now, wanted to be rich. So the Buddhist idols determined to get rid of the little fat fellow. How to do it was the question. At last they called Yemma, the judge of the lower regions, and gave him the power to destroy Daikoku.

Now Yemma had under him a whole legion of oni, some green, some black, others blue as indigo and others of a vermilion colour, which he usually sent on ordinary errands.

But for so important an expedition he now called Shino a very cunning old fellow, and ordered him to kill or remove Daikoku out of the way.

Shino made his bow to his master, tightened his tiger-skin belt around his loins and set off.

It was not an easy thing to find Daikoku, even though every one worshipped him. So the oni had to travel a long way, and ask a great many questions of people, and often lose his way before he got any clue. One day he met a sparrow who directed him to Daikoku's palace, where among all his money-bags and treasure piled to the ceiling, the fat and lop-eared fellow was accustomed to sit eating daikon radish, and amuse himself with his favourite pets, the rats. Around him was stored in straw bags his rice which he considered more precious than money.

Entering the gate, the oni peeped about cautiously but saw no one. He went further on till he came to a large store house standing alone and built in the shape of a huge rice-measure. Not a door or window could be seen, but climbing up a narrow plank set against the top edge he peeped over, and there sat Daikoku.

The oni descended and got into the room. Then he thought it would be an easy thing to pounce upon Daikoku. He was already chuckling to himself over the prospect of such wealth being his own, when Daikoku squeaked out to his chief rat.

'*Nedzumi-san*, (Mr Rat) I feel some strange creature must be near. Go chase him off the premises.'

Away scampered the rat to the garden and plucked a sprig of holly with leaves full of thorns like needles. With this in his fore-paw, he ran at the oni, whacked him soundly, and stuck him all over with the sharp prickles.

The oni yelling with pain ran away as fast as he could run. He was so frightened that he never stopped until he reached Yemma's palace, when he fell down breathless. He then told his master the tale of his adventure, but begged that he might never again be sent against Daikoku.

So the Buddhist idols finding they could not banish or kill Daikoku, agreed to recognize him, and so they made peace with him and to this day Buddhists and Shintoists alike worship the fat little god of wealth.

When people heard how the chief oni had been driven away by only a rat armed with holly, they thought it a good thing to keep off all oni. So ever afterward, even to this day, after driving out all the bad creatures with parched beans, they place sprigs of holly at their door-posts on New Year's Eve, to keep away the oni and all evil spirits.

BENKEI AND THE BELL

On one of the hills overlooking the blue sky's mirror of Lake Biwa, stands the ancient monastery of Miidera which was founded over 1,200 years ago, by the pious Mikado Tenchi.

Near the entrance, on a platform constructed of stoutest timbers, stands a bronze bell five and a half feet high. It has on it none of the superscriptions so commonly found on Japanese bells, and though its surface is covered with scratches it was once as brilliant as a mirror. This old bell, which is visited by thousands of people from all parts of Japan who come to wonder at it, is remarkable for many things.

Over two thousand years ago, say the bonzes, it hung in the temple of Gihon Shoja in India which Buddha built. After his death it got into the possession of the Dragon King of the World Under the Sea. When the hero Toda the Archer shot the enemy of the queen of the Underworld, she presented him with many treasures and among them this great bell, which she caused to be landed on the shores of the lake. Toda however was not able to remove it, so he presented it to the monks at Miidera. With great labour it was brought to the hill-top and hung in this belfry where it rung out daily matins and orisons, filling the lake and hill sides with sweet melody.

Now it was one of the rules of the Buddhists that no woman should be allowed to ascend the hill or enter the monastery of Miidera. The bonzes associated females and wicked influences together. Hence the prohibition.

A noted beauty of Kioto hearing of the polished face of the bell, resolved in spite of the law against her sex to ascend the hill to dress her hair and powder her face in the mirror-like surface of the bell.

So selecting an hour when she knew the priests would be too busy at study of the sacred rolls to notice her, she ascended the hill and entered the belfry. Looking into the smooth surface, she saw her own sparkling eyes, her cheeks, flushed rosy with exercise, her dimples playing, and then her whole form reflected as in her own silver mirror, before which she daily sat. Charmed as much by the vastness as the brilliancy of the reflection, she stretched forth her hand, and touching her finger-tips to the bell prayed aloud that she might possess just such a mirror of equal size and brightness.

But the bell was outraged at the impiety of the woman's touch, and the cold metal shrank back, leaving a hollow place, and spoiling the even surface of the bell. From that time forth the bell gradually lost its polish, and became dull and finally dark like other bells.

When Benkei was a monk, he was possessed of a mighty desire to steal this bell and hang it up at Hiyeisan. So one night he went over to Miidera hill and cautiously crept up to the belfry and unhooked it from the great iron link which held it. How to get it down the mountain was now the question.

Should he let it roll down, the monks at Miidera would hear it bumping over the stones. Nor could he carry it in his arms, for it was too big (around 16 feet) for him to grasp and hold. He could not put his head in it like a candle in a snuffer, for then he would not be able to see his way down.

So climbing into the belfry he pulled out the cross-beam with the iron link, and hanging on the bell put the beam on his shoulder to carry it in *tembimbo* style, that is, like a pair of scales.

The next difficulty was to balance it, for he had nothing but his lantern to hang on the other end of the beam to balance the bell. It was a prodigiously hard task to carry his burden the six or seven miles distance to Hiyeisan. It was 'trying to balance a bronze bell with a paper lantern.'

The work made him puff and blow and sweat until he was as hungry as a badger, but he finally succeeded in hooking it up in the belfry at Hiyeisan.

Then all the fellow priests of Benkei got up, though at night, to welcome him. They admired his bravery and strength and wished to strike the bell at once to show their joy.

'No, I won't lift a hammer or sound a note till you make me some soup. I am terribly hungry,' said Benkei, as he sat down on a cross piece of the belfry and wiped his forehead with his cowl.

Then the priests got out the iron soup-pot, five feet in diameter, and kindling a fire made a huge mess of soup and served it to Benkei. The lusty monk sipped bowl after bowl of the steaming nourishment until the pot was empty.

'Now,' said he, 'you may sound the bell.'

Five or six of the young bonzes mounted the platform and seized the rope that held the heavy log suspended from the roof. The manner of striking the bell was to pull back the log several feet, then let go the rope, holding the log after the rebound.

At the first stroke the bell quivered and rolled out a most mournful and solemn sound which as it softened and died away changed into the distinct murmur:

'I want to go back to Miidera, I want to go back to Miidera, I want to go-o back to-o M-i-i-de-ra-ra-a-a-a.'

'Naru hodo' said the priests. 'What a strange bell. It wants to go back. It is not satisfied with our ringing.'

'Ah! I know what is the matter' said the aged abbot. 'It must be sprinkled with holy water of Hiyeisan. Then it will be happy with us. Ho! page bring hither the deep sea shell full of sacred water.'

So the pure white shell full of the consecrated water was brought, together with the holy man's brush. Dipping it in the water the abbot sprinkled the bell inside and out.

'I dedicate thee, oh bell, to Hiyeisan. Now strike,' said he, signalling to the bell-pullers.

Again the young men mounted the platform, drew back the log with a lusty pull and let fly.

'M-m-m-mi-mi-de-de-ra-ra ye-e-e-e-ko-o-o-o-o' '(*Miidera ye ko*, I want to go back to Miidera)' moaned out the homesick bell.

This so enraged Benkei that he rushed to the rope, waved the monks aside and seizing the rope strained every muscle to jerk the beam its entire length afield, and then let fly with force enough to crack the bell. For a moment the dense volume of sound filled the ears of all like a storm, but as the vibrations died away, the bell whined out:

'Miidera-mi-mi-de-de-ra-a-a ye-e-e-ko-o-o-o-o.' 'I want to go back to Miidera,' sobbed the bell.

Whether struck at morning, noon or night the bell said the same words. No matter when, by whom, how hard or how gently it was struck, the bell moaned the one plaint as if crying, 'I want to go back to Miidera.' 'I want to go back to Miidera.'

At last Benkei in a rage unhooked the bell, shouldered it beam and all, and set off to take it back. Carrying the bell to the top of Hiyeisan, he set it down, and giving it a kick rolled it down the valley toward Miidera, and left it there. Then the Miidera bonzes hung it up again. Since that time the bell has completely changed its note, until now it is just like other bells in sound and behavior.

LITTLE SILVER'S DREAM OF THE SHOJI

Ko-gin-san (Miss Little Silver) was a young maid who did not care for strange stories of animals, so much as for those of wonder-creatures in the form of human beings. Even of these, however, she did not like to dream, and when the foolish old nurse would tell her ghost stories at night, she was terribly afraid they would appear to her in her sleep.

To avoid this, the old nurse told her to draw pictures of a tapir, on the sheet of white paper, which, wrapped round the tiny pillow, makes the pillow-case of every young lady, who rests her head on two inches of a bolster in order to keep her well-dressed hair from being mussed or rumpled.

Old grannies and country folks believe that if you have a picture of a tapir under the bed or on the paper pillow-case, you will not have unpleasant dreams, as the tapir is said to eat them.

So strongly do some people believe this that they sleep under quilts figured with the device of this long-snouted beast. If in spite of this precaution one should have a bad dream, he must cry out on awaking, 'tapir, come eat, tapir, come eat'; when the tapir will swallow the dream, and no evil results will happen to the dreamer.

Little Silver listened with both eyes and open mouth to this account of the tapir, and then making the picture and wrapping it around her pillow, she fell asleep. I suspect that the *kowameshi* (red rice) of which she had eaten so heartily at supper time, until her waist strings tightened, had something to do with her travels in dream-land.

She thought she had gone down to Ozaka, and there got on a junk and sailed far away to the southwest, through the Inland Sea. One night the water seemed full of white ghosts of men and women. Some of them were walking on, and in, the water. Some were running about. Here and there groups appeared to be talking together. Once in a while the junk would run against one of them; and when Little Silver looked to see if he were hurt or knocked over, she could see nothing until the junk passed by, when the ghost would appear standing in the same place, as though the ship had gone through empty air.

Occasionally a ghost would come up to the side of the ship, and in a squeaky voice ask for a dipper. While she would be wondering what a ghost wanted to do with a dipper, a sailor would quietly open a locker, take out a dipper having no bottom, and give one every time he was asked for them. Little Silver noticed a large bundle of these dippers ready. The ghosts would then begin to bail up water out of the sea to empty it in the boat. All night they followed the junk, holding on with one hand to the gunwale, while they vainly dipped up water with the other, trying to swamp the boat. If dippers with bottoms in them had been given them, the sailors said, the boat would have been sunk. When daylight appeared the shadowy host of people vanished.

In the morning they passed an island, the shores of which were high rocks of red coral. A great earthen jar stood on the beach, and around it lay long-handled ladles holding a half-gallon or more, and piles of very large shallow red lacquered wine cups, which seemed as big as the full moon. After the sun had been risen some time, there came down from over the hills a troop of the most curious looking people. Many were short, little wizen-faced folks, that looked very old; or rather, they seemed old before they ought to be. Some were very aged and crooked, with hickory-nut faces, and hair of a reddish grey tint. All the others had long scarlet locks hanging loose over their heads, and streaming down their backs. Their faces were flushed as if by hard drinking, and their pimpled noses resembled huge red barnacles. No sooner did they arrive at the great earthen jar than they ranged themselves round it. The old ones dipped out ladles full, and drank of the wine till they reeled. The younger ones poured the liquor into cups and drank. Even the little infants guzzled quantities of the yellow saké from the shallow cups of very thin red-lacquered wood.

Then began the dance, and wild and furious it was. The leather-faced old sots tossed their long reddish-grey locks in the air, and pirouetted round the big saké jar. The younger ones of all ages clapped their hands, knotted their handkerchiefs over their foreheads, waved their dippers or cups or fans, and practised all kinds of antics, while their scarlet hair streamed in the wind or was blown in their eyes.

The dance over, they threw down their cups and dippers, rested a few minutes and then took another heavy drink all around.

'Now to work' shouted an old fellow whose face was redder than his half-bleached hair, and who having only two teeth like tusks left looked just like an oni (imp). As for his wife, her teeth had long ago fallen out and the skin of her face seemed to have added a pucker for every year since a half century had rolled over her head.

Then Little Silver looked and saw them scatter. Some gathered shells and burned them to make lime. Others carried water and made mortar, which they thickened by a pulp made of paper, and a glue made by boiling fish skin. Some dived under the sea for red coral, which they hauled up by means of straw ropes, in great sprigs as thick as the branches of a tree. They quickly ran up a scaffold, and while some of the scarlet-headed plasterers smeared the walls, others below passed up the tempered mortar on long shell shovels, to the hand mortar-boards. Even at work they had casks and cups of saké at hand, while children played in the empty kegs and licked the gummy sugar left in some of them.

'What is that house for?' asked Little Silver of the sailors.

'Oh, that is the Kura (storehouse) in which the king of the Shoji stores the treasures of life, and health, and happiness, and property, which men throw away, or exchange for the saké, which he gives them, by making funnels of themselves.'

'Oh, Yes,' said Little Silver to herself, as she remembered how her father had said of a certain neighbour who had lately been drinking hard, 'he swills saké like a Shoji.'

She also understood why picnic or 'chow-chow' boxes were often decorated with pictures of Shoji, with their cups and dippers. For, at these picnics, many men get drunk; so much so indeed, that after a while the master of the feast orders very poor and cheap wine to be served to the guests. He also replaces the delicate wine cups of egg-shell porcelain, with big thick tea-cups or wooden bowls, for the guests when drunk, do not know the difference.

She also now understood why it was commonly said of a Mr Matsu, who had once been very rich but was now a poor sot, 'His property has all gone to the Shoji.'

Just then the ship in which she was sailing struck a rock, and the sudden jerk woke up Little Silver, who cried out, 'Tapir, come eat; tapir, come eat.'

No tapir came, but if he had I fear Little Silver would have been more frightened than she was by her dream of the ghosts; for next morning she laughed to think how they had all their work a-dipping water for nothing, and at her old nurse for thinking a picture of a tapir could keep off dreams.

THE TENGUS, OR THE ELVES WITH
LONG NOSES

Curious creatures are the tengus, with the head of a hawk and the body of a man. They have very hairy hands or paws with two fingers, and feet with two toes. They are hatched out of eggs, and have wings and feathers, until full grown. Then their wings moult, and the stumps are concealed behind their dress, which is like that of a man. They walk, when grown up, on clogs a foot high, which are like stilts, as they have but one support instead of two, like the sort which men wear. The tengus strut about easily on these, without stumbling.

The Dai Tengu, or master, is a solemn-faced, scowling individual with a very proud expression, and a nose about eight finger-breadths long. When he goes abroad, his retainers march before him, for fear he might break his nose against something. He wears a long grey beard down to his girdle, and moustaches to his chin. In his left hand he carries a large fan made of seven wide feathers. This is the sign of his rank. He has a mouth, but he rarely opens it. He is very wise, and rules over all the tengus in Japan.

The Karasu or crow-tengu is a black fellow, with a long beak, in the place where his nose and mouth ought to be. He looks as if some one had squeezed out the lower part of his face, and pulled his nose down so as to make a beak like a crow's. He is the Dai Tengu's lictor. He carries the axe of authority over his left shoulder, to chop bad people's heads off. In his right fist is his master's book of wisdom, and roll of authority. Even these two highest in authority in Tengu-land are servants of the great lord Kampira, the long-haired patron of sailors and mountaineers.

The greatest of the Dai Tengu lived in Kurama mountain and taught Yoshitsune. This lad, while a pupil in the monastery, would slip out in the evening, when the priests thought him asleep, and come to the king of the Tengus, who instructed him in the military arts, in cunning, magic and wisdom. Every night the boy would spread the roll of wisdom before him, and sit at the feet of the hoary-headed tengu, and learn the strange letters in which tengu wisdom is written, while the long-nosed servant tengus, propped up on their stilt-clogs, looked on. The boy was not afraid, but quickly learned the knowledge which birds, beasts and fishes have, how to understand their language and to fly, swim and leap like them.

When a tengu stumbles and falls down on his nose, it takes a long while to heal, and if he breaks it, the doctor puts it in splints like a broken arm, until it straightens out and heals up again.

Some of the amusements in Tengu-land are very curious. A pair of young tengus will fence with their noses as if they were foils. Their faces are well protected by masks, for if one tengu should 'poke his nose' into the other's eye he might put it out, and a blind tengu could not walk about, because he would be knocking his nose against everything.

Two old tengus with noses nearly two feet long, sometimes try the strength of their face-handles. One fellow has his beak straight up in the air like a supporting post, while the other sits a yard off with his elastic nose stretched across like a tight-rope, and tied with twine at the top of the other one's nose.

On this tight nose-rope a little tengu boy, with a tiny pug only two inches long, dances a jig. He holds an umbrella in his hand, now dancing, and now standing upon one foot. The tengu-daddy, whose nose serves as a tent-pole, waves his fan and sings a song, keeping time to the dance.

There is another tengu who sometimes quarrels with his wife, and when angry boxes her ears with his nose.

A lady-tengu who is inclined to be literary and sentimental, writes poetry. When the mood seizes her she ties the pen to her nose, dips it in ink and writes a poem on the wall.

A tengu-painter makes a long-handled brush to whitewash the ceiling, by strapping it to his nose.

Sometimes the little tengus get fighting, and then the feathers fly as they tear each other with their little claws which have talons on them shaped like a chicken's, but which when fully grown look like hands.

All the big tengus are fond of trying the strength of their noses, and how far they can bend them up and down without breaking. They have two favourite games of which they sometimes give exhibitions. The player has long strings of iron cash (that is, one hundred of the little iron coins, with a square hole in the centre). Several of these he slides on a rope like buttons on a string, or counters on a wire. Then he lifts them off with the tip of his nose. Sometimes his nose bends so much under the weight that the coins slip off. Whichever tengu can pick off the greater number of strings without letting any slip, wins the game, and is called *O-hana* (The King of Noses).

Another balances hoops and poles on his nose and throws balls through the hoops; or he poises a saucer of water on the tip of his nose without spilling a drop. Another fellow hangs a bell from the ceiling. Then, with a handkerchief tied loosely round his head, he pulls his nose back like a snapping-turtle's beak, and then suddenly lets go. His nose then strikes the bell and rings it. It hurts very much, but he does not mind it.

The tengus have one great fault. They love liquor too much. They often get drunk. They buy great casks of rice-wine, sling them round their necks, and drink out of long cups shaped like their faces, using the nose for a handle. A drunken tengu makes a funny sight, as he staggers about with his big wings drooping and flapping around him, and the feathers trailing in the mud, and his long nose limp, pendulous and groggy.

When the master of the tengus wishes to 'see the flowers,' which means to go on a picnic, he punishes his drunken servant by swinging the box of eatables over the fellow's red nose. Putting the end over his shoulders, he compels the sot to come along. It sobers the fellow, for the weight on his nose and the pulling on it hurts dreadfully, and often makes him squeal.

Oyama, a mountain near Tokio, is said to be full of these long-nosed elves, but many other mountains are inhabited by them, for they like lonely places away from men.

Dancers often put on masks like the tengu's face and dance a curious dance which they call the tengu's quadrille.

The tengus are very proud fellows, and think themselves above human beings. They are afraid of brave men, however, and never dare to hurt them. They scare children, especially bad boys. They watch a boy telling lies and catch him. Then the tengus pull out his tongue by the roots, and run away with it.

When a tengu walks, he folds his arms, throws back his head till his nose is far up in the air, and struts around as if he were a daimio. When a man becomes vain and carries his nose too high, the people say 'He has become a tengu.'

KINTARO, OR THE WILD BABY

Long, long ago, when the tallest fir trees on the Hakone mountains were no higher than a rice-stalk, there lived in that part of the range called Ashigara, a little ruddy boy, whom his mother had named Kintaro, or Golden Darling. He was not like other boys, for having no children to play with, he made companions of the wild animals of the forest.

He romped with the little bears, and often when the old she bear would come for her cubs to give them their supper and put them to bed, Kintaro would jump on her back and have a ride to her cave. He also put his arms around the neck of the deer, which were not afraid of him. He was prince of the forest, and the rabbits, wild boars, squirrels and martens, pheasants and hawks were his servants and messengers.

Although not much more than a fat baby, Kintaro wielded a big axe, and could chop a snake to pieces before he had time to wriggle.

Kintaro's father had been a brave soldier in Kioto, who through the malice of enemies at court, had fallen into disgrace. He had loved a beautiful lady whom he married. When her husband died she fled eastward to the Ashigara mountains, and there in the lonely forests in which no human being except poor woodcutters ever came, her boy was born.

She lived in a cave, nourishing herself on roots and herbs. The woodcutters soon learned about the strange pair living wild but peacefully in the woods, though they did not dream of her noble rank. The boy was known among them as 'Little Wonder,' and the woman as 'the old nurse of the mountain.'

Thus, all alone, the little fellow grew up, exercising himself daily, so that even though a child he could easily wrestle with a bear. Among his retainers were the tengus, though they were often rebellious and disobedient, not liking to be governed by a boy.

One day, an old mother-tengu, who had always laughed at the idea of obeying a little dumpling of a fellow like Kintaro, flew up to her nest in a high fir tree. Kintaro watched to see where it was, and waited till she left it to go and seek for food. Then going up to the tree, he shook it with all his might, until the nest came tumbling down, and the two young squabs of tengus with it.

Now it happened that just at that time the great hero and imp-killer, Raiko, was marching through the mountains on his way to Kioto. Seeing that the ruddy little fellow was no ordinary child, he found out the mother and heard her story. He then asked for the child and adopted him as his own.

So Kintaro went off with Raiko and grew up to be a brave soldier, and taking his father's name, he was known as Sakata Kintoki. His mother, however, remained in the mountains, and living to an extreme old age, was always known as 'the old nurse of the mountains.'

To this day, Kintaro is the hero of Japanese boys, and on their huge kites will usually be seen a picture of the little black-eyed ruddy boy of the mountains, with his axe, while around him are his wild playmates, and the young tengus rubbing their long noses, which were so nearly broken by their fall.

JIRAIYA, OR THE MAGIC FROG

Ogata was the name of a castle-lord who lived in the Island of the Nine Provinces, (Kiushiu). He had but one son, an infant, whom the people in admiration nicknamed Jiraiya (Young Thunder). During one of the civil wars, this castle was taken, and Ogata was slain; but by the aid of a faithful retainer, who hid Jiraiya in his bosom, the boy escaped and fled northward to Echigo. There he lived until he grew up to manhood.

At that time Echigo was infested with robbers. One day the faithful retainer of Jiraiya being attacked, made resistance, and was slain by the robbers. Jiraiya now left alone in the world went out from Echigo and led a wandering life in several provinces.

All this time he was consumed with the desire to revive the name of his father, and restore the fortunes of his family. Being exceedingly brave, and an expert swordsman, he became chief of a band of robbers and plundered many wealthy merchants, and in a short time he was rich in men, arms and booty. He was accustomed to disguise himself, and go in person into the houses and presence of men of wealth, and thus learn all about their gates and guards, where they slept, and in what rooms their treasures were stored, so that success was easy.

Hearing of an old man who lived in Shinano, he started to rob him, and for this purpose put on the disguise of a pilgrim.

Shinano is a very high table-land, full of mountains, and the snow lies deep in winter. A great snow storm coming on, Jiraiya took refuge in a humble house by the way. Entering, he found a very beautiful woman, who treated him with great kindness. This, however, did not change the robber's nature. At midnight, when all was still, he unsheathed his sword, and going noiselessly to her room, he found the lady absorbed in reading.

Lifting his sword, he was about to strike at her neck, when, in a flash, her body changed into that of a very old man, who seized the heavy steel blade and broke it in pieces as though it were a stick. Then he tossed the bits of steel away, and thus spoke to Jiraiya, who stood amazed but fearless:

'I am a man named Senso Dojin, and I have lived in these mountains many hundred years, though my true body is that of a huge frog. I can easily put you to death but I have another purpose. So I shall pardon you and teach you magic instead.'

Then the youth bowed his head to the floor, poured out his thanks to the old man and begged to be received as his pupil.

Remaining with the old man of the mountain for several weeks, Jiraiya learned all the arts of the mountain spirits; how to cause a storm of wind and rain, to make a deluge, and to control the elements at will.

He also learned how to govern the frogs, and at his bidding they assumed gigantic size, so that on their backs he could stand up and cross rivers and carry enormous loads.

When the old man had finished instructing him he said 'Henceforth cease from robbing, or in any way injuring the poor. Take from the wicked rich, and those who acquire money dishonestly, but help the needy and the suffering.' Thus speaking, the old man turned into a huge frog and hopped away.

What this old mountain spirit bade him do, was just what Jiraiya wished to accomplish. He set out on his journey with a light heart. 'I can now make the storm and the waters obey me, and all the frogs are at my command; but alas! the magic of the frog cannot control that of the serpent. I shall beware of his poison.'

From that time forth the oppressed poor people rejoiced many a time as the avaricious merchants and extortionate money lenders lost their treasures. For when a poor farmer, whose crops failed, could not pay his rent or loan on the date promised, these hard-hearted money lenders would turn him out of his house, seize his beds and mats and rice-tub, and even the shrine and images on the god-shelf, to sell them at auction for a trifle, to their minions, who resold them at a high price for the money-lender, who thus got a double benefit. Whenever a miser was robbed, the people said, 'The young thunder has struck,' and then they were glad, knowing that it was Jiraiya, (Young Thunder). In this manner his name soon grew to be the poor people's watchword in those troublous times.

Yet Jiraiya was always ready to help the innocent and honest, even if they were rich. One day a merchant named Fukutaro was sentenced to death, though he was really not guilty. Jiraiya hearing of it, went to the magistrate and said that he himself was the very man who committed the robbery. So the man's life was saved, and Jiraiya was hanged on a large oak tree. But during the night, his dead body changed into a bull-frog which hopped away out of sight, and off into the mountains of Shinano.

At this time, there was living in this province, a young and beautiful maiden named Tsunade. Her character was very lovely. She was always obedient to her parents and kind to her friends. Her daily task was to go to the mountains and cut brushwood for fuel. One day while thus busy singing at the task, she met a very old man, with a long white beard sweeping his breast, who said to her:

'Do not fear me. I have lived in this mountain many hundred years, but my real body is that of a snail. I will teach you the powers of magic, so that you can walk on the sea, or cross a river however swift and deep, as though it were dry land.'

Gladly the maiden took daily lessons of the old man, and soon was able to walk on the waters as on the mountain paths. One day the old man said, 'I shall now leave you and resume my former shape. Use your power to destroy wicked robbers. Help those who defend the poor. I advise you to marry the celebrated man Jiraiya, and thus you will unite your powers.'

Thus saying, the old man shrivelled up into a snail and crawled away.

'I am glad,' said the maiden to herself, 'for the magic of the snail can overcome that of the serpent. When Jiraiya, who has the magic of the frog, shall marry me, we can then destroy the son of the serpent, the robber named Dragon-coil (Orochimaru).'

By good fortune, Jiraiya met the maiden Tsunade and being charmed with her beauty, and knowing her power of magic, sent a messenger with presents to her parents, asking them to give him their daughter to wife. The parents agreed, and so the young and loving couple were married.

Hitherto when Jiraiya wished to cross a river he changed himself into a frog and swam across; or, he summoned a bull-frog before him, which increased in size until as large as an elephant. Then standing erect on his warty back, even though the wind blew his garments wildly, Jiraiya reached the opposite shore in safety. But now, with his wife's powers, the two, without any delay, walked over as though the surface was a hard floor.

Soon after their marriage, war broke out in Japan between the two famous clans of Tsukikage and Inukage. To help them fight their battles, and capture the castles of their enemies, the Tsukikage family besought the aid of Jiraiya, who agreed to serve them and carried their banner in his back. Their enemies, the Inukage, then secured the services of Dragon-coil.

This Orochimaru, or Dragon-coil, was a very wicked robber whose father was a man, and whose mother was a serpent that lived in the bottom of Lake Takura. He was perfectly skilled in the magic of the serpent, and by spurting venom on his enemies, could destroy the strongest warriors.

Collecting thousands of followers, he made great ravages in all parts of Japan, robbing and murdering good and bad, rich and poor alike. Loving war and destruction he joined his forces with the Inukage family.

Now that the magic of the frog and snail was joined to the one army, and the magic of the serpent aided the other, the conflicts were bloody and terrible, and many men were slain on both sides.

On one occasion, after a hard fought battle, Jiraiya fled and took refuge in a monastery, with a few trusty vassals, to rest a short time. In this retreat a lovely princess named Tagoto was dwelling. She had fled from Orochimaru, who wished her for his bride. She hated to marry the offspring of a serpent, and hoped to escape him. She lived in fear of him continually. Orochimaru hearing at one time that both Jiraiya and the princess were at this place, changed himself into a serpent, and distilling a large mouthful of poisonous venom, crawled up to the ceiling in the room where Jiraiya and his wife were sleeping, and reaching a spot directly over them, poured the poisonous venom on the heads of his rivals. The fumes of the prison so stupefied Jiraiya's followers, and even the monks, that Orochimaru, instantly changing himself to a man, profited by the opportunity to seize the Princess Tagoto, and make off with her.

Gradually the faithful retainers awoke from their stupor to find their master and his beloved wife delirious, and near the point of death, and the princess gone.

'What can we do to restore our dear master to life?' This was the question each one asked of the others, as with sorrowful faces and weeping eyes they gazed at the pallid forms of their unconscious master and his consort. They called in the venerable abbot of the monastery to see if he could suggest what could be done.

'Alas!' said the aged priest, 'there is no medicine in Japan to cure your lord's disease, but in India there is an elixir which is a sure antidote. If we could get that, the master would recover.'

'Alas! alas!' and a chorus of groans showed that all hope had fled, for the mountain in India, where the elixir was made, lay five thousand miles from Japan.

Just then a youth named Rikimatsu, one of the pages of Jiraiya, arose to speak. He was but fourteen years old, and served Jiraiya out of gratitude, for he had rescued his father from many dangers and saved his life. He begged permission to say a word to the abbot, who, seeing the lad's eager face, motioned to him with his fan to speak.

'How long can our lord live,' asked the youth.

'He will be dead in thirty hours,' answered the abbot, with a sigh.

'I'll go and procure the medicine, and if our master is still living when I come back, he will get well.'

Now Rikimatsu had learned magic and sorcery from the tengus, or long-nosed elves of the mountains, and could fly high in the air with incredible swiftness. Speaking a few words of incantation, he put on the wings of a tengu, mounted a white cloud and rode on the east wind to India, bought the elixir of the mountain spirits, and returned to Japan in one day and a night.

On the first touch of the elixir on the sick man's face he drew a deep breath, perspiration glistened on his forehead, and in a few moments more he sat up.

Jiraiya and his wife both got well, and the war broke out again. In a great battle Dragon-coil was killed and the princess rescued. For his prowess and aid Jiraiya was made daimio of Idzu.

Being now weary of war and the hardships of active life, Jiraiya was glad to settle down to tranquil life in the castle and rear his family in peace. He spent the remainder of his days in reading the books of the sages, in composing verses, in admiring the flowers, the moon and the landscape, and occasionally going out hawking or fishing. There, amid his children and children's children, he finished his days in peace.

HOW THE JELLYFISH LOST ITS SHELL

Parts of the seas of the Japanese Archipelago are speckled with thousands of round white jellyfish, that swim a few feet below the surface. One can see the great steamer go ploughing through them as through a field of frosted cakes. The huge paddle-wheels make a perfect pudding of thousands of them, as they are dashed against the paddle-box and whipped into a froth like white of eggs or churned into a thick cream by the propeller blades. Sometimes the shoals are of great breadth, and then it veritably looks as though a crockery shop had been upset in the ocean, and ten thousand white dinner-plates had broken loose. Around the bays and harbours the Japanese boys at play drive them with paddles into shoals, and sometimes they poke sticks through them. This they can do easily, because the jellyfish has no jacket of shell or bone like the lobster, nor any skin like a fish, and so always has to swim naked, exposed to all kinds of danger. Sometimes great jellyfishes, two or three feet in diameter, sail gaily along near the shore, as proud as the long-handled-umbrella of a daimio, and as brilliantly coloured as a Japanese parasol. Floating all around their bodies, like the streamers of a temple festival, or a court lady's ribbons, are their long tentacles or feelers. No peacock stretching his bannered tail could make a finer sight, or look prouder than these floating sun-fishes, or bladders of living jelly.

But alas for all things made of water! Let but a wave of

unusual force, or a sudden gust of wind come, and this lump of pride lies collapsed and stranded on the shore, like a pancake upset into a turnover, in which batter and crust are hopelessly mixed together. When found fresh, men often come down to the shore and cutting huge slices of blubber, as transparent as ice, they eat the solid water with their rice, in lieu of drink.

A jellyfish as big as an umbrella, and weighing as much as a big boy, will, after lying a few hours in the sun leave scarcely a trace on the spot for their bodies are little more than animated masses of water. At night, however where a jellyfish has stranded, the ground seems to crawl and emit a dull fire of phosphorescence which the Japanese call 'dragon's light.'

But the jellyfish once had a shell, and was not so defenceless, say the fairy tales. How it lost it is thus told.

In the days of old, the jellyfish was one of the retainers in waiting upon the Queen of the World Under the Sea, at her palace in Riu Gu. In those days he had a shell, and as his head was hard, no one dared to insult him, or stick him with their horns, or pinch him with their claws, or scratch him with their nails, or brush rudely by him with their fins. In short, this fish instead of being a lump of jelly, as white and helpless as a pudding, as we see him now, was a lordly fellow that could get his back up and keep it high when he wished to. He waited on the queen and right proud was he of his office. He was on good terms with the king's dragon, which often allowed him to play with his scaly tail but never hurt him in the least.

One day the queen fell sick, and every hour grew worse. The king became anxious, and her subjects talked about nothing else but her sickness. There was grief all through the water-world; from the mermaids on their beds of sponge, and the dragons in the rocky caverns, down to the tiny gudgeons in the rivers, that were considered no more than mere bait. The jolly cuttle-fish stopped playing his drums and guitar, folded his six arms and hid away moping in his hole. His servant the lobster in vain lighted his candle at night, and tried to induce him to come out of his lair. The dolphins and porpoises wept tears, but the clams, oysters and limpets shut up their shells and did not even wiggle. The flounders and skates lay flat on the ocean's floor, never even lifting up their noses. The squid wept a great deal of ink, and the jellyfish nearly melted to pure water. The tortoise was patient and offered to do anything for the relief of the queen.

But nothing could be done. The cuttle-fish who professed to be 'a kind of a' doctor, offered the use of all his cups to suck out the poison, if that were the trouble.

But it wasn't. It was internal, and nothing but medicine that could be swallowed would reach the disease.

At last some one suggested that the liver of a monkey would be a specific for the royal sickness, and it was resolved to try it. The tortoise, who was the queen's messenger, because he could live on both land and water, swim or crawl, was summoned. He was told to go upon earth to a certain mountain, catch a monkey and bring him alive to the Underworld.

Off started the tortoise on his journey to the earth, and going to a mountain where the monkeys lived, squatted down at the foot of a tree and pretended to be asleep though keeping his claws and tail out. There he waited patiently, well knowing that curiosity and the monkey's love of tricks would bring one within reach of his talons. Pretty soon, a family of chattering monkeys came running along among the branches overhead, when suddenly a young *saru* (monkey) caught sight of the sleeping tortoise.

'Naru hodo' (Is it possible?) said the long-handed fellow,

'here's fun; let's tickle the old fellow's back and pull his tail.'

All agreed, and forthwith a dozen monkeys, joining hand over hand, made a long ladder of themselves until they just reached the tortoise's back. (They didn't use their tails, for Japanese monkeys have none, except stumps two inches long). However, he who was to be the tail end of this living rope, when all was ready, crawled along and slipped over the whole line, whispering as he slid:

'Sh! don't chatter or laugh, you'll wake the old fellow up.'

Now the monkey expected to hold on the living pendulum by one long hand, and swinging down with the other, to pull the tortoise's tail, and see how near he could come to his snout without being snapped up. For a monkey well knew that a tortoise could neither jump off its legs nor climb a tree.

Once! Twice! The monkey pendulum swung back and forth without touching.

Three! Four! The monkey's finger-nails scratched the tortoise's back. Yet old Hard Shell pretended to be sound asleep.

Five! Six! The monkey caught hold of the tortoise's tail and jerked it hard. Old Tortoise now moved out its head a little, as if still only half awake.

Seven! Eight! This time the monkey intended to pull the tortoise's head, when just as he came within reach, the tortoise snapped him, held him in his claws, and as the monkey pendulum swung back he lost his hold. In an instant he was jerked loose, and fell head-foremost to the ground, half stunned.

Frightened at the loss of their end link, the other monkeys of the chain wound themselves up like a windlass over the branches, and squatting on the trees, set up a doleful chattering.

'Now,' says the tortoise, 'I want you to go with me. If you don't, I'll eat you up. Get on my back and I'll carry you; but I must hold your paw in my mouth so you won't run away.'

Half frightened to death, the monkey obeyed, and the tortoise trotted off to the sea, swam to the spot over the queen's palace, and in a fillip of the finger was down in the gardens of Riu Gu.

Here, let me say, that according to another version of this story the monkeys assembled in force when they suspected what the tortoise had come after, and catching him napping turned him over on his back so that he could not move or bite. Then they took his under shell off, so that he had to travel back to Riu Gu and get another one. This last version however is uncertain and it looks like a piece of invention to suppose that the monkeys had a sufficient medical knowledge to make them suspicious of the design of the tortoise on the monkey's liver. I prefer the regular account.

The queen hearing of the monkey's arrival thanked the tortoise, and commanded her cook and baker to feed him well and treat him kindly, for the queen felt really sorry because he was to lose his liver.

As for the monkey he enjoyed himself very much, and ran around everywhere amusing the starfishes, clams, oysters and other pulpy creatures that could not run, by his rapid climbing of the rocks and coral bushes, and by rolling over the sponge beds and cutting all manner of antics.

They had never before seen anything like it. Poor fellow! he didn't suspect what was to come.

All this time however the jellyfish pitied him in his heart, and could hardly keep what he knew to himself. Seeing that the monkey, lonely and homesick was standing by the shore of a pond, the jellyfish squeezed himself up near him and said:

'Excuse my addressing you, I feel very sorry for you because you are to be put to death.'

'Why?' said the monkey, 'What have I done?'

'Oh, nothing,' said the jellyfish, 'only our queen is sick and she wants your liver for medicine.'

Then if ever any one saw a sick looking monkey it was this one. As the Japanese say 'his liver was smashed.' He felt dreadfully afraid. He put his hands over his eyes, and immediately began to plan how to save both his liver and his life.

After a while the rain began to fall heavily, and the monkey ran in out of the garden, and standing in the hall of the queen's palace began to weep bitterly. Just then the tortoise, passing by, saw his captive.

'What are you crying about?'

'Aita! aita!' cried the monkey, 'When I left my home on the earth, I forgot to bring my liver with me, but hung it upon a tree, and now it is raining and my liver will decay and I'll die. Aita! aita!' and the poor monkey's eyes became red as a tai fish, and streamed with tears.

When the tortoise told the queen's courtiers what the monkey had said, their faces fell.

'Why, here's a pretty piece of business. The monkey is of no use without his liver. We must send him after it.'

So they dispatched the tortoise to the earth again, the monkey sitting a-straddle of his back. They came to the mountain again, and the tortoise being a little lazy, waited at the foot while the monkey scampered off, saying he would be back in an hour. The two creatures had become so well acquainted that the old Hard Shell fully trusted the lively little fellow.

But instead of an hour the tortoise waited till evening. No monkey came. So finding himself fooled, and knowing all the monkeys would take the alarm, he waddled back and told the queen all about it.

'Then,' said the queen after reprimanding her messenger for his silly confidence, 'the monkey must have got wind of our intention to use his liver, and what is more, some one of my retainers or servants must have told him.'

Then the queen issued an order commanding all her subjects to appear before the Dragon King of the Sea. Whoever did this wicked thing, Kai Riu O would punish him.

Now it happened that all the fish and sea animals of all sorts, that swam, crawled, rolled or moved in any way, appeared before Kai Riu O, the Dragon King, and his queen—all except the jellyfish. Then the queen knew the jellyfish was the guilty one. She ordered the culprit to be brought into her presence. Then publicly, before all her retainers and servants, she cried out:

'You leaky-tongued wretch, for your crime of betraying the confidence of your sovereign, you shall no longer remain among shell-fish. I condemn you to lose your shell.'

Then she stripped off his shell, and left the poor jellyfish entirely naked and ashamed.

'Be off, you tell-tale. Hereafter all your children shall be soft and defenceless.'

The poor jellyfish blushed crimson, squeezed himself out, and swam off out of sight. Since that time jellyfishes have had no shells.

LORD CUTTLEFISH GIVES A CONCERT

Despite the loss of the monkey's liver, the Queen of the World Under the Sea, after careful attention and long rest, got well again, and was able to be about her duties and govern her kingdom well. The news of her recovery created the wildest joy all over the Underworld, and from tears and gloom and silence, the caves echoed with laughter, and the sponge-beds with music. Every one had on a 'white face.' Drums, flutes and banjos, which had been hung up on coral branches, or packed away in shell boxes, were taken down, or brought out, and right merrily were they struck or thrummed with the ivory *hashi* (plectrum). The pretty maids of the queen put on their ivory thimble-nails, and the queen again listened to the sweet melodies on the koto, (flat harp), while down among the smaller fry of fishy retainers and the scullions of the kitchen, were heard the constant thump of the *tsutsumi* (shoulder-drum), the bang of the *taiko* (big drum), and the loud cries of the dancers as they struck all sorts of attitudes with hands, feet and head.

No allusion was openly made either to monkeys, tortoises or jellyfish. This would not have been polite. But the jellyfish, in a distant pool in the garden, could hear the refrain, 'The rivers of China run into the sea, and in it sinks the rain.'

Now in the language of the Underworld people the words for 'river,' and 'skin,' (or 'covering,') and 'China,' and 'shell,' and 'rain,' and 'jelly,' are the same. So the chorus, which was nothing but a string of puns, meant, 'The skin of the jellyfish runs to the sea, and in it sinks the jelly.'

But none of these musical performances were worthy of the queen's notice; although as evidences of the joy of her subjects, they did very well. A great many entertainments were gotten up to amuse the finny people, but the queen was present at none of them except the one about to be described. How and why she became a spectator shall also be told.

One night the queen was sitting in the pink drawing-room, arrayed in her queenly robes, for she was quite recovered and expected to walk out in the evening. Everything in the room, except a vase of green and golden coloured sponge-plant, and a plume of glass-thread, was of a pink colour. Then there was a pretty rockery made of a pyramid of pumice, full of embossed rosettes of living sea-anemones of scarlet, orange, grey and black colours, which were trained to fold themselves up like an umbrella, or blossom out like chrysanthemums, at certain hours of the day, or when touched, behaving just like four o'clocks and sensitive plants.

All the furniture and hangings of the rooms were pink. The floor was made of mats woven from strips of shell-nacre, bound at the sides with an inch border of pink coral. The ceiling was made of the rarest of pink shells wrought into flowers and squares. The walls were decorated with the same material, representing sea-scenes, jewels and tortoise shell patterns. In the *tokonoma*, or raised space, was a bouquet of sea-weed of richest dyes, and in the nooks was an open cabinet holding several of the queen's own treasures, such as a tiara which looked like woven threads of crystal (Euplectella), and a toilet box and writing case made of solid pink coral. The gem of all was a screen having eight folds, on which was depicted the palace and throne-room of Riu Gu, the visit of Toda, and the procession of the queen, nobles and grandees that escorted the brave archer, when he took his farewell to return to earth.

The queen sat on the glistening sill of the wide window looking out over her gardens, her two maids sitting at her feet. The sound of music wafted through the coral groves and crystal grottoes reached her ear.

'*O medzurashi gozarimasu!*' '(How wonderful this is!)' exclaimed the queen, half aloud. 'What strange music is this? It is neither guitar, nor hand, nor shoulder drum, nor singing. It seems to be a mixture of all. Hear! It sounds as if a band with many instruments was playing to the accompaniment of a large choir of voices.'

True enough! It was the most curious music ever heard in Riu Gu, for to tell the truth the voices were not in perfect accord, though all kept good time. The sound seemed to issue from the mansion of Lord Cuttlefish, the palace physician. The queen's curiosity was roused.

'I shall go and see what it is,' said she, as she rose up. Suddenly she recollected, and exclaimed:

'O, no, it would not be proper for me to be seen in public at this hour of the evening, and if it is in Lord Cuttlefish's mansion, I could not enter without a retinue, No, it won't do for me, it's beneath my dignity,' said her majesty to herself as she went over to touch her anemones, while her maids fanned her, seeing their mistress flushed with excitement, and fearing a relapse.

Curiosity got the better of the queenly lady, and off she started with only her two maids who held aloft over her head, the long pearl-handled fans made of white shark's fins.

'Besides,' thought she, 'perhaps the concert is outside, in the garden. If so, I can look down and see from the great green rock that overlooks it, and my lord Kai Riu O need not know of it.'

The queen walked over her pebbled garden walk, avoiding the great high road paved with white coral rock, and taking a by-path trimmed with fan-coral. The sound of the drums and voices grew louder, until as she reached the top of a green rock back of Lord Cuttlefish's garden, the whole performance was open to her view.

It was so funny, and the queen was so overcome at the comical sight, that she nearly fell down and got the hysterics, laughing so heartily. She utterly forgot her dignity, and laughed till the tears ran down her face. She was so afraid she would scream out, that she nearly choked herself to death with her sleeve, while her alarmed maids, though meaning nothing by their acts but friendly help, slapped her back to give her breath.

There, at the top of a high green rock, all covered with barnacles, on a huge tuft of sponge, sat Lord Cuttlefish, playing on three musical instruments at once. His great warty speckled head, six feet high, like a huge bag upside down, was bent forward to read the notes of his music book by the light of a wax candle, which was stuck in the feelers of a prickly lobster, and patiently held. Of his six pulpy arms one long one ran down like the trunk of an elephant, fingering along the pages of a music book. Two others were used to play the guitar, one to grasp the handle and pinch the strings, and the other to hold the ivory stick to strike the strings. The tsutsumi (small double drum) was held on his shoulder and neck, while still another arm curled up in a bunch, punched it like a fist. Below him was a another, a bass drum, set in a frame, and in his last leg, or arm, was clutched a heavy drum-stick, which pounded out tremendous noise, if not music. There the old fellow sat with his head bobbing, and all his six cuppy arms in motion, his rolling blue eyes ogling the notes, and his mouth like an elephant's, screeching out the song, which was made up of puns on 'tortoises,' 'monkeys,' 'jellyfishes,' 'livers' and 'shell,' though the real words made an entirely different sense.

All this time, in front of Lord Cuttlefish, sat the lobster holding up the light, like the *kurombo*, or black fellows who hold candles at the end of long-handled candle-sticks on the stage of the theatres so that the people may see the faces of the actors.

But the audience, or rather the orchestra was the funniest part of all. They could hardly be called listeners, for they were all performers. On the left was the lusty red-faced tai fish with its gills wide open, singing at the top, or rather at the bottom, of his throat, and beating time by flapping his wide fins. Just back of him was a little gudgeon, silent and fanning himself with a blue flat fan, having disgracefully broken down on a high note. Next behind, on the right, was a long-nosed gar-fish singing alto, and proud of her slender form, with the last new thing in folding fans held in her fin. In the foreground squatted a great fat frog with big bulging eyes, singing base, and leading the choir by flapping his webbed fingers up and down with his frightful cavern of a mouth wide open. Next, sat the stately and dignified mackerel who was rather scandalized at the whole affair, and kept very still, refusing to join in. At the mackerel's right fin, squeaked out the stupid flat-headed *fugu* fish with her big eye impolitely winking at the servant-maid just bringing in refreshments; for the truth was, she was thirsty after so much vocal exercise. The fugu was very vain and always played the coquette around the hooks of the fishermen who always liked to eat her because she was so sweet, yet her flesh was poison.

'How strange it is that men will angle after that ugly hussy, when she poisons them,' was the oft-repeated remark of the gar-fish.

Just behind the herring, with one eye on Lord Cuttlefish

and one on the coming refreshments, was the skate. The truth must be told that the entire right wing of the orchestra was very much demoralized by the smell of the steaming tea and eatables just about to be served. The *suppon*, (tortoise with a snout like a bird's beak,) though he continued to sing, impolitely turned his head away from Lord Cuttlefish, and his back to the frog that acted as precentor. The sucker, though very homely, and bloated with fat, kept on in the chorus, and pretended not to notice the waiter and her tray and cups. Indeed, Madame Sucker thought it quite vulgar in the tortoise to be so eager after the cakes and wine.

In truth the concert had been long, and all were thirsty and ready for a bite and a drink.

Suddenly the music ceased, and the long clatter on the drum announced the end. Lord Cuttlefish kicked over his drum, unscrewed his guitar, and packed it away in his music box. He then slid along on his six slippery legs to the refreshments, and actually amused the company by standing on his head, and twirling his six cuppy arms around.

At this Miss Mackerel was quite shocked, and whispered under her fan to the gar-fish, 'It is quite undignified. What would the queen say if she saw it?' not knowing that the queen was looking on.

Then all sat down on their tails, propped upright on one fin, and produced their fans to cool themselves off. The lobster pulled off the candle stump and ate it up, wiped his feelers, and joined the party.

The liquid refreshments consisted of sweet and clear saké (rice beer) tea, and cherry-blossom water. The solids were thunder-cakes, egg-cracknels, boiled rice, daikon radishes and macaroni, lotus-root, *taro*, and side-dishes piled up with flies, worms, bugs and all kinds of bait for the small fry—the finny brats that were to eat at the second table. The tea was poured by the servants of Lord Cuttlefish. These were the funniest little green *kappas*, or creatures half way between a monkey and a tortoise, with yellow eyes, hands like an ape, hair clipped short on their heads, eyes like frogs, and a mouth that stretched from ear to ear. Poor creatures! they were only too happy to know that though they looked like monkeys their livers would not do for medicine.

The queen did not wait to see the end of the feast, but laughing heartily, returned to her palace and went to sleep.

After helping himself with all the cups of his arms out of the tub of boiled rice, until Miss Mackerel made up her mind that he was an *omeshi gurai*, (rice glutton,) and drinking like a shoal of fishes, Lord Cuttlefish went home, coiled himself up into a ball, and fell asleep. He had a headache next morning.

YORIMASA, THE BRAVE ARCHER

Genzan Yorimasa was a brave warrior and a very useful man who lived more than eight thousand moons ago. On account of his valour and skill in the use of the bow he was called to Kioto, and promoted to be chief guard of the imperial palace. At that time the emperor, Narahito, could not sleep at night, because his rest was disturbed by a frightful beast, which scared away even the sentinels in armour who stood on guard.

This dreadful beast had the wings of a bird, the body and claws of a tiger, the head of a monkey, a serpent tail and the crackling scales of a dragon. It came after night, upon the roof of the palace, and howled and scratched so dreadfully, that the poor mikado losing all rest, grew weak and thin. None of the guards dare face it in hand-to-hand fight, and none had skill enough to hit it with an arrow in the dark, though several of the imperial corps of archers had tried again and again. When Yorimasa received his appointment, he strung his bow carefully, and carefully honing his steel-headed arrows, stored his quiver, and resolved to mount guard that night with his favourite retainer.

It chanced to be a stormy night. The lightning was very vivid, and Kaminari, the thunder-god was beating all his drums. The wind swirled round frightfully, as though Fuden the wind-god was emptying all his bags. Toward midnight, the falcon eye of Yorimasa saw, during a flash of lightning, the awful beast sitting on the 'devil's tile' at the tip of the ridge-pole, on the north-east end of the roof. He bade his retainer have a torch of straw and twigs ready to light at a moment's notice, to loosen his blade, and wet its hilt-pin, while he fitted the notch of his best arrow into the silk cord of his bow.

Keeping his eyes strained, he pretty soon saw the glare now of one eye, now two eyes, as the beast with swaying head crept along the great roof to the place on the eaves directly under the mikado's sleeping-room. There it stopped.

This was Yorimasa's opportunity. Aiming about a foot to the right of where he saw the eye glare, he drew his yard-length shaft clear back to his shoulder, and let fly. A dull thud, a frightful howl, a heavy bump on the ground, and the writhing of some creature among the pebbles, told in a few seconds' time that the shaft had struck flesh. The next instant Yorimasa's retainer rushed out with blazing torch and joined battle with his dirk. Seizing the beast by the neck, he quickly despatched him, by cutting his throat. Then they flayed the monster, and the next morning the hide was shown to his majesty.

All congratulated Yorimasa on his valour and marksmanship. Many young men, sons of nobles and warriors, begged to become his pupils in archery. The mikado ordered a noble of very high rank to present to Yorimasa a famous sword named *Shishi-no-o*, (King of Wild Boars), and to give him a lovely maid of honour named Ayami, to wife. And so the brave and the fair were married, and to this day the fame of Yorimasa is like the '*ume-take-matsu*,' (plum-blossom, bamboo and pine), fragrant, green and ever-during.

WATANABE CUTS OFF THE ONI'S ARM

When the capital of Japan was the city of Kioto, and the mikado dwelt in it with all his court, there lived a brave captain of the guard named Yorimitsu, who belonged to the famous Minamoto family. He was also called Raiko, and by this name he is best known to all the boys and girls in Great Japan. Under Captain Raiko were three brave guardsmen, one of whom was named Watanabe Tsuna. The duty of these men-at-arms was to watch at the gates leading to the palace.

It had come to pass that the blossom capital had fallen in a dreadful condition, because the guards at the other gates had been neglected. Thieves were numerous and murders were frequent, so that every one in the city was afraid to go out into the streets at night. Worse than all else, was the report that oni or imps were prowling around in the dark to seize people by the hair of the head. Then they would drag them away to the mountains, tear the flesh off their bones, and eat them up.

The worst place in the city, to which the horned imps came oftenest, was at the south-western gate called the Rajo-mon.

To this post of danger, Raiko sent Tsuna, the bravest of his guards.

It was on a dark, rainy and dismal night, that Tsuna started, well-armed, to stand sentinel at the gate. His trusty helmet was knotted over his chin, and all the pieces of his armour were well laced up. His sandals were girt tight to his feet, and in his belt was thrust the trusty sword, freshly ground, until its edge was like a razor's, and with it the owner could cut asunder a hair floating in the air.

Arriving at the red pillar of the gate, Tsuna paced up and down the stone way with eyes and ears wide open. The wind was blowing frightfully, the storm howled and the rain fell in such torrents that soon the cords of Tsuna's armour and his dress were soaked through.

The great bronze bell of the temples on the hills boomed out the hours one after another, until a single stroke told Tsuna it was the hour of the Rat (midnight).

Two hours passed, and the hour of the Bull sounded (2 a.m.,) still Tsuna was wide awake. The storm had lulled, but it was darker than ever.

The hour of the Tiger (3 o'clock) rung out, and the soft mellow notes of the temple bell died away like a lullaby wooing one to sleep, spite of will and vow.

The warrior, almost without knowing it, grew sleepy and fell into a doze. He started and woke up. He shook himself, jingled his armour, pinched himself, and even pulled out his little knife from the wooden scabbard of his dirk, and pricked his leg with the point of it to keep awake, but all in vain. Unconsciously overcome, he leaned against the gate-post, and fell asleep.

This was just what the imp wanted. All the time he had been squatting on the cross-piece at the top of the gate waiting his opportunity. He now slid down as softly as a monkey, and with his iron-like claws grabbed Tsuna by the helmet, and began to drag him into the air.

In an instant Tsuna was awake. Seizing the hairy wrist of the imp with his left hand, with his right he drew his sword, swept it round his head, and cut off the demon's arm. The oni, frightened and howling with pain, leaped up the post and disappeared in the clouds.

Tsuna waited with drawn sword in hand, lest the oni might come again, but in a few hours morning dawned. The sun rose on the pagodas and gardens and temples of the capitol and the nine-fold circle of flowery hills. Everything was beautiful and bright. Tsuna returned to report to his captain, carrying the oni's arm in triumph. Raiko examined it, and loudly praised Tsuna for his bravery, and rewarded him with a silken sash.

Now it is said that if an oni's arm be cut off it cannot be made to unite with the body again, if kept apart for a week. So Raiko warned Tsuna to lock it up, and watch it night and day, lest it be stolen from him.

So Tsuna went to the stone-cutters who made idols of Buddha, mortars for pounding rice, and coffers for burying money in to be hidden away in the ground, and bought a strong box cut out of the solid stone. It had a heavy lid on it, which slid in a groove and came out only by touching a secret spring. Then setting it in his bed chamber, he guarded it day and night, keeping the gate and all his doors locked. He allowed no one who was a stranger to look at the trophy.

Six days passed by, and Tsuna began to think his prize was sure, for were not all his doors tight shut? So he set the box out in the middle of the room, and twisting some rice-straw fringe in token of sure victory and rejoicing, he sat down in ease before it. He took off his armour and put on his court robes. During the evening, but rather late, there was a feeble knock like that of an old woman at the gate outside.

Tsuna cried out, 'Who's there?'

The squeaky voice of his aunt (as it seemed), who was a very old woman, replied 'Me, I want to see my nephew, to praise him for his bravery in cutting the oni's arm off.'

So Tsuna let her in and carefully locking the door behind

her, helped the old crone into the room, where she sat down on the mats in front of the box and very close to it. Then she grew very talkative, and praised her nephew's exploit, until Tsuna felt very proud.

All the time the old woman's left shoulder was covered with her dress while her right hand was out. Then she begged earnestly to be allowed to see the limb. Tsuna at first politely refused, but she urged, until yielding affectionately he slid back the stone lid just a little.

'This is my arm' cried the old hag, turning into an oni, and dragging out the arm.

She flew up to the ceiling, and was out of the smoke-slide through the roof in a twinkling. Tsuna rushed out of the house to shoot her with an arrow, but he saw only a demon far off in the clouds grinning horribly. He noted carefully however that the direction of the imps' flight was to the north-west.

A council was now held by Raiko's band, and it was decided that the lurking-place of the demons must be in the mountains of Oye in the province of Tango. It was resolved to hunt out and destroy the imps.

WATANABE KILLS THE GREAT SPIDER

During the time in which Watanabe was forming his plan to destroy the onis that lurked in the Oye mountains, the brave Raiko fell sick, and daily grew weaker and paler. When the demons found this out they sent the three-eyed imp called Mitsume Kozo, to plague him.

This imp, which had a snout like a hog's, three monstrous blue eyes, and a mouth full of tusks, was glad that the brave soldier could no longer fight the onis. He would approach the sick man in his chamber, leer horribly at him, loll out his tongue, and pull down the lids of his eyes with his hairy fingers, until the sight sickened Raiko more and more.

But Raiko, well or ill, always slept with his trusty sword under his pillow, and pretending to be greatly afraid, and to cower under the bed-clothes, the kozo grew bolder and bolder. When the imp was near the bed, Raiko drew his blade, and cut the oni across his huge double nose. This made the demon howl, and he ran away, leaving tracks of blood.

When Tsuna and his band heard of their brave master's exploit, they came to congratulate him, and offered to hunt out the demon and destroy him.

They followed the red drops until they came to a cavern in the mountains. Entering this they saw in the gloom a spider six feet high, with legs as long as a fishing-pole, and as thick as a daikon radish. Two great yellow eyes glared at them like lamps. They noticed a great gaping wound as if done by a sword-cut on his snout.

It was a horrible, nasty hairy thing to fight with swords, since to get near enough, they would be in danger of the creature's claws. So Tsuna went and chopped down a tree as thick as a man's leg, leaving the roots on, while his comrades prepared a rope to tie up the monster like a fly in a web. Then with a loud yell Tsuna rushed at the spider, felled him with a blow, and held him down with the tree and roots so he could not bite or use his claws. Seeing this, his comrades rushed in, and bound the monster's legs tight to his body so that he could not move. Drawing their swords they passed them through his body and finished him. Returning in triumph to the city, they found their dear captain recovered from his illness.

Raiko thanked his brave warriors for their exploits, made a feast for them, and gave them many presents. At this feast Captain Raiko told them that he had received orders from the mikado to march against the oni's den in Tango, slaughter them all, and rescue the prisoners he should find there. Then he showed them his commission written in large letters,

'I command you, Raiko, to chastise the onis.'

He also allowed them to examine the gold brocade bag, in which it was kept, and which one of the fair ladies of the court had made for him with her own tapering fingers.

At this time many families in Kioto were grieving over the loss of their children, and even while Tsuna had been away, several lovely damsels had been seized and taken to the demon's den.

Lest the onis might hear of their coming, and escape, the four trusty men disguised themselves as *Komuso* or wandering priests of the mountains. They put on over their helmets, huge hats like wash-bowls, made of straw, woven so tightly that no one could see their faces. They covered their armour with very cheap and common clothes, and then after worshipping at the shrines, began their march.

RAIKO AND THE SHI-TEN DOJI

Quite pathless were the desolate mountains of Tango, for no one ever went into them except once in a while a poor woodcutter or charcoal-burner; yet Raiko and his men set out with stout hearts. There were no bridges over the streams, and frightful precipices abounded. Once they had to stop and build a bridge by felling a tree, and walking across it over a dangerous chasm. Once they came to a steep rock, to descend which they must make a ladder of creeping vines. At last they reached a dense grove at the top of a cliff, far up to the clouds, which seemed as if it might contain the demon's castle.

Approaching, they found a pretty maiden washing some clothes which had spots of blood on them. They said to her, 'Sister, Miss, why are you here, and what are you doing?'

'Ah,' said she, with a deep sigh, 'you must not come here. This is the haunt of demons. They eat human flesh and they will eat yours.' 'Look there' said she pointing to a pile of white bones of men, women and children, 'You must go down the mountain as quickly as you came.' Saying this she burst into tears.

But instead of being frightened or sorrowful, the brave fellows nearly danced for joy. 'We have come here for the purpose of destroying the demons by the mikado's orders,' said Raiko, patting his breast, where inside his dress in the damask bag was the imperial order.

At this the maiden dried her tears and smiled so sweetly

that Raiko's heart was touched by her beauty.

'But how came you to live among these cannibal demons,' asked Raiko.

She blushed deeply as she replied sadly 'Although they eat men and old women, they keep the young maidens to wait on them.'

'It's a great pity' said Raiko, 'but we shall now avenge our fellow subjects of the mikado, as well as your shame and cruel treatment, if you will show us the way up the cliff to the den.'

They began to climb the hill but they had not gone far before they met a young oni who was a cook in the great doji's kitchen. He was carrying a human limb for his master's lunch. They gnashed their teeth silently, and clutched their swords under their coats. Yet they courteously saluted the cook-demon, and asked for an interview with the chief. The demon smiled in his sleeve, thinking what a fine dinner his master would make of the four men.

A few feet forward, and a turn in the path brought them to the front of the demon's castle. Among tall and mighty boulders of rock, which loomed up to the clouds, there was an opening in the dense groves, thickly covered with vines and mosses like an arbour. From this point, the view over the plains below commanded a space of hundreds of miles. In the distance the red pagodas, white temple-gables and castle towers of Kioto were visible.

Inside the cave was a banqueting hall large enough to seat one hundred persons. The floor was neatly covered with new, clean mats of sea-green rice-straw, on which tables, silken cushions, arm-rests, drinking-cups, bottles and many other articles of comfort lay about. The stone walls were richly decorated with curtains and hangings of fine silken stuffs.

At the end of the long hall, on a raised dais, our heroes

presently observed, as a curtain was lifted, the chief demon, Shi-ten doji, of august, yet frightful appearance. He was seated on a heap of luxurious cushions made of blue and crimson crape, stuffed with swan's down. He was leaning on a golden arm-rest. His body was quite red, and he was round and fat like a baby grown up. He had very black hair cut like a small boy's, and on the top of his head, just peeping through the hair were two very short horns. Around him were a score of lovely maidens—the fairest of Kioto—on whose beautiful faces was stamped the misery they dared not fully show, yet could not entirely conceal. Along the wall other demons sat or lay at full length, each one with his handmaid seated beside him to wait on him and pour out his wine. All of them were of horrible aspect, which only made the beauty of the maidens more conspicuous. Seeing our heroes walk in the hall led by the cook, each one of the demons was as happy as a spider, when in his lurking hole he feels the jerk on his web-thread that tells him a fly is caught. All of them at once poured out a fresh saucer of saké and drank it down.

Raiko and his men separated, and began talking freely with the demons until the partitions at one corner were slid aside, and a troop of little demons who were waiter-boys entered. They brought in a host of dishes, and the onis fell to and ate. The noise of their jaws sounded like the pounding of a rice mill.

Our heroes were nearly sickened at the repast, for it consisted chiefly of human flesh, while the wine-cups were made of empty human skulls. However, they laughed and talked and excused themselves from eating, saying they had just lunched.

As the demons drank more and more they grew lively, laughed till the cave echoed, and sang uproarious songs. Every time they grinned, they showed their terrible tusks, and teeth like fangs. All of them had horns, though most of these were very short.

The doji became especially hilarious, and drank the health of every one of his four guests in a skull full of wine. To supply him there was a tub full of saké at hand, and his usual drinking-vessel was a dish which seemed to Tsuna to be as large as a full moon.

Raiko now offered to return the courtesies shown them by dancing 'the Kioto dance,' for which he was famous. Stepping out into the centre of the hall, with his fan in one hand, he danced gracefully and with such wonderful ease, that the onis screamed with delight, and clapped their hands in applause, saying they had never seen anything to equal it. Even the maidens, lost in admiration of the polished courtier, forgot their sorrow, and felt as happy for the time as though they were at home dancing.

The dance finished, Raiko took from his bosom a bottle of saké, and offered it to the chief demon as a gift, saying it was the best wine of Sakai. The delighted doji drank and gave a sip to each of his lords saying, 'This is the best liquor I ever tasted, you must drink the health of our friends in it.'

Now Raiko had bought, at the most skilful druggists' in the capital, a powerful sleeping potion, and mixed it with the wine, which made it taste very sweet. In a few minutes all the demons had dropped off asleep, and their snores sounded like the rolling thunder of the mountains.

Then Raiko rose up and gave the signal to his comrades. Whispering to the maidens to leave the room quietly, they drew their swords, and with as little noise as possible cut the throats of the demons. No sound was heard but the gurgling of blood that ran out in floods on the floor. The doji lying like a lion on his cushions was still sleeping, the snores issuing out of his nose like thunder from a cloud. The four warriors approached him and like loyal vassals as they were, they first turned their faces towards Kioto, reverenced the mikado, and prayed for the blessing of the gods who made Japan. Raiko then drew near, and measuring the width of the doji's neck with his sword found that it would be short. Suddenly, the blade lengthened of itself. Then lifting his weapon, he smote with all his might and cut the neck clean through.

In an instant, the bloody head flew up in the air gnashing its teeth and rolling its yellow eyes, while the horns sprouted out to a horrible length, the jaws opening and shutting like the edges of an earthquake fissure. It flew up and whirled round the room seven times. Then with a rush it flew at Raiko's head, and bit through the straw hat and into the iron helmet inside. But this final effort exhausted its strength, its motions ceased and it fell heavily to the floor.

Anxiously the comrades helped their fallen leader to rise, and examined his head. But he was unhurt,—not a scratch was on him. Then the heroes congratulated each other and after despatching the smaller demons, brought out all the treasure and divided it equally. Then they set the castle on fire and buried the bones of the victims, setting up a stone to mark the spot. All the maidens and captives were assembled together, and in great state and pomp they returned to Kioto. The virgins were restored to their parents, and many a desolate home was made joyful, and many mourning garments taken off. Raiko was honoured by the mikado in being made a *kuge* (court noble,) and was appointed Chief of the entire garrison of Kioto. Then all the people were grateful for his valour.

THE SAZAYE AND THE TAI

Sazaye is a shell-fish, which is very proud of its shell. This is high, full of points like towers, and thick like a castle wall. When feeding, enjoying itself or moving around, its long neck and body are stretched out before it, armed with its hard operculum, which is like an iron shield, or the end of a battering ram. The operculum fits the entrance to its shell like a trap door. As soon as any danger is near it pulls in its head, and slams itself shut with a loud noise.

On account of the hardness and thickness of his shell, the sazaye is the envy of the soft-bodied fishes that covet his security. But on the other hand the sazaye, though a slow moving creature, is apt to be too proud of his defence and trust too much to his fancied security.

One day a tai (red fish) and a herring were looking at the strong shell of the sazaye, and becoming quite envious, the tai said:

'What a mighty strong castle you do live in, Mr Sazaye. When you once shut up your shell no one need even try to touch you. You are to be envied sir.'

The sazaye was tickled at the flattery, but pretending to be very humble, shook his head and said:

'It is very kind in you, my lords, to say so, but my little hut is nothing but a shell; yet I must say that when I lock my door I do not feel any anxiety, and I really pity you poor fellows who have no shell at all.'

He had hardly got the last word out of his grisly throat, when suddenly there was a great splash, and away darted the tai and herring, never resting their fins or tails a moment till safe out of danger.

The Sazaye drew in his flap in the twinkling of an eye, and keeping as quiet as possible, wondered what the noise was. Was it a stone, or a net, or a fish-hook? He wondered if the tai and herring were caught.

'Surely they must be,' thought he. 'However I'm safe, thanks to my castle shell,' he muttered.

So drawing his trap tighter he took a long nap. When he woke up, quite refreshed, he cautiously loosened his trap and peeped out.

'How strange every thing looks, am I dreaming?' said he as he saw piles of fish, clams, prawns and lobsters lying on a board all around him.

'Ugh, what is that?' clapping himself shut as a great black-nosed and long-whiskered dog poked his muzzle near him.

Poor shell-fish! There he lay in a fishmonger's shop, with a slip of paper marked 'ten cash,' (one-tenth of a cent,) on his back. A few hours later, purchased by a labourer's wife for his dinner, he was stewing along with several of his relatives in his own juice. The castle, of which he was so proud, serving first as a dinner-pot, then as a saucer, after which it was thrown away in a heap and burned into lime.

SMELLS AND JINGLES

Yedo people are very fond of broiled eels. A rich merchant, named Kisaburo, who was very miserly with his money, once moved his quarters next door to the shop of one Kichibei, who caught and cooked eels for a living. During the night Mr Kichibei caught his stock in trade, and in the day-time served them, smoking hot, to his customers. Cut into pieces three or four inches long, they were laid to sizzle on a grid-iron over red hot charcoal, which was kept in a glow by constant fanning.

Kisaburo, wishing to save money, and having a strong imagination, daily took his seat at meal time close to his neighbour's door. Eating his boiled rice, and snuffing in the odors of the broiled eels, as they were wafted in, he enjoyed with his nose, what he would not pay for to put in his mouth. In this way, as he flattered himself, he saved much money, and his strong box grew daily heavier.

Kichibei, the eel-broiler, on finding this out, thought he would charge his stingy neighbour for the smell of his eels. So, making out his bill he presented it to Kisaburo, who seemed to be much pleased. He called to his wife to bring his iron-bound money box, which was done. Emptying out the shining mass of *kobans* (oval gold pieces, worth five or six dollars), *ichi-bu* and *ni-bu* (square silver pieces, worth a quarter and a half dollar respectively) he jingled the coins at a great rate, and then touching the eel-man's bill with his fan, bowed, low and said with a smile:

'All right, neighbour Kichibei, we are square now.'

'What!' cried the eel-frier, 'are you not going to pay me?'

'Why yes, I have paid you. You have charged me for the smell of your eels, and I have paid you with the sound of my money.'

THE LAKE OF THE LUTE AND THE
MATCHLESS MOUNTAIN

Of all the beautiful objects in 'the land of the holy gods,' as the Japanese call their country, none are more beautiful than Fuji Mountain and Lake Biwa. The one is a great cone of white snow, the other is a sheet of heaven-blue water, in shape like a lute with four strings.

Sweeping from twenty square leagues of space out of the plain and rising twelve thousand feet in air, Fuji, or Fusi Yama, casts its sunset shadow far out on the ocean, and from fourteen provinces gleams the splendour of its snowy crest. It sits like a king on his throne in the heart of Suruga Province.

One hundred and thirty miles to the west as the crane wings her flight, in the heart of Omi, is Biwa Ko, the lake of the lute. It is sixty miles long and as blue as the sky whose mirror it is. Along its banks rise white-walled castles and stretch mulberry plantations. On its bosom rise wooded islands, white, but not with frost; for thousands of herons nestle on the branches of the trees, like lilies on their stems. Down under the blue depths, say the people, is the Dragon shrine (Riu Gu), where dwell the dragon-helmed Kai Riu O, and his consort, the shell-crowned Queen of the World Under the Sea.

Why do the pilgrims from all over the empire exclaim joyfully, while climbing Fuji's cinder-beds and lava-blocks, 'I am a man of Omi'? Why, when quenching their thirst with the melted snow-water of Fuji crater, do they cry out 'I am drinking from Lake Biwa'? Why do the children clap their hands, as they row or sail over Biwa's blue surface, and say: 'I am on top of Fujiyama'?

To these questions the Japanese legend gives answer.

When Heaven and earth were first created, there was neither Lake of Biwa nor Mountain of Fuji. Suruga and Omi were both plains. Even for long after men inhabited Japan and the mikados had ruled for centuries there was neither earth so nigh to heaven nor water so close to the Underworld as the peaks of Fuji and the bottom of Biwa. Men drove the plow and planted the rice over the very spot where crater and deepest depth now are.

But one night in the ancient times there was a terrible earthquake. All the world shook, the clouds lowered to the earth, floods of water poured from the sky, and a sound like the fighting of a myriad of dragons filled the air. In the morning all was serene and calm. The sky was blue. The earth was as bright and all was as 'white-faced' as when the Sun Goddess first came out from her hiding in the cave.

The people of Omi awoke, scarce expecting to find either earth or heaven, when lo! they looked on what had yesterday been tilled land or barren moor, and there was a great sheet of blue. Was it sky? Had a sheet of the 'blue field of heaven' fallen down? Was it the ocean? They came near it, tasted it. It was fresh and sweet as a fountain-rill. They looked at it from the hill-tops, and, seeing its outline, called it 'the lake of the four-stringed lute.' Others, proud of their new possession, named it the Lake of Omi.

Greater still was the surprise of the Suruga people. The sailors, far out at sea, rubbed their eyes and wondered at the strange shape of the towering white cloud. Was it the Iwakura, the eternal throne of Heaven, come down to rest on earth out of the many piled white clouds of heaven? Some thought they had lost their reckoning; but were assured when they recognized familiar landmarks on shore. Many a cottager woke up to find his house, which lay in a valley the day before, was now far up on the slope, with the distant villages and the sea visible; while far, far above shone the snowy head of a mountain, whose crown lay in the blue sky. At night the edges of the peak, like white fingers, seemed to pluck the stars from the Milky Way.

'What shall we call this new-born child of the gods?' said the people. And various names were proposed.

'There is no other mountain so beautiful in all the earth, there's not its equal anywhere; therefore call it Fuji, (no two such), the peerless, the matchless mountain,' said one.

'It is so tall, so comely, so grand, call it Fuji, (rich scholar, the lordly mountain),' said another.

'Call it Fuji, (never dying, the immortal mountain),' said a third.

'Call it, after the festal flower of joy, Fuji' (Wistaria) said another, as he decked the peak of his hat with the drooping clusters of the tender blue blossom. 'It looks blue and purple in the distance, just like the fuji flower.' Various as the meanings of the name were, they sounded all alike to the ear. So, without any quarreling, all agreed to call it Fuji and each to choose his own meaning. To this day, though many a learned dispute and the scratching of the written character on the sand with walking stick, or on paper with pencil, or on the palm of the hand with forefinger takes place, all pronounce the name alike as they rave on the beauties of Fujiyama.

So went forth into the countries bounding 'the four seas' the belief that there was a white mountain of perfect form in Japan, and that whoever ascended it would live long and even attain immortality; and that somewhere on the mountain was hidden the elixir of immortality, which if any one drank he would live forever. Now in one of the kingdoms of far-off China there lived a rich old king, who had abundance of treasures, health and many children. But he did not wish to die, and, hence, spent his days in studying the lore and arts of the alchemists, who believed they would finally attain to the transmutation of lead into gold, find the universal solvent of all things, the philosophers' stone, the elixir of life, and all the wondrous secrets which men in Europe long afterward laboured to discover.

Among the king's sages was one old man of mighty wisdom, who had heard of the immortal mountain of Japan, and, learning of the manner of its appearance, concluded that the Japan Archipelago contained the Fortunate Isles and in it was the true elixir of life. He divulged his secret to the king, and advised him to make the journey to the Land of the Rising Sun.

Overjoyed at the good news and the faithfulness of his loyal sage, the king loaded him with gifts and honours. He selected five hundred of the most beauteous youths and virgins of his kingdom, and, fitting out a fleet, sailed away to the Happy Isles of the East. Coasting along the shore until they recognized the glorious form of the mountain, they landed and began the ascent. Alas! for the poor king. The rough sea and severe storms had worn on his aged frame and the fatigues of the ascent were so great, that before reaching the top he fainted away, and before the head of the procession had set foot on the crater edge the monarch was dead. Sadly they gave up the search for the elixir of life, and, descending the mountain, buried their master in the Province of Kii. Then, in their exuberance of youth and joy, thinking little of the far future and wishing to enjoy the present, they separated in couples, married, and, disposing of their ship and cargo, settled in the country, and colonized the eastern part of Japan.

Long afterward, when Buddhist believers came to Japan, one of them, climbing Fuji, noticed that around its sunken crater were eight peaks, like the petals of their sacred lotus flower. Thus, it seemed to them, Great Buddha had honoured Japan, by bestowing the sacred symbol of Nirvana, or Heaven, on the proudest and highest part of Japan. So they also named it Fuji, 'the sacred mountain'; and to this day all the world calls this sacred mountain Fuji, or Fusi Yama, while the Japanese people believe that the earth which sunk in Omi is the same which, piled to the clouds, is the lordly mountain of Suruga.

THE WATERFALL OF YORO, OR THE FOUNTAIN OF YOUTH

Long, long, ago, when the oldest stork was young, there lived an aged woodcutter and his son on the slopes of the mountain Tagi, in the province of Mino. They gained a frugal livelihood by cutting brushwood on the hill-side, and carrying it in bundles on their back to sell in the nearest market town; for they were too poor to own an ox. With the money thus received they bought rice and radishes, their daily food.

Only once or twice a year, at New Year's and on the mikado's birthday, could they afford to treat themselves to a mess of bean-curd or fresh fish. Yet the old man was very fond of rice-wine, and every week bought a gourd full to keep his old blood warm.

As the years rolled on the aged father's limbs became so stiff that he was unable any longer to climb the mountains. So his son, now grown to be a sturdy man, cut nearly double the quantity of wood and thus kept the family larder full. The old man was so proud of his son that he daily stood at sunset in front of his rustic gate to welcome him back. And to see the old daddy and the young stripling remove their headkerchiefs, and bow with hands on knees in polite fashion, bending their backs and sucking in their breath, out of respect to each other, and to hear them inquiring after one another's health, showering mutual compliments all the time, one would have thought they had not seen each other for eight years, instead of eight hours.

One winter the snow fell long and thick, until all the ground in field and forest was covered several feet over. The bamboo branches bent with their weight of white, the pine boughs broke under their load, and even the stone idols along the wayside were covered up. At first, even with the hardest work, the young woodcutter could scarcely get and sell wood to buy enough food to keep them both alive. He often went hungry himself, so that his father might have his warm wine.

One day he went by another path up one of the mountain dells with his rope basket strapped to his back, and the empty gourd-bottle at his belt. While gloomily grieving over his hard luck, the faint odor of rice-wine seemed borne on the breeze.

He snuffed the air. It was no mistake. 'Here's luck, surely,' said he, throwing down his bundle.

Hurrying forward he saw a foaming waterfall tumbling over the rocks in a thick stream.

As he drew near, some of the spray fell on his tongue. He tasted it, smacked his lips and throwing down his cord and basket to the ground, filled his gourd and hastened home to his father.

Every day, till the end of his father's life, did he come to this wonderful cascade of wine, and thus the old man was nourished for many a long year.

The news of this fountain of youth spread abroad until it reached the court. The mikado, hearing of it, made a journey to Mino to see the wonderful waterfall. In honour of this event, and as a reward of filial piety, the name of the year-period was changed to Yoro, (Nourishing Old Age).

To this day, many people young and old go out to enjoy picnic parties at the foot of the waterfall; which now, however, runs honest water only, which makes the cheeks red; and not the wonderful wine that once tipped the old daddy's nose with perpetual vermilion.

THE EARTHQUAKE FISH

*M*ukashi, mukashi, (as most Japanese stories begin), long, long ago, when the gods came down from heaven to subdue the earth for the mikados, and civilize the country, there were a great many earthquakes, and nothing to stop them. The world continually rocked, and men's houses and lives were never safe.

Now the two gods who were charged with the work of subduing the northeastern part of the world were Kashima and Katori. Having done their work well, and quieted all the enemies of the Sun Goddess, they came to the province of Hitachi. Kashima, sticking his sword into the earth, ran it through to the other side, leaving the hilt above the ground. In the course of centuries this mighty sword shrunk and turned to stone, and the people gave it the name of *Kaname ishi*, (The rock of Kaname).

Now Kaname means the rivet in a fan, that holds all the sticks together, and they gave the name 'rivet-rock,' because it is the rivet that binds the earth together. No one could ever lift this rock except Kashima the mighty one who first set it in the earth.

Yet even Kashima never raises it, except to stop an earthquake of unusual violence. When the earth quivers, it is because the great earthquake-fish or *jishin-uwo* is restless or angry. This jishin-uwo is a great creature something like a catfish. It is about seven hundred miles long, and holds the world on its back. Its tail is at Awomori in the north, and the base of its head is at Kioto, so that all Japan lies on top of it. To his mouth are attached huge twirling feelers, which are just like the hideous moustaches which the hairy-faced men from beyond the Tai-kai (Pacific Ocean) wear on their lips. As soon as these begin to move, it is a sign that the monster is in wrath. When he gets angry, and flaps his tail or bumps his head, there is an earthquake. When he flounders about or rolls over, there is terrible destruction of life and property on the surface of the earth above.

In order to keep the earthquake-fish quiet, the great giant Kashima is appointed to watch him. His business is to stand near by, and when the monster becomes violent Kashima must jump up and straddle him, and hold his gills, put his foot on his fin; and when necessary lift up the great rock of Kaname and hold him down with its weight. Then he becomes perfectly quiet, and the earthquake ceases. Hence the people sing this earthquake verse:

'No monster can move the Kaname rock
Though he tug at it never so hard,
For over it stands, resisting the shock,
The Kashima Kami on guard.'

Another verse they sing as follows:

'These are things
An earthquake brings;
At nine of the bell they sickness fortell,
At five and seven betoken rain,
At four the sky is cleared thereby,
At six and eight comes wind again.'

THE DREAM STORY OF GOJIRO

Only a few years ago there was a gentleman in Fukui, Japan, who had a son, a bright lad of twelve, who was very diligent at school and had made astonishing progress in his studies. He was especially quick at learning Chinese characters, of which every Japanese gentleman who wishes to be called educated must know at least two thousand. For, although the Chinese and Japanese are two very different languages, yet the Japanese, Coreans and Chinese use the same letters to write with, just as English, Germans, French and Spaniards all employ one and the same alphabet.

Now Gojiro's father had promised him that when he read through five volumes of the *Nihongi*, or Ancient History of Japan, he would give him for a present a book of wonderful Chinese stories. Gojiro performed his task, and his father kept his promise. One day on his return from a journey to Kioto, he presented his son with sixteen volumes, all neatly silk-bound, well illustrated with wood-cuts, and printed clearly on thin, silky mulberry paper, from the best wooden blocks. It will be remembered that several volumes of Japanese literature make but one of ours, as they are much lighter and thinner than ours.

Gojiro was so delighted with the wonderful stories of heroes and warriors, travellers and sailors, that he almost felt himself in China. He read far into the night, with the lamp inside of his musquito curtain; and finally fell asleep, still undressed, but with his head full of all sorts of Chinese wonders.

He dreamed he was far away in China, walking along the banks of the great Yellow River. Everything was very strange. The people talked an entirely different language from his own; had on different clothes; and, instead of the nice shaven head and top-knot of the Japanese, every one wore a long pigtail of hair, that dangled at his heels. Even the boats were of a strange form, and on the fishing smacks perched on projecting rails, sat rows of cormorants, each with a ring around his neck. Every few minutes one of them would dive under the water, and after a while come struggling up with a fish in its mouth, so big that the fishermen had to help the bird into the boat. The game was then flung into a basket, and the cormorant was treated to a slice of raw fish, by way of encouragement and to keep the bird from the bad habit of eating the live fish whole. This the ravenous bird would sometimes try to do, even though the ring was put around his neck for the express purpose of preventing him from gulping down a whole fish at once.

It was springtime, and the buds were just bursting into flower. The river was full of fish, especially of carp, ascending to the great rapids or cascades. Here the current ran at a prodigious rate of swiftness, and the waters rippled and boiled and roared with frightful noise. Yet, strange to say, many of the fish were swimming up the stream as if their lives depended on it. They leaped and floundered about; but every one seemed to be tossed back and left exhausted in the river, where they panted and gasped for breath in the eddies at the side. Some were so bruised against the rocks that, after a few spasms, they floated white and stiff, belly up, on the water, dead, and were swept down the stream. Still the shoal leaped and strained every fin, until their scales flashed in the sun like a host of armoured warriors in battle. Gojiro, enjoying it as if it were a real conflict of wave and fishes, clapped his hands with delight.

Then Gojiro inquired, by means of writing, of an old white-bearded sage standing by and looking on: 'What is the name of this part of the river?'

'We call it Lung Men,' said the sage.

'Will you please write the characters for it,' said Gojiro, producing his ink-case and brush-pen, with a roll of soft mulberry paper.

The sage wrote the two Chinese characters, meaning 'The Gate of the Dragons,' or 'Dragons' Gate,' and turned away to watch a carp that seemed almost up into smooth water.

'Oh! I see,' said Gojiro to himself. 'That's pronounced Riu Mon in Japanese. I'll go further on and see. There must be some meaning in this fish-climbing.' He went forward a few rods, to where the banks trended upward into high bluffs, crowned by towering firs, through the top branches of which fleecy white clouds sailed slowly along, so near the sky did the tree-tops seem. Down under the cliffs the river ran perfectly smooth, almost like a mirror, and broadened out to the opposite shore. Far back, along the current, he could still see the rapids shelving down. It was crowded at the bottom with leaping fish, whose numbers gradually thinned out toward the centre; while near the top, close to the edge of level water, one solitary fish, of powerful fin and tail, breasted the steep stream. Now forward a leap, then a slide backward, sometimes further to the rear than the next leap made up for, then steady progress, then a slip, but every moment nearer, until, clearing foam and ripple and spray at one bound, it passed the edge and swam happily in smooth water.

It was inside the Dragon Gate.

Now came the wonderful change. One of the fleecy white clouds suddenly left the host in the deep blue above, dipped down from the sky, and swirling round and round as if it were a water spout, scratched and frayed the edge of the water like a fisher's troll. The carp saw and darted toward it. In a moment the fish was transformed into a white dragon, and, rising into the cloud, floated off toward Heaven. A streak or two of red fire, a gleam of terrible eyes, and the flash of white scales was all that Gojiro saw. Then he awoke.

'How strange that a poor little carp, a common fish that lives in the river, should become a great white dragon, and soar up into the sky, to live there,' thought Gojiro, the next day, as he told his mother of his dream.

'Yes,' said she; 'and what a lesson for you. See how the carp persevered, leaping over all difficulties, never giving up till it became a dragon. I hope my son will mount over all obstacles, and rise to honour and to high office under the government.'

'Oh! oh! now I see!' said Gojiro. 'That is what my teacher means when he says the students in Tokio have a saying, 'I'm a fish to day, but I hope to be a dragon to-morrow,' when they go to attend examination; and that's what Papa meant when he said: 'That fish's son, Kofuku, has become a white dragon, while I am yet only a carp.''

So on the third day of the third month, at the Feast of Flags, Gojiro hoisted the *nobori*. It was a great fish, made of paper, fifteen feet long and hollow like a bag. It was yellow, with black scales and streaks of gold, and red gills and mouth, in which two strong strings were fastened. It was hoisted up by a rope to the top of a high bamboo pole on the roof of the house. There the breeze caught it, swelled it out round and full of air. The wind made the fins work, and the tail flap, and the head tug, until it looked just like a carp trying to swim the rapids of the Yellow River—the symbol of ambition and perseverance.

THE PROCESSION OF LORD LONG-LEGS

Lovely and bright in the month of May, at the time of rice-planting, was the day on which the daimio, Lord Long-legs, was informed by his chamberlain, Hop-hop, that on the morrow his lordship's retinue would be in readiness to accompany their worshipful Lord Long-legs on his journey. This Lord Long-legs was a daimio who ruled over four acres of rice-field in Echizen, whose revenue was ten thousand rice-stalks. His retainers, who were all grasshoppers, numbered over six thousand, while his court consisted only of nobles, such as Mantis, Beetle and Pinching-bug. The maids of honour who waited on his queen Katydid, were ladybugs, butterflies and goldsmiths, and his messengers were fireflies and dragonflies. Once in a while a beetle was sent on an errand; but these stupid fellows had such a habit of running plump into things, and bumping their heads so badly that they always forgot what they were sent for. Besides these, he had a great many servants in the kitchen—such as grubs, spiders, toads, etc. The entire population of his dominion, including the common folks, numbered several millions, and ranked all the way from horse-flies down to ants, mosquitoes and ticks.

Many of his subjects were very industrious and produced fine fabrics, which, however, were seized and made use of by great monsters, called men. Thus the grey worms kept spinning-wheels in their heads. They had a fashion of eating mulberry leaves, and changing them into fine threads, called silk. The wasps made paper, and the bees distilled honey. There was another insect which spread white wax on the trees. These were all retainers or friendly vassals of Lord Long-legs.

Now it was Lord Long-legs' duty once a year to go up to Yedo to pay his respects to the great Tycoon and to spend several weeks in the eastern metropolis. I shall not take the time nor tax the patience of my readers in telling about all the bustle and preparation that went on in the *yashiki* (mansion) of Lord Long-legs for a whole week previous to starting. Suffice it to say that clothes were washed and starched, and dried on a board, to keep them from shrinking; trunks and baskets were packed; banners and umbrellas were put in order; the lacquer on the brass ornaments; shields and swords and spears were all polished; and every little item was personally examined by the daimio's chief inspector. This functionary was a black-and-white-legged mosquito, who, on account of his long nose, could pry into a thing further and see it easier than any other of his lordship's officers; and, if anything went wrong, he could make more noise over it than any one else. As for the retainers, down to the very last lackey and coolie, each one tried to outshine the other in cleanliness and spruce dress.

The Bumblebee brushed off the pollen from his legs; and the humbler Honeybee, after allowing his children to suck his paws, to get the honey sticking to them, spruced up and listened attentively to the orders read to him by the train-leader, Sir Locust, who prided himself on being seventeen years old, and looked on all the others as children. He read from a piece of wasp-nest paper: 'No leaving the line to suck flowers, except at halting-time.' The Blue-tailed Fly washed his hands and face over and over again. The ladybugs wept many tears, because they could not go with the company; the crickets chirped rather gloomily, because none with short limbs could go on the journey; while Daddy Long-legs almost turned a somersault for joy when told he might carry a bundle in the train. All being in readiness, the procession was to start at six o'clock in the morning. The exact minute was to be announced by the time-keeper of the mansion, Flea-san, whose house was on the back of Neko, a great black cat, who lived in the porter's lodge of the castle, near by. Flea-san was to notice the opening or slits in the monster's moony-green eyes, which when closed to a certain width would indicate six o'clock. Then with a few jumps she was to announce it to a mosquito friend of hers, who would fly with the news to the gate-keeper of the yashiki, one Whirligig by name.

So, punctually to the hour, the great double gate swung wide open, and the procession passed out and marched on over the hill. All the servants of Lord Long-legs were out, to see the grand sight. They were down on their knees, saying: 'Oshidzukani,' (please go slowly). When their master's palanquin passed, they bowed their heads to the dust, as was proper. The ladies, who were left behind, cried bitterly, and soaked their paper handkerchiefs with tears, especially one fair brown creature, who was next of kin to Lord Long-legs, being an ant on his mother's side.

The procession was closed by six old daddies (spiders), marching two by two, who were a little stupid and groggy, having had a late supper, and a jolly feast the night before. When the great gate slammed shut, one of them caught the end of his foot in it, and was lamed for the rest of the journey. This old Daddy Long-legs, hobbling along, with a bundle on his back, was the only funny thing in the procession, and made much talk among bystanders on the road.

This is the order and the way they looked. First there went

out, far ahead, a plump, tall Mantis, with a great long baton of grass, which he swung to and fro before him, from right to left, (like a drum-major), crying out: '*Shitaniro*, down on your knees! Get down with you!' Whereat all the ants, bugs and lizards at once bent their forelegs, and the toads, which were already squatting, bobbed their noses in the dust. Even the mud-turtles poked their heads out of the water to see what was going on. All the worms and grubs who lived up in trees or tall bushes had to come down to the ground. It was forbidden to any insect to remain on a high stalk of grass, lest he might look down on His Highness. Even the Inch-worm had to wind himself up and stop measuring his length, while the line was passing. And in case of grubs or moths in the nest or cocoon, too young to crawl out, the law compelled their parents to cover them over with a leaf. It would be an insult to Lord Long-legs to look down on him. Next followed two lantern-bearers, holding glow-worms for lanterns in their fore-paws. These were wrapped in cases made of leaves, which they took off at night. Behind were six fireflies, well supplied with self-acting lamps, which they kept hidden somewhere under their wings. Next marched four abreast the band of little weevils, carrying the umbrellas of state, which were morning-glories—some open, some shut. Behind them strutted four green grasshoppers, who were spear-bearers, carrying pink blossoms. Just before the palanquin were two tall dandies, high lords themselves and of gigantic stature and imposing bellies, who, with arms akimbo and feelers far up in the air, bore aloft high over all the insignia of their Lord Long-legs. All these fellows strutted along on their hind legs, their backs as stiff as a hemp stalk, their noses pointing to the stars, and their legs striding like stilts. The priest in his robes, a praying beetle, who was chaplain, walked on solemnly.

Meanwhile a great crowd of spectators lined the path; but

all were on their knees. Frogs and toads blinked out of the sides of their heads. The pretty red lizards glided out, to see the splendid show; worms stopped crawling; and all kinds of bugs ceased climbing, and came down from the grass and flower-stalks, to bow humbly before the train of Lord Long-legs. Bug mothers hastened, with their bug babies on their backs, down to the road, and, squatting down, taught their little nits to put their fore-paws politely together and bow down on their front knees. No one dared to speak out loud; but the mole-cricket, nudging his fellow under the wing, said: 'Just look at that green Mantis! He looks as though "he would rush out with a battle-axe on his shoulder to meet a chariot." See how he ogles his fellow!'

'Yes; and just behold that bandy-legged hopper, will you? I could walk better than that myself,' said the other.

'Sh!' said the mole-cricket. 'Here comes the palanquin.'

Everybody now cast a squint up under their eyebrows, and watched the palanquin go by. It was made of delicately-woven striped grass, bound with bamboo threads, lacquered, and finished with curtains of gauze, made of dragonfly wings, through which Lord Long-legs could peep. It was borne on the shoulders of four stalwart hoppers, who, carrying rest-poles of grass, trudged along, with much sweat and fuss and wiping of their foreheads, stopping occasionally to change shoulders. At their side walked a bodyguard of eight hoppers, armed with pistils, and having side-arms of sword-grass. They were also provided with poison-shoots, in case of trouble. Other bearers followed, keeping step and carrying the regalia, consisting of chrysanthemum stalks and blossoms. Then followed, in double rank, a long string of wasps, who were for show and nothing more. Between them, inside, carefully saddled, bridled, and in full housings, was a horsefly, led by a snail, to keep the restive animal from going at a too rapid pace.

Three big, gawky helmet-headed beetles next followed, bearing rice-sprouts, with full heads of rice.

'Oh! oh! look there!' cried a little grub at the side of the road. 'See the little grasshopper riding on his father's back!'

'Hai,' said Mother Butterfly, putting one paw on her baby's neck, for fear of being arrested for making a noise.

It was so. The little 'hopper, tired of long walking, had climbed on his father's back for a ride, holding on by the feelers and seeing everything.

Finally, toward the end of the procession, was a great crowd of common 'hoppers, beetles, and bugs of all sorts, carrying the presents to be given in Yedo, and the clothing, food and utensils for the use of Lord Long-legs on the journey; for the hotels were sometimes very poor on the Tokaido high road, and the daimio liked his comforts. Besides, it was necessary for Lord Long-legs to travel with proper dignity, as became a daimio. His messengers always went before and engaged lodging-places, as the fleas, spiders and mosquitoes from other localities, who traveled up and down the great high road, sometimes occupied the places first. The procession wound up by the rear-guard of Daddy Long-legs, who prevented any insult or disrespect from the rabble. After the line had passed, insects could cross the road, traffic and travel were resumed, and the road was cleared, while the procession faded from view in the distance.

KIYOHIME, OR THE POWER OF LOVE

Quiet and shady was the spot in the midst of one of the loveliest valley landscapes in the empire, near the banks of the Hidaka River, where stood the tea-house kept by one Kojima. It was surrounded on all sides by glorious mountains, ever robed with deep forests, silver-threaded with flashing water-falls, to which the lovers of nature paid many a visit, and in which poets were inspired to write stanzas in praise of the white foam and the twinkling streamlets. Here the bonzes loved to muse and meditate, and anon merry picnic parties spread their mats, looped their canvas screens, and feasted out of nests of lacquered boxes, drinking the amber saké from cups no larger nor thicker than an egg-shell, while the sound of guitar and drum kept time to dance and song.

The garden of the tea-house was as lovely a piece of art as the florist's cunning could produce. Those who emerged from the deep woods of the lofty hill called the Dragon's Claw, could see in the tea-house garden a living copy of the landscape before them. There were mimic mountains, (ten feet high), and miniature hills veined by a tiny path, with dwarfed pine groves, and tiny bamboo clumps, and a patch of grass for meadow, and a valley just like the great gully of the mountains, only a thousand times smaller, and but twenty feet long. So perfect was the imitation that even the miniature irrigated rice-fields, each no larger than a chequer-board, were in full sprout. To make this little gem of nature in art complete, there fell from over a rock at one end a lovely little waterfall two feet high, which after an angry splash over the stones, rolled on over an absurdly small beech, all white-sanded and pebbled, threading its silver way beyond, until lost in fringes of lilies and aquatic plants. In one broad space imitating a lake, was a lotus pond, lined with iris, in which the fins of gold fish and silver carp flashed in the sunbeams. Here and there the nose of a tortoise protruded, while on a rugged rock sat an old grandfather surveying the scene with one or two of his grand-children asleep on his shell and sunning themselves.

The fame of the tea-house, its excellent fare, and special delicacy of its mountain trout, sugar-jelly and well-flavored rice-cakes, drew hundreds of visitors, especially poetry-parties, and lovers of grand scenery.

Just across the river, which was visible from the verandah of the tea-house, stood the lofty firs that surrounded the temple of the Tendai Buddhists. Hard by was the pagoda, which painted red peeped between the trees. A long row of paper-windowed and tile-roofed dwellings to the right made up the monastery, in which a snowy eye-browed but rosy-faced old abbot and some twenty bonzes dwelt, all shaven-faced and shaven-pated, in crape robes and straw sandals, their only food being water and vegetables.

Not the least noticeable of the array of stone lanterns, and bronze images with aureoles round their heads, and incense burners and holy water tanks, and dragon spouts, was the belfry, which stood on a stone platform. Under its roof hung the massive bronze bell ten feet high, which, when struck with a suspended log like a trip-hammer, boomed solemnly over the valley and flooded three leagues of space with the melody which died away as sweetly as an infant falling in slumber. This mighty bell was six inches thick and weighed several tons.

In describing the tea-house across the river, the story of its sweetest charm, and of its garden the fairest flower must not be left untold. Kiyo, the host's daughter, was a lovely maiden of but eighteen, as graceful as the bamboo reed swaying in the breeze of a moonlit summer's eve, and as pretty as the blossoms of the cherry-tree. Far and wide floated the fame of Kiyo, like the fragrance of the white lilies of Ibuki, when the wind sweeping down the mountain heights, comes perfume-laden to the traveler.

As she busied herself about the garden, or as her white socks slipped over the mat-laid floor, she was the picture of grace itself. When at twilight, with her own hands, she lighted the gay lanterns that hung in festoons along the eaves of the tea-house above the verandah, her bright eyes sparkling, her red petticoats half visible through her semi-transparent crape robe, she made many a young man's heart glow with a strange new feeling, or burn with pangs of jealousy.

Among the priests that often passed by the tea-house on their way to the monastery, were some who were young and handsome.

It was the rule of the monastery that none of the bonzes should drink saké (wine) eat fish or meat, or even stop at the tea-houses to talk with women. But one young bonze named 'Lift-the-Kettle' (after a passage in the Sanscrit classics) had rigidly kept the rules. Fish had never passed his mouth; and as for saké, he did not know even its taste. He was very studious and diligent. Every day he learned ten new Chinese characters. He had already read several of the sacred sutras, had made a good beginning in Sanskrit, knew the name of every idol in the temple of the 3,333 images in Kioto, had twice visited the sacred shrine of the Capital, and had uttered the prayer '*Namu mio ho ren ge kio*,' ('Glory be to the sacred lotus of the law'), counting it on his rosary, five hundred thousand times. For sanctity and learning he had no peer among the young neophytes of the bonzerie.

Alas for 'Lift-the-Kettle!'. One day, after returning from a visit to a famous shrine in the Kuanto, (Eastern Japan), as he was passing the tea-house, he caught sight of Kiyohime, (the 'lady' or 'princess' Kiyo), and from that moment his pain of heart began. He returned to his bed of mats, but not to sleep. For days he tried to stifle his passion, but his heart only smouldered away like an incense-stick.

Before many days he made a pretext for again passing the house. Hopelessly in love, without waiting many days he stopped and entered the tea-house.

His call for refreshments was answered by Kiyohime herself!

As fire kindles fire, so priest and maiden were now consumed in one flame of love. To shorten a long story, 'Lift-the-Kettle' visited the inn oftener and oftener, even stealing out at night to cross the river and spend the silent hours with his love.

So passed several months, when suddenly a change come over the young bonze. His conscience began to trouble him for breaking his vows. In the terrible conflict between principle and passion, the soul of the priest was tossed to and fro like the feathered seed-ball of a shuttlecock.

But conscience was the stronger, and won.

He resolved to drown his love and break off his connection with the girl. To do it suddenly, would bring grief to her and a scandal both on her family and the monastery. He must do it gradually to succeed at all.

Ah! how quickly does the sensitive love-plant know the finger-tip touch of cooling passion! How quickly falls the silver column in the crystal tube, at the first breath of the heart's chill even though the words on the lip are warm! Kiyohime marked the ebbing tide of her lover's regard, and then a terrible resolve of evil took possession of her soul. From that time forth, she ceased to be a pure and innocent and gentle virgin. Though still in maiden form and guise, she was at heart a fox, and as to her nature she might as well have worn the bushy tail of the sly deceiver. She resolved to win over her lover, by her importunities, and failing in this, to destroy him by sorcery.

One night she sat up until two o'clock in the morning, and then, arrayed only in a white robe, she went out to a secluded part of the mountain where in a lonely shrine stood a hideous scowling image of Fudo, who holds the sword of vengeance and sits clothed in fire. There she called upon the god to change her lover's heart or else destroy him.

Thence, with her head shaking, and eyes glittering with anger like the orbs of a serpent, she hastened to the shrine of Kampira, whose servants are the long-nosed sprites, who have the power of magic and of teaching sorcery. Standing in front of the portal she saw it hung with votive tablets, locks of hair, teeth, various tokens of vows, pledges and marks of sacrifice, which the devotees of the god had hung up. There, in the cold night air she asked for the power of sorcery, that she might be able at will to transform herself into the terrible *ja*,—the awful dragon-serpent whose engine coils are able to crack bones, crush rocks, melt iron or root up trees, and which are long enough to wind round a mountain.

It would be too long to tell how this once pure and happy maiden, now turned to an avenging demon went out nightly on the lonely mountains to practise the arts of sorcery. The mountain-sprites were her teachers, and she learned so diligently that the chief goblin at last told her she would be able, without fail, to transform herself when she wished.

The dreadful moment was soon to come. The visits of the

once lover-priest gradually became fewer and fewer, and were no longer tender hours of love, but were on his part formal interviews, while Kiyohime became more importunate than ever. Tears and pleadings were alike useless, and finally one night as he was taking leave, the bonze told the maid that he had paid his last visit. Kiyohime then utterly forgetting all womanly delicacy, became so urgent that the bonze tore himself away and fled across the river. He had seen the terrible gleam in the maiden's eyes, and now terribly frightened, hid himself under the great temple bell.

Forthwith Kiyohime, seeing the awful moment had come, pronounced the spell of incantation taught her by the mountain spirit, and raised her T-shaped wand. In a moment her fair head and lovely face, body, limbs and feet lengthened out, disappeared or became demon-like, and a fire-darting, hissing-tongued serpent, with eyes like moons trailed over the ground towards the temple, swam the river, and scenting out the track of the fugitive, entered the belfry, cracking the supporting columns made of whole tree-trunks into a mass of ruins, while the bell fell to the earth with the cowering victim inside.

Then began the winding of the terrible coils round and round the metal, as with her wand of sorcery in her hands, she mounted the bell. The glistening scales, hard as iron, struck off sparks as the pressure increased. Tighter and tighter they were drawn, till the heat of the friction consumed the timbers and made the metal glow hot like fire.

Vain was the prayer of priest, or spell of rosary, as the bonzes piteously besought great Buddha to destroy the demon. Hotter and hotter grew the mass, until the ponderous metal melted down into a hissing pool of scintillating molten bronze; and soon, man within and serpent without, timber and tiles and ropes were nought but a few handfuls of white ashes.

THE FISHERMAN AND
THE MOON-MAIDEN

Pearly and lustrous white, like a cloud in the far-off blue sky, seemed the floating figure of the moon-maiden, as she flew to earth. She was one of the fifteen glistening virgins that wait attendant upon the moon in her chambers in the sky. Looking down from her high home to the earth, she became enraptured with the glorious scenery of Suruga's ocean shore, and longed for a bath in the blue waters of the sea.

So this fairy maid sped to the earth one morning early, when the moon having shone through the night was about to retire for the day. The sun was rising bright and red over the eastern seas, flushing the mountains and purpling the valleys. Out amid the sparkling waves the ships sailed toward the sun, and the fishermen cast their nets.

It was in early spring, when the air was full of the fragrance of plum blossoms, and the zephyrs blew so softly that scarce a bamboo leaf quivered, or a wave lapsed with sound on the silvery shore.

The moon-maiden was so charmed with the scenery of earth, that she longed to linger above it to gaze tranquilly. Floating slowly through the air, she directed her course to the pine groves that fringe the strand near Cape Miwo. Lying at the base of Fuji mountain, whose snowy crown glistens above, fronting the ocean, whose blue plain undulates in liquid glory till it meets the bending sky, the scenery of Miwo is renowned everywhere under the whole heavens, but especially in the land which the mikado's reign blesses with peace.

Full of happiness, the fairy maiden played sweet music from her flute, until the air was full of it, and it sounded to the dweller on earth like the sweet falling of rain drops on the thirsty ground. Her body shed sweet fragrance through the air, and flowers fell from her robes as she passed. Though none saw her form, all wondered.

Arriving over a charming spot on the sea shore, she descended to the strand, and stood at the foot of a pine tree. She laid her musical instrument on a rock near by, and taking off her wings and feathered suit hung them carefully on the pine tree bough. Then she strolled off along the shore to dip her shining feet in the curling waves.

Picking up some shells, she wondered with innocent joy at the rich tints, which seemed more beautiful than any colour in the moon-world. With one, a large smooth scallop, she was particularly pleased; for inside one valve was a yellow disc, and on its mate was a white one.

'How strange,' said she. 'Here is the sun, and there is the moon. I shall call this the *Tsuki-hi-kai*—"sun and moon shell",' and she put them in her girdle.

It chanced that near the edge of the pine grove, not far away, there dwelt a lone fisherman, who, coming down to the shore, caught a whiff of sweet perfume such as had never before delighted his nostrils. What could it be? The spring zephyrs, blowing from the west, seemed laden with the sweet odor.

Curiosity prompted him to seek the cause. He walked toward the pine tree, and looking up, caught sight of the feathery suit of wings. Oh! how his eyes sparkled. He danced for joy, and taking down the robe carried it to his neighbours.

All were delighted, and one old man said that the fairy must herself be near by. He advised the man to seek until he found her.

So with feathered robe in hand the fisherman went out again to the strand, and took his place near the pine tree. He had not waited long before a lovely being, with rose-tinted white skin and of perfect form, appeared.

'Please good sir, give me back my feathered robe,' said she, in a sad voice of liquid sweetness, though she seemed greatly frightened.

'No, I must keep it as a sacred treasure, a relic from a heavenly visitor, and dedicate it in the shrine yonder as a memorial of an angel's visit' said the fisherman.

'Oh, wicked man, what a wretched and impious thing to rob an inhabitant of heaven of the robe by which she moves. How can I fly back to my home again?'

'Give me your wings, oh ye wild geese that fly across the face of the moon, and on tireless pinions seek the icy shores in spring time, and soar unwearied homeward in autumn. Lend me your wings.'

But the wild geese overhead only whirred and screamed, and bit their sprays of pine which they carried in their mouth.

'Oh, ye circling gulls, lend me but for a day your downy wings. I am prisoner here', cried the weeping fairy.

But the graceful gulls hovering for a moment swept on in widening circles out to farther sea.

'Oh, breezes of the air which blow whither ye list! Oh, tide of ocean which ebbs and flows at will! Ye may move all, but I am prisoner here, devoid of motion. Oh, good sir have pity and give me back my wings,' cried the moon-maiden, pressing her hands together in grief.

The fisher's heart was touched by the pathos of her voice

and the glittering of her tears.

'I'll give back your winged-robe if you'll dance and make music for me', said he.

'Oh, yes, good sir, I will dance and make music, but first let me put on my feather-robe for without it I have no power of motion.'

'Oh, yes', said the suspicious mortal, 'If I give you back your wings you'll fly straight to heaven.'

'What! can you not believe the word of a heavenly being, without doubting? Trust me in good faith and you'll lose nothing.'

Then with shamed face the fisherman handed to the moon-maiden her feathered robe, which she donned and began to dance. She poured out such sweet strains from her upright flute that with eye and ear full of rapture, the fisherman imagined himself in heaven. Then she sang a sweet song in which she described the delights of life in the moon and the pleasure of celestial residence.

The fisherman was so overjoyed that he longed to detain the fairy. He begged her to dwell with him on earth, but in vain. As he looked, he saw her rising. A fresh breeze, rippling the face of the sea, now sprang up, and wafted the pearly maiden over the pine-clad hills and past Fuji mountain. All the time sweet music rained through the air until, as the fisherman strained his eyes toward the fresh-fallen snow on Fuji's crest, he could no longer distinguish the moon-maiden from the fleecy clouds that filled the thin air.

Pondering long upon the marvellous apparition, the fisherman resolved to mark the spot where the fairy first descended to earth. So he prevailed upon the simple villagers to build a railing of stone around the now sacred pine.

Daily they garlanded the old trunk with festoons of tasseled and twisted rice-straw. Long after, when by the storms of centuries the old pine, in spite of bandages and crutches, and tired of wrestling with the blast, fell down like an old man, to rise no more, a grateful posterity cleared the space and built the shrine of Miwo, which still dots with its sacred enclosure the strand of Suruga on which the fairy danced.

THE JEWELS OF THE EBBING AND THE FLOWING TIDE

Chiuai was the fourteenth mikado of the Land of the Gods (Japan). His wife, the empress, was named Jingu, or Godlike Exploit. She was a wise and discreet lady and assisted her husband to govern his dominions. When a great rebellion broke out in the south island called Kiushiu, the mikado marched his army against the rebels. The empress went with him and lived in the camp. One night, as she lay asleep in her tent, she dreamed that a heavenly being appeared to her and told her of a wonderful land in the west, full of gold, silver, jewels, silks and precious stones. The heavenly messenger told her if she would invade this country she would succeed, and all its spoil would be hers, for herself and Japan.

'Conquer Corea!' said the radiant being, as she floated away on a purple cloud.

In the morning the empress told her husband of her dream, and advised him to set out to invade the rich land. But he paid no attention of her. When she insisted, in order to satisfy her, he climbed up a high mountain, and looking far away towards the setting sun, saw no land thither, not even mountain peaks. So, believing that there was no country in that direction he descended, and angrily refused to set out on the expedition. Shortly after, in a battle with the rebels the mikado was shot dead with an arrow.

The generals and captains of the host then declared their loyalty to the empress as the sole ruler of Japan. She, now having the power, resolved to carry out her daring plan of invading Corea. She invoked all the *kami* or gods together, from the mountains, rivers and plains to get their advice and help. All came at her call. The kami of the mountains gave her timber and iron for her ships; the kami of the fields presented rice and grain for provisions; the kami of the grasses gave her hemp for cordage; and the kami of the winds promised to open his bag and let out his breezes to fill her sails toward Corea. All came except Isora, the kami of the sea shore. Again she called for him and sat up waiting all night with torches burning, invoking him to appear.

Now, Isora was a lazy fellow, always slovenly and ill-dressed, and when at last he did come, instead of appearing in state in splendid robes, he rose right out of the sea-bottom, covered with mud and slime, with shells sticking all over him and sea-weed clinging to his hair. He gruffly asked what the empress wanted.

'Go down to Riu Gu and beg his majesty Kai Riu O, the Dragon King of the World Under the Sea, to give me the two jewels of the tides,' said the imperial lady.

Now among the treasures in the palace of the Dragon King of the World Under the Sea were two jewels having wondrous power over the tides. They were about as large as apples, but shaped like apricots, with three rings cut near the top. They seemed to be of crystal, and glistened and shot out dazzling rays like fire. Indeed, they appeared to seethe and glow like the eye of a dragon, or the white-hot steel of the sword-forger. One was called the Jewel of the Flood-Tide, and the other the Jewel of the Ebb-Tide. Whoever owned them had the power to make the tides instantly rise or fall at his word, to make the dry land appear, or the sea overwhelm it, in the fillip of a finger.

Isora dived with a dreadful splash, down, down to Riu Gu, and straightway presented himself before Kai Riu O. In the name of the empress, he begged for the two tide-jewels.

The Dragon King agreed, and producing the flaming globes from his casket, placed them on a huge shell and handed them to Isora, who brought the jewels to Jingu, who placed them in her girdle.

The empress now prepared her fleet for Corean invasion. Three thousand barges were built and launched, and two old kami with long streaming grey hair and wrinkled faces, were made admirals. Their names were Suwa Daimio Jin (Great Illustrious, Spirit of Suwa) and Sumiyoshi Daimio Jin, the kami who lives under the old pine tree at Takasago, and presides over nuptial ceremonies.

The fleet sailed in the tenth month. The hills of Hizen soon began to sink below the horizon, but no sooner were they out of sight of land than a great storm arose. The ships tossed about, and began to butt each other like bulls, and it seemed as though the fleet would be driven back; when lo! Kai Riu O sent shoals of huge sea-monsters and immense fishes that bore up the ships and pushed their sterns forward with their great snouts. The *shachihoko*, or dragon-fishes, taking the ship's cables in their mouths towed them forward, until the storm ceased and the ocean was calm. Then they plunged downwards into the sea and disappeared.

The mountains of Corea now rose in sight. Along the shore were gathered the Corean army. Their triangular fringed banners, inscribed with dragons, flapped in the breeze. As soon as their sentinels caught sight of the Japanese fleet, the signal was given, and the Corean line of war galleys moved gaily out to attack the Japanese.

The empress posted her archers in the bows of her ships and waited for the enemy to approach. When they were within a few hundred sword-lengths, she took from her girdle the Jewel of the Ebbing Tide and cast the flashing gem into the sea. It blazed in the air for a moment, but no sooner did it touch the water, than instantly the ocean receded from under the Corean vessels, and left them stranded on dry land. The Coreans, thinking it was a tidal wave, and that the Japanese ships were likewise helpless in the undertow, leaped out of their galleys and rushed over the sand, and on to the attack. With shouting and drawn swords their aspect was terrible. When within range of the arrows, the Japanese bowmen opened volleys of double-headed, or triple-pronged arrows on the Coreans, and killed hundreds.

But on they rushed, until near the Japanese ships, when the empress taking out the Flood-Tide Jewel, cast it in the sea. In a snap of the finger, the ocean rolled up into a wave many tens of feet high and engulfed the Corean army, drowning them almost to a man. Only a few were left out of the ten thousand. The warriors in their iron armour sank dead in the boiling waves, or were cast along the shore like logs. The Japanese army landed safely, and easily conquered the country. The king of Corea surrendered and gave his bales of silk, jewels, mirrors, books, pictures, robes, tiger skins and treasures of gold and silver to the empress. The booty was loaded on eighty ships, and the Japanese army returned in triumph to their native country.

KAI RIU O, OR THE DRAGON KING OF THE WORLD UNDER THE SEA

Soon after her arrival at home, the empress Jingu gave birth to a son, whom she named Ojin. He was one of the fairest children ever born of an imperial mother, and was very wise and wonderful even when an infant. He was a great favourite of Takenouchi, the prime minister of the empress. As he grew up, he was full of the Yamato Damashii, or the spirit of unconquerable Japan.

This Takenouchi was a very venerable old man, who was said to be three hundred and sixty years old. He had been the counsellor of five mikados. He was very tall, and as straight as an arrow, when other old men were bent like a bow. He served as a general in war and a civil officer in peace. For this reason he always kept on a suit of armour under his long satin and damask court robes. He wore the bear-skin shoes and the tiger-skin scabbard which were the general's badge of rank, and also the high cap and long fringed strap hanging from the belt, which marked the court noble. He had moustaches, and a long beard fell over his breast like a foaming waterfall, as white as the snows on the branches of the pine trees of Ibuki mountain.

Now the empress, as well as Takenouchi, wished the imperial infant Ojin to live long, be wise and powerful, become a mighty warrior, be invulnerable in battle, and to have control over the tides and the ocean as his mother once had. To do this it was necessary to get back the Tide Jewels.

So Takenouchi took the infant Ojin on his shoulders, mounted the imperial war-barge, whose sails were of gold-embroidered silk, and bade his rowers put out to sea. Then standing upright on the deck, he called on Kai Riu O to come up out of the deep and give back the Tide Jewels to Ojin.

At first there was no sign on the waves that Kai Riu O heard. The green sea lay glassy in the sunlight, and the waves laughed and curled above the sides of the boat. Still Takenouchi listened intently and waited reverently. He was not long in suspense. Looking down far under the sparkling waves, he saw the head and fiery eyes of a dragon mounting upward. Instinctively he clutched his robe with his right hand, and held Ojin tightly on his shoulder, for this time not Isora, but the terrible Kai Riu O himself was coming.

What a great honour! The Sea King's servant, Isora, had appeared to a woman, the empress Jingu, but to her son, the Dragon King of the World Under the Sea deigned to come in person.

The waters opened; the waves rolled up, curled, rolled into wreaths and hooks and drops of foam, which flecked the dark green curves with silvery bells. First appeared a living dragon with fire-darting eyes, long flickering moustaches, glittering scales of green all ruffled, with terrible spines erect, and the joints of the fore-paws curling out jets of red fire. This living creature was the helmet of the Sea King. Next appeared the face of awful majesty and stern mien, as if with reluctant condescension, and then the jewel robes of the monarch. Next rose into view a huge haliotis shell, in which, on a bed of rare gems from the deep sea floor, glistened, blazed and flashed the two Jewels of the Tides.

Then the Dragon-King spoke, saying:

'Quick, take this casket, I deign not to remain long in this upper world of mortals. With these I endow the imperial prince of the Heavenly line of the mikados of the Divine country. He shall be invulnerable in battle. He shall have long life. To him I give power over sea and land. Of this, let these Tide-Jewels be the token.'

Hardly were these words uttered when the Dragon-King disappeared with a tremendous splash. Takenouchi standing erect but breathless amid the crowd of rowers who, crouching at the boat's bottom had not dared so much as to lift up their noses, waited a moment, and then gave the command to turn the prow to the shore.

Ojin grew up and became a great warrior, invincible in battle and powerful in peace. He lived to be one hundred and eleven years old, and was next to the last of the long lived mikados of Everlasting Great Japan.

To this day Japanese soldiers honour him as the patron of war, and pray to him as the ruler of battle.

When the Buddhist priests came to Japan they changed his name to *Hachiman Dai Bosatsu*, or the 'Great Buddha of the Eight Banners.' On many a hill and in many a village of Japan may still be seen a shrine to his honour. Often when a soldier comes back from war, he will hang up a tablet or picture-frame, on which is carved a painting or picture of the two-edged short sword like that which Ojin carried. Many of the old soldiers who fought in armour wore a little silver sword of Ojin set as a frontlet to their helmets, for a crest of honour. On gilded or lacquered Japanese cabinets and shrines, and printed on their curious old, and new greenback paper money, are seen the blazing Jewels of the Tides. On their gold and silver coins the coiled dragon clutches in his claws the Jewels of the Ebbing and the Flowing Tide. One of the iron-clad war ships of the imperial Japanese navy, on which floats proudly the red sun-banner of the Empire of the Rising Sun, is named *Kogo* (Empress) after the Amazon empress who in the third century carried the arms of the Island Empire into the main land of Asia, and won victory by her mastery over the ebbing and the flowing tides.

THE CREATION OF HEAVEN AND EARTH

Of old the Heavens and the Earth were not separated. Land and water, solids and gases, fire and stone, light and darkness were mixed together. All was liquid and turbid chaos.

Then the mighty mass began to move from within. The lighter particles of gas and air began to rise, forming the sky and heavens. The heavy parts sank and cohered, becoming the earth. The water formed the four seas. Then there appeared something like a white cloud floating between heaven and earth. Out of this came forth three beings—The Being of the Middle of Heaven, The High August Being, and The Majestic Being. These three 'hid their bodies.'

Out of the warm mould of the earth something like a rush sprouted up. It was clear and bright like crystal. From this rush-sprout came forth a being whose title is 'The Delightful and Honourable Rush-Sprout.' Next appeared another being out of the buds of the rush-sprout whose name is 'The Honourable Heaven-born.' These five beings are called 'the heavenly gods.'

Next came into existence four pairs of beings viz.: (1) The Being Sprung from the First Mud, and The Being of the Sand and Mud; (2) The Being with Hands and Feet Growing, and the Being Having Breath; (3) The Male Being, and the Female Being of the Great Place (the earth); (4) The Being of Complete Perfection, and the Being who cried out 'Strange and Awful' to her mate.

Thus the last pair that came into existence were the first man and woman called Izanagi and Izanami.

It is said that the other pairs of beings before Izanagi and Izanami were only their imperfect forms or the processes through which they passed before arriving at perfection.

These two beings lived in the Heavens. The world was not yet well formed, and the soil floated about like a fish in the water, but near the surface; and was called 'The Floating Region.' The sun, earth and moon were still attached to each other like a head to the neck, or arms to the body. They were little by little separating, the parts joining them growing thinner and thinner. This part, like an isthmus, was called 'Heaven's Floating Bridge.' It was on this bridge that Izanagi and Izanami were standing when they saw a pair of wagtails cooing and billing sweetly together. The heavenly couple were so delighted with the sight that they began to imitate the birds. Thus began the art of love, which mortals have practised to this day.

While talking together on this Bridge of Heaven, they began to wonder if there was a world beneath them. They looked far down upon the green seas, but could see nothing! Then Izanagi took his long jewelled spear and plunged it into the turbid mass, turning it round and round. As he lifted it up, the drops which trickled from it hardened into earth of their own accord; and thus dry land was formed. As Izanagi was cleansing his spear the lumps of muck and mud which had adhered to it flew off into space, and were changed into stars and comets.

[It is said that by turning his spear round and round, Izanagi set the Earth revolving in daily revolutions].

To the land thus formed, they gave the name of 'The Island of the Congealed Drop,' because they intended to create a large archipelago and wished to distinguish this as the first island.

They descended from Heaven on the floating bridge and landed on the island. Izanagi struck his tall spear in the ground making it the axis of the world. He then proceeded to build a palace around the spear which formed the central pillar. [This spot was formerly at the North pole, but is now at Eshima, off the central eastern coast of Japan]. They then resolved to walk round the island and examine it. This done, they met together. Izanami cried out, 'What a lovely man!' But Izanagi rebuked her for speaking first, and said they must try it again. Then they walked round the island once more. When they met, Izanami held her tongue while Izanagi said, 'What a lovely woman!'

Being now both in good humour, they began the work of creating Japan. The first island brought up out of the water was Awaji; and then the main island. After that, eight large islands were created, whence comes one of the names of Japan, 'The Empire of the Eight Great Islands.' Six smaller islands were also produced. The several thousand islets which make up the archipelago of Everlasting Great Japan were formed by the spontaneous consolidation of the foam of the sea.

After the country was thus formed the divine pair created eight millions of earthly gods or kami, and the ten thousand different things on the earth. Vegetation sprang up over all the land, which was however still covered with mist. So Izanagi created with his breath the two gods, male and female of the wind. All these islands are the children of Izanagi and Izanami, and when first born were small and feeble, but gradually grew larger and larger, attaining their present size like human beings, which are at first tiny infants.

As the gradual separation of the land and sea went on, foreign countries were formed by the congealing of the foam of the sea. The god of fire was then born of Izanami, his mother. This god often got very angry at any one who used unclean fire. Izanami then created by herself the gods of metals, of clay and of fresh water. This latter was told always to keep the god of fire quiet, and put him out when he began to do mischief.

Izanagi and Izanami, though married but a short time, began to quarrel, for Izanami had once told her husband not to look at her when she hid herself. But Izanagi did not do what she requested, but intruded on her privacy when she was unwell, and stared at her when she wished to be alone. Izanami then got very angry, and went down to the lower world of darkness, and disappeared.

In the dark world under the earth Izanami stayed a long time, and after long waiting, Izanagi went after her. In the darkness of the Underworld he was horrified at what he saw, and leaving his consort below, tried to escape to the earth again.

In his struggles several gods were created, one of them coming out of his staff. When he got up to daylight, he secured a large rock to close up the hole in the earth. Turning this rock into a god, he commanded him to watch the place. He then rushed into the sea and continued washing for a long time to purify himself. In blowing out from his lungs the polluted air inhaled in the Underworld, the two evil gods sprang forth from his breath. As these would commit great harm and wickedness, Izanagi created two other gods to correct their evil. But when he had washed his eyes and could see clearly again, there sprang out two precious and lovely beings; one from his left eye, being a rare and glistening maiden, whom he afterwards named Amaterasu, or 'The Heaven Illuminating Spirit.' From his right eye appeared Susa no O, the 'Ruler of the Moon.' Being now pure again, and having these lovely children, Izanagi rejoiced and said, 'I have begotten child upon child, and at the end of my begetting, I have begotten me two jewel-children.' Now the brightness of the person of the maiden Amaterasu was beautiful, and shone through Heaven and Earth. Izanagi, well pleased, said: 'Though my children are many, none of them is like this wonder-child. She must not be kept in this region.' So taking off the necklace of precious stones from his neck and rattling it, he gave it to her, saying, 'Rule thou over the High Plain of Heaven.'

At that time the distance between Heaven and Earth was not very great, and he sent her up to the blue sky by the Heaven-uniting Pillar, on which the Heavens rested like a prop. She easily mounted it, and lived in the sun, illuminating the whole Heavens and the Earth. The Sun now gradually separated from the Earth, and both moved farther and farther apart until they rested where they now are.

Izanagi next spoke to Susa no O the Ruler of the Moon, and said, 'Rule thou over the new-born Earth and the blue Waste of the Sea, with its Multitudinous Salt Waters.'

[So then the Heavens and the Earth and Moon were created and inhabited. And as Japan lay directly opposite the sun when it separated from the Earth, it is plain that Japan lies on the summit of the globe. It is easily seen that all other countries were formed by the spontaneous consolidation of the ocean foam, and the collection of mud in the various seas. The stars were made to guide warriors from foreign countries to the court of the mikado, who is the true Son of Heaven.]

HOW THE SUN GODDESS WAS ENTICED OUT OF HER CAVE

When the far-shining goddess, on account of the evil pranks of her brother, Susa no O, the Ruler of the Moon, hid herself in a cave, there was no more light, and heaven and earth were plunged into darkness.

A council of all the gods was held in the dry bed of one of the rivers [which we call the Milky Way] in the fields of Heaven. The question of how to appease the anger of the goddess was discussed. A long-headed and very wise god was ordered to think out a plan to entice her forth from the cave.

After due deliberation, it was resolved that a looking-glass should be made to tempt her to gaze at herself, and that tricks should be played to arouse her curiosity to come out and see what was going on.

So setting to work with a will, the gods forged and polished a mirror, wove cloth for beautiful garments, built a pavilion, carved a necklace of jewels, made wands, and tried an augury.

All being ready, the fat and rosy-cheeked goddess of mirth with face full of dimples, and eyes full of fun, named Uzume, was selected to lead the dance. She had a flute made from a bamboo cane by piercing holes between the joints, while every god in the great orchestra had a pair of flat hard wood clappers, which he struck together.

She bound up her long flowing sleeves with a creeper vine,

and made for herself a baton of twigs of bamboo grass, by which she could direct the motions of the musicians. This she held in one hand while in the other was a spear wound round with grass, on which small bells tinkled. Great bonfires were lighted in front of the cave, so that the audience of gods could see the dance. A large circular box which resounded like a drum when trod on, was set up for Uzume to dance upon. The row of cocks now began to crow in concert.

All being ready, the Strong-handed god who was to pull the Sun Goddess out of the cave, as soon as overcome by her curiosity she should peep forth, hid himself beside the stone door of the cave. Uzume mounted the box and began to dance. As the drum-box resounded, the spirit of folly seized her, and she began to chant a song.

Becoming still more foolish, Uzume waved her wand wildly, loosened her dress, and danced till she had not a stitch of clothing left on her. The gods were so amused at her foolishness that they all laughed, until the heavens shook as with claps of thunder.

The Sun Goddess within the cave heard all these strange noises; the crowing of the cocks, the hammering on the anvil, the chopping of wood, the music of the koto, the clappering of the hard wood, the tinkling of the bells, the shouting of Uzume and the boisterous laughter of the gods. Wondering what it all meant, she peeped out.

As she did so the Doubly Beautiful goddess held up the mirror.

The Far-Shining one seeing her own face in it was greatly astonished. Curiosity got the better of fear. She looked far out. Instantly the strong-handed god pulled the rocky door open, and seizing her hand, dragged her forth. Then all the heavens and earth were lightened, the trees and grass became green again, and the goddess of colours resumed her work of tinting the flowers. The gloom fled from all eyes, and human beings again became 'white-faced.'

Thus the calamity which had befallen heaven and earth, by the Sun Goddess hiding in the cave became a means of much benefit to mortals. For by their necessity the gods were compelled to invent the arts of metal-working, weaving, carpentry, jewelling and many other useful appliances for the human race. They also on this occasion first made use of music, dancing, the Dai Kagura (The comedy which makes the gods laugh) and many of the games which the children play at the present time.

www.ingramcontent.com/pod-product-compliance
Lightning Source LLC
Chambersburg PA
CBHW030034030726
47500CB00001B/102